The WHITE CITY

The WHITE CITY

Alec Michod

St. Martin's Press · Publishers of Many Books · New York, NY

www.stmartins.com

Illustration on page 169 by Rick Michod

Book design by Jonathan Bennett

Library of Congress Cataloging-in-Publication Data

Michod, Alec.
    The White City / Alec Michod.—1st ed.
        p. cm.
    ISBN 0-312-31397-7
        1. World's Columbian Exposition (1893 : Chicago, Ill.)—Fiction.
    2. Serial murders—Fiction.   3. Chicago (Ill.)—Fiction.   4. Kidnapping—
    Fiction.   5. Architects—Fiction.   I. Title.

    PS3613.I346W47 2004
    813'.6—dc22

                                                    2003058181

First Edition: January 2004

10 9 8 7 6 5 4 3 2 1

For my family,
great Chicagoans

DIRECT LINE
• VERY LOW RATE EXCURSIONS •
TO **WORLD'S FAIR** EVERY WEEK

One

Chicago in October. The wind off the lake is already blistering. It sneaks along the shore and then turns sharply inland, funneled between the massive buildings, then settles, before striking again, more blustery than before. Some find respite just outside the Electricity Building; others head for the Wooded Island, which, despite being surrounded by lagoons, remains largely serene. The Women's Building, if approached from the west, blocks the wind temporarily. But there is no real cover. Lips chap. Eyes tear up. Skin crackles. The Stock Exhibit will close early today, on account of the wind distressing the livestock and summoning up the soil. There are rumors that this afternoon's parade might be rescheduled, Buffalo Bill's Wild West Extravaganza postponed, and the Movable Sidewalk, which juts out into Lake Michigan, damaged permanently. Ferris's Wheel, which has revolved without stopping since the fair opened back in May, came to a grinding halt just before sunrise; the fear was that the wind might detach one of the cars, large as any house, and send it plummeting to earth, killing hundreds. Today's World's Fair specials are twice as infrequent, due to the gale-force waves the wind's drudged up, and the Alley El, which loops downtown before heading south, runs at half speed, the elevated tracks buckling in the wind, so that, overall, attendance is down. High above the White City, the sun's piercing—a sun not of October but of July. Not a cloud in the sky, not yet.

It is late morning, a Monday. The year is 1893.

Even inside, wind batters the windows from their panes. Pipes clang. The hanging paintings rattle. And everyone's scrambling for cover, because at any moment, they fear, the Palace of Fine Arts could crumble, since, like every other building in the White City, it's made only of white staff, a plaster of Paris and fibrous jute-cloth admixture. Even the austerity of the ceiling, a sweeping gilded cupola imported from a hillside Umbrian monastery, cannot calm such fears, although Elizabeth Rockland would like to believe so and to convince her son of this as well. To this end, she says, "The sky's too taupe for my liking," but Billy is more interested in over-heard whisperings—there's been another killing this morning, the third in as many days.

William Rockland, a wide, buttery man with wide, buttery jowls, doesn't mind the windows rattling. In fact, he doesn't hear them, so determined is he, leading his wife and son ever onward through the crowd, gesticulating wildly, his eyes restless. He is not a consoling guide in such times, being anxious by nature. His cheeks redden, per-spiration drips from his brow, and the man nearly collapses from shortness of breath if you so much as look at him. Billy, following obediently, shrivels from embarrassment. His father's intentions are good—they're going to be late for lunch with Potter Palmer, and nobody's late for lunch with Potter Palmer—but everyone's looking, so he soon finds his way into the hoop of his mother's dress and hides.

Bombastically, "William!" Like William Rockland, Potter Palmer is a portly man, with the mustache of a walrus concealing his facial chub and, on account of a top-heavy torso and spindly legs, a rather noticeable wobble. Billy likes to watch Palmer walk, but Palmer talking is even more amusing, with his ruddy cheeks jiggling spittle, so he peekaboos his head out from beneath the dress. Nobody notices. "I don't have much of an appetite just yet," Palmer is saying, "so why don't you and I off to hear Mr. Douglass"—the abolitionist, who's speaking this noon—"and the ladies can do as they wish, and we'll all just eat later. How's that?"

"Boo!" Billy shoots out from under the dress, prances around, wagging his tongue. His hair, which is longer than it should be, droops over his entire face, covering both eyes. Mother Rockland spent a full hour with him in preparation for today's luncheon— puffing out his hair; insuring that each curl sits in its right, smart place; powdering his cheeks; ringing his eyes with color and rouging his lips. The results are phantasmagoric, conjuring the spirit of a lost, imagined daughter.

Finally, William Rockland pats his son on a shoulder and says, "Off you go."

But where? Billy looks confused, so he says, "Where?"

Down the marble staircase and out into the sun-streaked day. Mother leads, offers a hand, but Billy bats it away. Behind them treads Mrs. Palmer, opening a sun umbrella. Just as soon as it's opened, however, the wind turns it inside out and launches it from her hands. Bertha Palmer sniggers, embarrassed.

Columbian Guards, walking stiffly, tip their hats.

They walk directly into the wind, bracing their coiffures, while Billy darts in and out of the crowd, flirting with throwing himself into North Pond, skidding to a stop, sprinting straight at Mother till she leaps, from fright, out of the way and into the arms of a passing gentleman with wiry hair bulging out from beneath his bowler and wearing a purple velvet jacquard. They pass a portly man with a spotless cream-color suit and vest and an equally spotless hat the color of snow before it goes ashen. Melodies and fragments from minstrel songs drift in off the Midway, a mile-long slag of shanty exhibit huts geared toward entertainment, not instruction. There you'll find the Moorish Palace, Hagenbeck's Animal Show, a Turkish Village, a German Village, a Street in Cairo replete with dancing girls, and perched loftily over all, Ferris's gigantic wheel. Here in the White City, however, the buildings are tall and distantly placed, everything's set off in a glass case or hung on a wall, and the people walk around with blank faces saying nothing, searching for the eleven-ton cheese or the fifteen-hundred-pound chocolate Venus de Milo. Aside from the Electricity Building, with its illumined dynamos, there's nothing here Billy has a desire to see.

Soon, they stand before the Women's Building. Outside, halfway up the front steps, a young Negro woman is passing out a broadside entitled "The Reason Why the Colored American Is Not in the World's Columbian Exposition." Bertha Palmer takes one, smiling a wide thanks, and says, "I do think Miss Wells is quite fantastic."

The Negro woman, though a smile crosses her face, says, "It is by Mr. Douglass, ma'am."

The Women's Building is located to the immediate left of the lip of the lagoon, just north of the all-glass Horticulture. High above sits a creature, neither fowl nor marsupial, but some ghastly blend of the two. The structure itself is hulking, despite its medium size, and as a whole more masculine than feminine, more brawn than bust—the steps out front are as steep as any, and one invariably breaks into a sweat in ascending.

A chirpy Bertha Palmer says, "Oh, well, I knew that."

"Dear, you're dripping," says Mother Rockland. She bats the air directly in front of Billy's face.

They're halfway up the second flight of stairs when Mrs. Palmer halts dead in her tracks and laughs. A woman in an ornamental black hoop dress with dernier-cri buttons along the front side and a smile that's bigger than the Sahara appears before them.

Bertha Palmer says hello: "It is such a beautiful day."

"It is," the woman replies. She regards Mother Rockland and says, "Hello, I'm Jane Addams. How do you do?" And then turns to Billy, offers a hand, and says, "Hello, young man. How do you do?"

Billy says nothing. Grunting, he sits on a step toward the top and rests his head in the trowel of his hands.

Mother says, "This'll just take but one moment, dear."

Jane Addams, whose Hull-House made *kindergarten* a household word, says, "Excuse me, but I am actually running late." Mrs. Rockland nods. Before Jane Addams hurries off, she says, referencing the boy, "Keep him in your sight at all times." Again Mrs. Rockland nods. Jane Addams turns to Bertha Palmer and says, "We wouldn't want another to go missing." A momentary pause. "See you soon, I hope. Tomorrow?" And with that, she's off.

Mother Rockland's hand closes around young Billy's and squeezes. She yanks him up and drags him along—up, and inside.

Inside, no wind. All's silent, save for the sounds of scuttling fairgoers. Immediately he breaks her hold and skitters off to a bench with an ornate sloping back, where he sits, watching everything and everybody, eyes darting about as they will, impatiently. Displays in the Women's Building are of lace and embroidery, steeped in nostalgia. Included is a glassed-in copy of *Jane Eyre*—the book, not the personage. He's tired but can't sit still. He'd much rather be back in the Palace of Fine Arts, surrounded by the swirling seascapes of Homer, the naked torsos of Rodin. Here everything is so—lackluster. He hops afoot and approaches his mother, tugging at her dress in an attempt to distract her.

But she'll have nothing of it. She scowls, splitting her face in half, and then returns her attentions to Bertha Palmer.

Billy would like to know how it is possible to talk as much as they do, but he simply looks up at the Cassatt, the pastels blurring together. Instantaneously, he becomes dizzy. It appears, at first, as either sky or sea, a wash of blue that spreads horizon to horizon and becomes blurrier the longer he looks. A glance at Mother finds her still talking to Bertha Palmer, now laughing, now listening, her ears slanted. He does not mind, although he would like her to notice his latest trick—standing on his head. Presently, he does just this, placing the crown of his head upon the cement bench, arms outstretched, then kicking his feet up until they're balanced aloft. Upside down, everything appears smaller and blurrier, but perhaps that's on account of the lack of oxygen. The muscles in his legs and arms and stomach clench, and blood floods his face until it darkens and Billy gasps for air. Before too long, Billy can't hold it any longer and collapses over onto the ground, banging his head on the underside of the bench. It hurts, but he springs to his feet and nearly curtsies, checking to see if Mother has noticed. She has not; in fact, she's ambled off with Bertha Palmer, stands on the far side of the exhibition hall examining a statue, made by Alice Rideout, intended to represent Sacrifice. Has she forgotten about him entirely, or will she

return, more attentive than before? He has one more trick up his
sleeve—to skid across the floor and slide into her, tackling her. It
would be a risky endeavor, to be sure, but he's done it before, to tri-
umphant success (a few months ago; she was injured, her ankle
fractured, but such are the risks, Billy figured and figures still, of
being a mother). He is about to do just that, has gripped his hands
together into fists, set to run, when off in the distance, across the
hall, only a few feet from Mother and Bertha Palmer, he spots a man
who, though full-grown, nevertheless stands no taller than Billy
Rockland. A midget. He's heard of them, yet hasn't seen one. More
than Mother's attentions, he'd like a gander. Perhaps he'll find a
friend, or be guided out of the current hell he's in—guided off and to
Electricity. That would be ideal, so he's off after the small man,
hoping he's headed for the Electricity Building. Soon enough,
they're down the stairs and out, back into the day.

Outside, the sun's sharper, the wind's stronger, with gusts that
freeze the fluid in Billy's nose upon contact.

The small man zigs in and out of shadows, zagging left and then
right, so pursuit is difficult. Still, Billy tails him around the bank of a
wading pool and alongside a lagoon, then over a footbridge. Two
women scantily dressed in lace affixed with jangling ornaments pass
by, one saying to the other, "What I'd really love to see is the Dead
Letter Office."

Billy swivels around, enrapt. Once he's spun a full circle, he realizes that he's lost the small man. Woods surround him, shading out
the sun. Fear ripples up his spine, causing him to want to retrace his
steps back to the Palace of Fine Arts. He'd like to return. He'd like to
find Mother. Instead, he makes his way deeper onto the Wooded
Island. The Wooded Island has hidden away on its modest acreage
two rather captivating rarities: a Japanese Ho-o-o Den and the
Hunter's Cabin, monument to Davy Crockett and Daniel Boone.
Swans and mallard ducks float on the leafy water of the lagoon and
come to shore searching out shade and respite, for this onslaught of
people, even for a duck, can be somewhat onerous. Davy Crockett
and Daniel Boone, especially the latter, have for long been heroes
who have fertilized the Rockland boy's imagination with yearnings

for adventure if not in fact a fast-paced life perennially on the lam, and for this reason Billy Rockland decides to postpone his trip to the Electricity Building.

High above, an owl hoots. Wind shrills.

He sprints off into woodland, rustling leaves underfoot and sticks and twigs too slight to bear his weight, which is willowy, so that with each step there's a snap. Trails crisscross the island, and every now and again there's a park bench for the relaxation of fair-goers, a few of whom are indeed here, relaxing, though not too many, for clouds have advanced upon the day. Carefree, he treads on the few flowers that remain and on various shrubbery. He steps into muck. Soon it's advanced up his legs, covering first his shins and later his kneecaps, his knickers mud-splotched. The earth just gives way. He falls to the ground—on his face.

He lies in the mud and rolls over and over again. Then he's supine, pretending he has passed on from this world.

Sounds of birds in the tops of the trees, a duck quacking.

Sun clips the few clouds advancing off the lake and bakes the boy's muddied face. The mud hardens. He rolls onto his back and sets his head upon his cupped-together hands, reclining, and whistles to a melody he only just made up. After a time, he opens his eyes and is surprised, if not exactly frightened, to find a tall man with a black hat towering high above him blocking the light. Standing there tall as the heavens.

"Don't be frightened," the man says.

Just then, a rustling is heard in nearby shrubbery, then the splash of water as a mallard plops into the pond.

"Are you all right?"

The man's voice is lower than his father's. It just might be the deepest voice he has ever heard. Now that Billy has sat up, the man's no longer blocking the sun, and Billy must squint or shade his eyes with a hand.

But he does neither, just sits there staring up into the glaring sun.

"What are you up to?" The man holds out a hand, the very palm of which has the size, if not the malleability, of a pillow. "It'll be dark soon. I was taking a walk through here. Just visited that . . . *thing* over there," the man pointing lakeward, toward the Ho-o-o Den, "and then I spotted you. You should not be in here by yourself." He coughs. Mucus dribbles from between his lips. He winks. "But here you are. I like that," then doffs his hat. "Hannibal Skurlock's the name."

"Billy," says Billy.

A splashing sound in the water immediately to their left startles them both.

Skurlock furrows his brow and asks, "How old are you, son?"

Billy shrugs, saying nothing. Still, he reaches for the man's hand, to be helped up.

As he stands, the child's head spins. Everything spins. Eventually he says, "Thanks," and is set to leave. But then one of those monstrous hands clamps down on his left shoulder, detaining him.

Billy looks around, up at the man, and smiles.

Skurlock inquires, "Where are your parents?" His face, Billy notices, is jagged, uneven; it looks like an apricot mashed underfoot. Thunderously, Skurlock says, "How shall we locate them?"

Right behind them, a rustling in the thickets.

Billy anxiously shudders, says, "I have to go." But on account of Skurlock's grip, he can't.

"Where are they?" says Skurlock. "I'll take you to them."

"Electricity." It just slips out.

"We'll go together," and they're off together.

FINE VIENNA SAUSAGES 10¢

Two

The letters, all but one, are written on paper that's white as snow. Hundreds upon hundreds of letters received, many of them bearing little if any postage, within the past seven weeks, since the first killing. Letters fluttering up and then landing, blanketing her, but still the wind sends spikes upwards along her spine, jolting her awake. It is early morning, the sun having yet to pierce the horizon, but the room has lightened, even if her demeanor, habitually cheery, has not. Though she's never been a restless sleeper, especially whenever Professor James launched into one of his sinuous ramblings, this past week, since arriving in Chicago, Dr. Elizabeth Handley has felt all out of sorts—on account of the killings, yes, to say nothing of the nightmares the killings call forth, but mostly because of the letters. Anonymous letters written by anybody—your neighbor, a friend, a sister. Filled with hope or its contrary, dread. Why is it that tragedy, however wrought, brings people so seamlessly together?

There's not much else to go on, so she's read the letters over and over again, searching for even the smallest clue but finding nothing. Each wayward ink stain presents itself as a cipher, each elongated *e* as a coded message that bears nothing of substance. Maddening, to say the least. She's read Galton and Gross; she's enamored herself of the probings of Sherlock Holmes; she even brings her voluminous

notes from Professor James's lectures with her when she travels—yet
so far nothing's paid off. As the very first woman to graduate with a
doctor of psychology degree from Harvard University, Dr. Elizabeth
Handley is as well suited as anyone to track the killer the dailies have
come to call Clemantis, on account of what newspapermen have
posited must be his apparently brazen or showy nature. He is a man,
they say, on the make. Why? It is nothing but conjecture; nothing of
substance is known about the murderer other than the obvious: he
murders. Boys. Since he first struck seven weeks ago, there have
been three additional killings in three weeks, all except for the first
found somewhere on the grounds of the White City—one by the
Peristyle, another out on the Movable Sidewalk, and the last on the
far side of the Transportation Building. Just last week, though, three
more corpses were uncovered—the sons of a doctor, a stevedore, a
carriage-driver, all found in the Stock Pavilion, where they keep the
Percheron horses. That was when Chief Detective Simonds of the
Central Detective Detail wired a colleague in Boston, who
promptly sent out one of the finest sleuths he'd come across: a
wispy woman with something of a permanent limp, porcelain skin,
piercing gray eyes, and lips so full they appeared filled with air—not
to mention a mind equally capable of high-level mathematics and
bawdy barroom asides. There was no other word for her—Dr. Elizabeth Handley was a sleuth through and through. She deduced, sure,
but what made Handley a sleuth was her free-associative intuition.
Former students claimed she was nothing more than a trickster,
while Handley enthusiasts swore she was something of an alien. You
see, while only halfway through her studies at Harvard, Elizabeth
Handley had solved an investigation that would have made the
careers of investigators much more senior than she. Hudson Martin
had been an upstanding member of Cambridge society, a barber
and the father of three. When women on the campus began to disappear, nobody so much as bothered to suggest the remote possibility that perhaps somebody associated with the university could be
the abductor. His name appeared in print only once—he was said to
have been the illegitimate father of one of the victims—but he was
never questioned by authorities, wasn't even considered as a poten-

tial suspect until Handley came into the picture. Branching off on a lecture William James gave on whether consciousness is malleable or not, Handley decided that she wanted to spend some time with the local police, to study the personalities of criminals. She came upon his name almost as if by accident, while searching through the county's property deeds. The most recent girl to disappear in broad Cambridge daylight had been living with her mother in a building owned by one Hudson Martin. The name rang a bell, although Elizabeth Handley couldn't quite place it; then it hit her. Though the detectives on the case warned her against considering Mr. Martin a suspect, she repaired to his residence, where she discovered three girls, two living and one a week dead, entombed in his basement. The case made the next day's front page, FEMALE DR. SAVES THE DAMSELS, and though she would have preferred otherwise, the future Dr. Handley was something of a celebrity.

Soon, a knocking. She attempts to right herself but falls back into the bed, crunching the straw. Her head feels as if it weighs a metric ton; her body feels like elastic, spindly and brittle. The letters fly about her like autumn leaves falling. It's a comforting sound, the sound of paper fluttering. She falls, if only for a moment, back asleep, but is awakened by a second knocking, more thunderous than its predecessor. After a third try, she scuttles halfway across her hotel room when the door flies open of its own accord. Inspector Moreau, a small, shiftless man from the Northern Provinces, stomps in. His voice is but a waver; if you want to hear what he says, you'd best stand to his immediate right and form a cup with your hands around your ear and nod vigorously, to say nothing of sympathetically; otherwise, he might sulk. As he does now. Once the door's shut firmly behind him, she flops back into bed. This, after all, is the Palmer House, widely known to have the finest beds west of Paris.

"Dr. Handley?" Were her eyes opened, she'd see his scowl; had he spoken louder, she might hear the irritation in his voice. "I'm afraid I must wake you."

"Call me Elizabeth," says Handley. "Consider me awake," and up she pops, almost pirouetting once around the room, arms thrown wide, her smile wider. It's a talent practiced by Handleys since their arrival on these shores fourteen years before the arrival of the *Mayflower*—the ability to throw yourself into a job with abandon. The shameless display of energy frightens the rather staid Inspector Moreau.

"They've found another," he says.

"Where?" She mouths it.

"The Wooded Island."

She's been here only since the middle of last week and has yet to see the White City. That is, she's in her room more or less every day for the duration of the entire day, studying the facts of the case, reading the incoming letters. She'd like a day, just one, to wander the grounds as one's meant to, flabbergasted by the White City's many wonders. As it is, though, her work keeps her eyes averted from the White City's baser entertainments and her body far from nourishment. Perhaps she'll eat a bite of stale toast, or nibble on a wafer. She's learned, by default, to subsist directly on air. Downstairs in the lobby, without meaning to, she catches a glimpse of herself in a mirror and almost shrieks from fright, so alien-looking is her gaunt countenance.

"Let's go," he says. And they do.

Throughout her short career, Dr. Handley's seen the loam of human depravity, but only from afar or briefly—she's interviewed inmates at McClean, in Belmont; she's spent time at the infamous Cherry Hill penal colony in Philadelphia; she's lived in the Five Points district in New York City. She agrees with Lord Shaftesbury that one should reform and not terminate; she's read *Criminal Investigation* already half-a-dozen times, considers last year's *Fingerprints* to be brilliant, if flawed; and though she'd never admit it, she delights in the work of Sacher Masoch and still to this day reads the case files of Jack the Ripper. But it's always been at a distance. Nothing in the literature of madness could have prepared her for this.

Just over the footbridge and onto the Wooded Island, past Hunter's Cabin—that's where a crowd has gathered, an unusually large crowd, given the dwindling hour. How did so many people

find out about this so soon? The sun bleaches the sky an almost iri-
descent white. There is little wind, on account of the massive Manufactures and Liberal Arts Building directly to the east. Dr. Handley
carries with her at all times a doctor's bag, of the worn, tattered-
leather sort one might associate with physicians, not sleuths. In it
she keeps her camera, a large, bulky affair that easily might break
the back of any other carrier; the sight of Dr. Handley with her bag
is rather comical—that of a hunchback tugging a brimming cart.
Some days she tugs it in a barrow, but today she feels obligated to
carry it. Over her free shoulder she slings a bulky, three-legged tripod, which shoots up into the sky and very nearly decapitates those
she passes.

Inspector Moreau parts the crowd for Dr. Handley. Chief Detective Simonds of the Central Detective Detail, though he sent for
her, meets her here for the first time.

"Dr. Handley," the chief detective says. "At last, and under such,
well, sordid circumstances, I'm afraid." Simonds, a tall man with
broad shoulders and bushy eyebrows, feigns a smile; though anything but earnest, it passes for a felicitation.

"What is it?" Straightaway, Dr. Handley makes a move toward the
body.

The crowd parts, but then out steps a portly, buxom Columbian
Guard with a mustache that curlicues. He says, "I'm sorry, but you
really don't—"

"Actually, I do," says Dr. Handley. And with that, she pushes him
out of the way.

It's a dark shape, no bigger than a clumped-together shirt of
some sort. In fact, it's a Columbian Guard's wool jacket. Ah, so the
evidence has already been tampered with. Now nothing Dr. Handley finds, should she find anything at all, can be trusted. Uniqueness,
invariability, immutability—all have been molested, leaving her with
little to go on. It offends her in an almost personal way, but then she
understands that perhaps it was best, what the guard did—to mask,
to conceal. Whatever's underneath should never be seen by human
eyes. Nevertheless, without so much as a second thought, Dr. Handley hovers over the crime scene, down on her haunches, knees in

the mud, and with little conscious apprehension lifts the wool jacket.

Down by the lagoon, surrounded by mud that's yet to freeze over, that in fact steams in broad daylight, here's the corpse of a young boy. A frighteningly young boy, very nearly an infant. So young, in fact, it will be difficult to determine sex or age. The body, it appears, has been positioned tactfully, in nothing close to resembling a natural position—leastwise not one that Dr. Handley's familiar with—with its arms crossed up and over its head and legs as if bound, only without the binding. Still the face is a peaceful face, with eyes closed, as if only sleeping. Did its mother kiss it once before it disappeared? Was it loved? Will they be able to identify the boy? Will they ever find the boy's mother? Dr. Handley searches the area immediately proximate to the corpse for anything—a stray piece of fabric, a footprint; there won't be fingerprints, but perhaps the killer will have left a print of his foot. Alas, there are too many, so it will be difficult to determine which, if any, might belong to the killer.

Onlookers look on, curious but in a perverse way.

She is angry at the crowd for gathering, but also sympathetic. Death disgusts but also fascinates. Were she to see such a commotion while out for a morning stroll, she, too, might stop and gawk. But they stand there so dumbly, as if *waiting* for somebody to do something; well, why don't *they* do something. Though word of the murders has spread more quickly than even the Great Fire, certainly if these dozen-or-so onlookers were to canvass the city, going from neighborhood to neighborhood, some good might come of it. Fear might multiply, but so would knowledge. And knowledge would lead to the killer. Already more than a month, and still not a single clue.

She retrieves her camera from the bag and sets up the tripod overlooking the crime scene. Even though twenty-nine years have passed since Odelbrecht, in 1864, first advocated the use of photography for the documentation of evidence at a crime scene, there's still something inherently scandalous about photographing death, about a woman in the White City capturing the image of a cadaver for all eternity. Dr. Handley uses the dry-plate method so she doesn't have to develop her prints on-site. Dry-chemical plate-glass negatives are easy to transport, more sensitive to light and more consistent than wet-collodion negatives, but since Dr. Handley's a stickler for clarity, she lugs around large eleven-by-fourteen-inch negatives and a tripod heavy enough to support the unwieldly camera. It is, in truth, an eye-catching sight—at first people can't help but look at the corpse. Soon enough, however, curiosity fades, and people can't bear the sight. Some look away in disgust, others gasp. It's a lengthy process, one best accomplished alone and without a crowd. Perhaps the belief is that the soul of the dead will not be able to ascend to heaven, instead forever trapped in a photograph.

"Inspector," she calls out. Both Moreau and Chief Detective Simonds step closer to her, to better hear her. They don't need to; her words are clear enough, if not quite voluble. "Let's lose the spectacle, shall we?"

And without a word, Chief Detective Simonds and his Columbian Guard set about clearing the area, waving the onlookers away. It is as if they were only waiting to be asked, for everyone, save two, leaves at once, trudging off to a new day at the fair—maybe a ride on the wheel, a spin around the Movable Sidewalk, a glimpse of the twenty-two-thousand-pound Monster Canadian Cheese.

"Thank you." She captures the first photograph.

Too many questions remain. How many more boys will have to die for her insufficiencies? That's how she feels at times; other times she's a dolt blindly following her own personal delirium. Where does the killer go when he's not killing? Did the boy disappear during the day, or in the middle of the night? Does the killer (she refuses to call him Clemantis—such a beautiful flower, clematis, such a horrid fellow) keep them for a while before disposing of them? Does he have his way with them? Where does he keep them? That the killer is a he, even, isn't a known, indisputable fact. Were she to have a child, would it be a boy?

Dr. Handley is about to replace the Columbian Guard's jacket over the corpse when, to the left of the infant's left shoulder, she spots a darkened splotch in the mud. It is darker than the mud surrounding it, so she figures it might be blood, and with her left finger she probes, only to find that it has yet to dry. Whether it's actually blood, and whose, she can't say, but she thinks to overturn the infant to check its posterior side. A brazen, unflinching, utterly Handleyesque touch, to be sure.

"Jesus," from Chief Detective Simonds.

It appears that the infant, once flipped, has been partially deskinned, its left shoulder stripped. This is the worst thing she has ever seen, by far, but still Dr. Handley does not look away. The left shoulder has turned to umber, with riveted crevices shooting diagonally from right to left. Dr. Handley, without flinching, leans in to inspect. The incision appears to have been done by a professional, or someone who knows how to wield a knife. This changes things.

Dr. Handley captures a photograph.

Not a word is spoken on the way back to the temporary headquarters that's been set up specifically to deal with the killer the papers will now call the Husker. It is a small room set up in Public Comfort, at the northernmost edge of the White City by the Esquimaux Village. The elevated rail rumbles by, its cars only half-full on account of the still-early hour. Dr. Handley will turn thirty-two tomorrow, yet she's not told a soul and won't; she will receive a wire from her mother, back in Cambridge, but still, it won't even occur to her that it's her birthday. She pictures the killer in her mind, or tries to. Is he tall or short? Slim or hefty? Mustache, beard, or cleanly shaven? Would you know it, just by glancing in his eyes? Does madness, she wonders, have a recognizable face? Chief Detective Simonds is right behind her, with Inspector Moreau to his immediate right, everyone in silence.

Finally, "Any ideas?"

"I need to be alone," says Dr. Handley. And with that, Chief Detective Simonds takes his leave, off to gather together a task force. Inspector Moreau, although he worked on the infamous Royas case last year, is at a complete loss; he doesn't even know how to begin looking for a man capable of such malevolence. "We need to be vigilant, I suppose," Dr. Handley says, as much to herself as to the inspector. "But in a delicate way. We can't go around town rounding up all the usual suspects. This man is not your average killer. Perhaps he is European, but I believe him to be native or, at the least, familiar with the area. He is most likely a loner, of course, so that we likely won't learn much of him from others. Nobody's seen him, so he must be incognito, or perhaps he just moves about late at night. When were all the bodies found?" Before the inspector can say, Dr. Handley continues: "Early morning, with the exception of the first and this latest. The crimes themselves occurred most likely once darkness had settled, but I don't believe these were desperate killings. These were planned, perhaps long in advance. He didn't know these boys, no, but he grew to know them, perhaps even love them. Our killer, Inspector, will not be a typical ruffian. He is, perhaps, right under our noses, and we don't even know it. One thing's for certain, Inspector," she says. "This, I'm afraid, is the very beginning. Excuse me, but I have some photographs to develop."

Three

They are five if you count the midget, each in blackface. Fat men gather to watch, chomping on juicy sausages. Also mothers with their sons and daughters in tow, but today's fourth victim in as many hours is an orphan, by the looks of him. His name is Nix, Thom Nix. He has that doughy, distant look and a face fit for the stage—a pliant, chestnut-colored orb, with eyes as sapphires, only more lustrous. To the crowd's delight, he does not so much as snicker. This being the Midway, home of sideshow shills and carnies aplenty, it's not often the crowds are thrown for a loop. Here nothing surprises; everything beguiles. A man allegedly boxed and shipped himself C.O.D., only to be apprehended upon arrival for entering the fair without a ticket. There's Fahreda Mahzar, "the Bewitching Bellyrina." And Bernarr MacFadden, the strong man with the exercise machines. And the stuffed carcass of Comanche, the lone survivor of Custer's Last Stand. And a nineteen-year-old named Ehrich Weiss, half of the Brothers Houdini. But today it's the sight of an orphan about to be electrocuted by men in blackface, even if it's not entirely novel, that's been drawing crowds since earliest morning.

The stage is makeshift and might topple over at any moment. At the center of the stage sits a chair into which the victim's placed. "Electrocutions, every hour! See them sizzle! See them fry! Then see them revivify!" At once, standing front and center, a woman, elderly if she's still living, calls out, "We want *blood!*" Meanwhile, the crowd around her goes wild and hoots and howls and charges, like livestock pent up for months on end and granted sudden, unexpected freedom. He does not have much time to inspect his captors as they jostle about, occasionally sprinting, as fits their fashion, from one side of the stage to the other. The shadow of Ferris's Wheel, high as the heavens, crisscrosses the stage; and off to its side drifts the Captive Balloon, which appears this noon like a giant cherry intent on escape. There are trapeze artists, as well, if that excites. Off in the distance is the quiet ticking of Western Union's network of clocks; if it weren't for Hagenbeck's Trained Animals, one might be able to hear it. If, too, the black-faced men weren't playing instruments—a *kalangu* among them—and dancing about, brisk and frenzied.

Just then, a cord of some sort is affixed to the crown of Nix's head. The men in blackface, save for the midget, wait at the far side of the stage, hovering over a box with a T jutting up from it. Very soon the crowd quiets somewhat as the midget takes the stage, front and center. "We have it in us, ladies and gents, to set the world aflame. But there are, of course, inherent dangers." The voice is practiced, deep and brawny, musically measured. "Death, for instance, ladies and gentlemen, does not affect favorites. There are methods by which we can avoid it, and that, my friends, is why we are here today. Today, for your entertainment," dramatic pause, "you will witness this boy brought to the brink of death, then brought miraculously back again!"

Nix, strapped in, hooked up, scans the crowd, searching for faces he might know, or like to. He finds none.

Kabam!

Without his knowing it, they have electrocuted him, sent a pretend charge straight into his body. For but a moment he has forgotten to play dead; then he does, perfectly. His head flops to one side and seems to rest there, dangling in a way that's anything but natural. Something, however, is amiss, for the crowd has begun to mill about anxiously, and not on account of Nix's playacting. There are gasps and screeches; at first Nix thinks it can only be part of the act.

But then he sees the smoke. Rising all about him, spumes of soot black smoke so dark he's surrounded by blackness. Were this the White City, there'd be little worry, on account of the fireboats patrolling the lagoons and the alarms wired every couple of feet by Fire Marshal Murphy (this not having helped in the case of the Cold Storage Warehouse Fire, in early July); yet, this being the Midway and situated on the other side of Illinois Central and without fire alarms, everyone, seeing the faintest trace of smoke, runs, frantic, for safety, wherever they may find it. Everyone, that is, save Nix, who doesn't know what to do. He's strapped in, trapped. And feels hands all over him, feels the straps loosen, fall. Then sees the midget right up in his face, instructing, "Come now, let's off," before, without apology, throwing the boy off the edge of the stage and into the mud.

Safe, and alive, he's told, "Run!"

He does. And soon searches about for a hootchy-kootchy girl and finds one. No, finds three of them, running against the crowd and toward the White City. Feet squelch in the slag. Mud squirts up and splatters the boy's face. The girls slip between two big-bellied men with muttonchops and head for cover—away from the wheel, which revolves still. Nix, being smitten, follows, picking his trot up into a gallop. Weaving in and out of the crowd, kootch-dancing, they move as angels, and trail a spume of jasmine that's covered only by human smells as they pass the outhouses, which are but scarcely covered cavities in the earth.

Only later, standing at the western gate of the White City, does Nix realize that the hootchy-kootchy girls have vanished. Standing in their stead now is a veritable tub of a man, with rosy jowls from which drip beads of sweat the size of eggs. He wears gray flannel and like-colored pants that puff out into balloons before being tucked into his boots. His eyes, notices Nix, are neither blue nor brown; and the skin on his face is droopy, if coarse, and pocked. Nix finds it comical and would laugh, were it not for the man clamping a claw on the boy's shoulders. Nix gags for a time while the man says, in a weasely, stentorian voice, "And what, son, do you think you're doing?"

Nix, frozen, shrugs, replies, "Um."

At which moment from their left comes a scraping so loud it drones out all else—a terrifying, harrowing sound, and both man and boy jump, startled.

The man, it seems, knows what it is; not Nix.

"Steamer pier! Battleship," shouts a man with a funny, beaver-shaped hat. It is an elevated rail come, on schedule, to pick up its passengers. Men and women, whole families dressed in woolen black, exit, while like-dressed others enter, headed for an early trip home.

At once, the man leans down, hands still gripping the boy's shoulders. He is right up and in the boy's face, smelling alarmingly of liverwurst, saying, "Well, the parade is about to start, and you best get a move on." Standing, "Now, go," and verily he pats the boy on the head.

From the far-off, the sounds of the parade—the jeers, the drums, the squeals of surprise and elation. The boy squints, mud-faced. Presently, he runs off. To where, he has no idea. He'd like very much to locate the girls he'd earlier tailed, so he glances enterprisingly about but spots only dark-garbed men, women, and children. Even here you must be on the lookout. For evil, were it to strike, would do so anywhere, regardless of one's surroundings. People here, Nix notices, have shady eyes and shrewd foreheads, their skin a waxen shade of frosty white. It is not as if he's never seen white people before, yet never so many in one place. Still, the buildings tall as the heavens all around him, Nix feels quite safe, plus excited to be here. He's down a path that cuts between two large buildings, then passes a third, smaller one, on the far side of which is a lagoon with mallards skimming the surface.

In the center of the lagoon sits an island. Here fair-goers trample through purslane and pigweed and burdock. This is the Wooded Island, where, despite its central location, those from the Republic of Hayti, China, Ceylon, Java, and Siam come and mill about and wonder– about nothing, or everything. From across the lagoon, Nix watches a family of four stop at a crown-shaped tree. He watches as Father points up and instructs the others on foliage and trunkage. Nix wants to hear but can't; he wants to learn but won't. He wants to be there, to have a family like that, not like his own. When, however, the sudden urge to swim across the lagoon and join them comes, Nix goes. He continues on, ringing the lagoon. His head craned back and to the side in wonder, he bumps into folks. Rather often he has to skitter between a man's legs or tunnel under a woman's dress, just to get out of the way.

A man in top hat and overcoat humming a song Nix has heard already twice today.

"There's a place in—"

Then two men walking, each supported by canes made of ivory.

"France."

Nix cups his hands together, creating a bowl of sorts, and places his lips to a slight hole between his thumbs, blows. The men halt at once, uncertain whether it's science or an accident that trumpets such a warning. Luckily no ladies lurk about; otherwise, their reputations, to say nothing of their confidence, might be in question— for one's porcelain leanings are best kept in the privacy of one's own abode. Their eyes meet, men and boy, and hold for a moment before disengaging. Nix is off and running, the two men talking, saying, "Do you think it's at all possible?"

"Another one?"

Nodding, "That is what they are saying."

Nix has no idea what they are talking about, nor does he care, so he doubles his step. He dodges fair-goers, but then, as if propelled, he stops. There in front of him stands a tall man with a black hat, who's glowering, and a boy who, by the looks of him, might be a replication of Nix himself—only with hair the color of flames mid-fire. It is an odd, disconcerting moment, and Nix blinks, hoping that he might cleanse his eyes of hallucination. With no luck. He blinks again, even shakes his head in disbelief, and when they're still there, right there, across a parkway, no more than a hundred yards away, Nix understands that there's only one way to remedy the situation. He traverses the parkway, to inspect. But by the time he's crossed halfway, they're gone, off to explore the White City. Nix scans about for them, hoping to catch them in the corner of an eye midstride. He doesn't.

Wind gusts in off the Midway, bringing with it the smell of cindering wood.

He passes Choral and rings the southern edge of the lagoon, past Mines and Mining and Electricity, in front of which, following a feeling, Nix halts. He looks up and around, gasping aloud when his eyes set upon the mammoth building across North Canal. Though it's scarcely past noon, the building is lit up every color of the spectrum, from the deepest blues to the most impassioned reds. A slight wind comes in off the lake, between the buildings, where it picks up force and strikes Nix with almost enough force to lift him from his feet and propel him across the way. Nix feels small. Feels, oddly, afraid for the first time since setting foot in the White City. For this is but a building that might fall at any moment. What if Nix happens to be standing right there, where he's presently standing, when the building falls—would he die, or survive? Would anyone, were he to survive, care enough to seek him out? Or would he live out his days buried under that mountain of rubble, without a soul to comfort him, living or dead? Around him fountains, directed straight out of Pegasus's mouth, shoot colored water into the air, sprinkling Nix as he passes. Gondolas, their drivers in midarpeggio, glide by as downily as a hand grazing a well-fluffed cushion. Twelve men, maybe more, row a Roman ship. Behind Nix walk two other, younger men, one of whom says, "Myself, I'm fond of the Dead Letter Office." Were it not for his fright of the deep and what might lurk even in shallow waters, Nix might sneak aboard. However, suddenly, the sky darkens, evening having encroached, as it often does upon the White City, with stealth and guile, such that each light in synchrony comes flickering to life. He shudders, such is the surprise. It is colder—so cold that Nix, wearing little, shivers. He begins to trot, then to run, and then, slipping into a passageway with gargoyles looking down from on high, to sprint.

He runs as fast as he can, as far as he can. Until, abruptly, he's alone. Smells have thickened, so much so that Nix can scarcely breathe. A white wooden gate stands open before him; through it he now passes, finding himself in an ocean of animal droppings. This is the Stock Pavilion, yet even the animals themselves have been removed, the thinking being that, with fireworks scheduled for later this evening, the animals might buck up and wreak havoc on the fair. Mud cakes, on contact, to Nix's shoes; soon he is stuck. Wind has picked up, driving with all the force of Hades from in off the lagoons, around the obelisk, and right at him.

He's about to hunker over and pry his feet from their hold when he hears a barking coming from across the pavilion. He sees the eyes first, then the rabid dog's breath. Terrified, he imagines the dog charging him, ripping at him with sharpened fangs till all that's left is a nub of Nix. Nix, being Nix, and ever mindful of how to get out of a situation, hunkers over and endeavors to unlace then slip out of his boots, and run. He takes one step, then turns, espying that the dog has likewise fled, only in the dead opposite direction. He's safe, for the moment. He places both hands on his knees, catching his breath. Then he crosses the pavilion, looking over each shoulder to make sure nobody, or nothing, is following him. All is silent, except for an occasional jeer coming from the Midway.

A dark, folded-together shape about ten yards away lies crumpled on the ground. Perhaps, he thinks, someone lost a jacket. He feels that he needs to lie down and sleep for days; perhaps this would be a good place. He could use the jacket as a pillow, or a blanket, as need be. He approaches and looks around one last time to make sure he's not being followed. It grows colder as Nix lies down, flopped to the ground. He coils up to the jacket and suffocates it with his arms, squeezing once. Presently, as if struck by a lightning bolt, yet one of ice, Nix realizes that this is not a jacket, nor a blanket, nor anything of the sort. The texture's closer to butter than cotton, and the smell is worse than that of the dung that surrounds him, but even so he falls asleep, without a care in the world, strangle-cuddling the dead body as if it were a living brother.

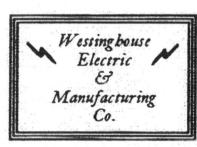

Westinghouse Electric & Manufacturing Co.

Four

From high above the White City comes the ringing of the New
Liberty Bell, a high, battle-cry sound. It has been ringing all
day and will continue well into the night. People keep time to it, and
to it some will sing. One lone cloud spots the deep blue sky, and the
temperature holds steady at a brisk fifty-two degrees on the Fahren-
heit scale. A cool noontime wind veers off the lagoon. They pass in
front of the glass-wonder of Horticulture and are halfway along
Transportation when the lagoon splits off in front of Mines and
Mining and Electricity, with its intricate frontal work and sharp-
tipped arches.

To a passing gondolier, "Espero!"

"Commandi signore," the half-sung response as the vessel closes
in on the shore.

In front of them hulks the Manufactures and Liberal Arts Building, their intended destination. The discussion at present is whether
they will go to the Dead Letter Office first or last or not at all. The
Dead Letter Office, they say, is something of a phantasmagoric
place, where waylaid love letters are perused, sometimes returned
to sender, often destroyed. There is something perverse about his
desire to go, he well knows, but still, Rockland preferring the latter,
Palmer has taken it upon himself to offer alternatives; he can always
go another time. Craning his neck back for the moment, then

endeavoring to procure a cigar from his breast pocket, Potter Palmer says, "I am open to suggestions, but I would like to make the lecture." That has been scheduled for later in the afternoon, around three, the hope being that those who attend will make it out in time for the Festival Hall Music Program, at four; the International Rope Ceremonies, at five; and at eight, fireworks, where the whole White City will be set ablaze, and not on account of a hapless cow.

"What else is there?" inquires Rockland of Manufactures, while still admiring Electricity.

"The Yerkes, I believe," says Palmer. The cigar is lit. "And a clavichord"—the former being a telescope, while the latter's thought to have once belonged to, and have been regularly played by, Bach.

"Hmmm." Rockland glances at Potter Palmer, whose mind, as happens, is elsewhere—on the fact that his debts are mounting almost as rapidly as dead boys are found, on account of the midsize house he recently purchased (on Prairie Avenue, where the Palmers used to live before moving to Lake Shore Drive), plus rumors of a strike, which would mean a rapid and ungovernable depletion in Palmer's resources, which in turn would mean an abrupt halt of the next P. Palmer project, to be called the Cosmopolitan. Designed after the world's first skyscraper, the Monadnock, right here in Chicago, and already, months before the ground has been broken, written up in half-a-dozen periodicals from Tulsa to Timbuktoo. The Cosmopolitan will be a hulking, sky-scraping beast, one dependent more on glass than on stone, and shaped as a carafe, taller than it has the base to be. As of now, all that exists of the project is a yawning trench, as big as a city block, that sits catty-corner from Palmer & Co., on State and Adams Streets. Needless to say, architectural purists have taken to ridiculing the project, one critic calling it "the very antidote to greed, a plaything for the wealthy." After this, Palmer, ever a believer in the politics of the instant, replaced his doubts with extra funding, and made a point of spending more time with his primary architect, William Rockland.

Over the calm waters of the lagoon skims a fireboat on layover. Passing, those onboard wave.

All of a sudden, they happen upon the parade. Floats bearing the titles COMMERCE and ELESTRA among them, as well as a steam-spouting electrical dragon, stream past, buoyed by a mob that's four-people-deep at its thinnest. First to pass by are the hussars—horses as big as houses ridden by men bedecked with silver and black. Then come the children, wearing clothes that range from vermilion to ochre. Girls dressed as sweet maidens and boys in threadbare uniforms, singing in unison, while a marching band plays a rousing processional. A man and woman, standing directly in front of them, begin to waltz, knocking into people. The man throws an elbow right up into William Rockland's face.

Potter Palmer wondering, "Bill?"

"There is," starts Rockland, "something about which I have been meaning to speak to you."

Potter Palmer thinking he knows what Rockland is about to say, says himself, "Not today, Bill. Let's just enjoy ourselves."

William Rockland, though, seems not to have heard and continues, "Right, but will they—"

"Strike?" Yes. "There is no doubt," says Potter Palmer. "But, Bill?" Palmer now has the elder Rockland's undivided attention. "While Mr. Armour," the meatpacking king, "has made it so that strikes are more than imminent, especially given last year's panic.

"It is a sure thing," he continues, "but it is not the end. We have no silver. Nothing with which to pay the laborers, but there are, Bill, always ways. Frankly, between you and me, I do not approve, not in the least. Silver? That is for the past," says Potter Palmer—the man who, after selling his P. Palmer and Co. store to Levi Leiter, of Maryland, and Marshall Field, of Massachusetts, came to symbolize the new prosperity and spent his consummate energies founding a Chicago dynasty; the man who was one of the first to see Chicago as a crossroads for the North and the South after the Civil War; the man who during the war dealt in cotton and land and who at the end of the war was worth more than seven million dollars; the man who, with his sufficient purse, erected the Palmer House as a gift for his wife; the man who, after losing his personal fortune when the city went up in flames, joined forces two years later in the construction of the Crystal Palace; the man who founded the Chicago Club ("Dogs, women, Democrats, and reporters need not apply"); the man who, despite his numerous trips to Europe, still had a thing for candied popped corn. "The future? There is nothing to worry about, Bill."

"You must—"

Both men, startled by the voice behind them, say, "What is it?"

The man is a Columbian Guard, or dressed as one, in brigand's leggings and a cavalier's cap, which he tips as he says, "There has been a slight altercation. Your wife, sir," whether to Rockland or Palmer isn't certain, "she's fainted."

SECURITY DEPARTMENT REPORT

Persons taken into custody for "petty pilfering"
and put off grounds on paying for goods taken *421*

Arrests *954*

Convictions *438*

Acquittals *94*

Five

All around them people jeer, slur, sneer. Before them is a pit, a circle of earthen slag large as all of downtown.

The man has him by the hand, tight. Billy's white knuckles are almost unnoticeable. Skurlock yanks him closer still, saying, "This is going to be fun."

"But it's not Electricity," Billy is quick to respond. He looks up. Skurlock does not return his look, but says, "You'll like this."

"What is it?"

"Do you," he says with a momentary glance, "know what a cowboy is?"

The boy's face brightens. A cowboy, as it happens, has since as far back as he can remember been what Billy has aspired to be; but he never thought cowboys existed, on account of his father's reminding him that they're a "fabrication, son. And as such will only disappoint, so get it out of your head as soon as you can, and you will be the better off for it." He nods, then says to the man with the black hat, "I do know what a cowboy is."

The sun, brighter now, snakes down from the azure blue sky. Out onto the stage come three bucking broncos, each of different hues—from soot black to golden brown, and each handled by a separate rider. The crowd jeers. There are yips and yaps as the riders circle round and round. Very soon the lead bronco rears back on its

hind legs, its twiggy front legs kicking at clouds of dust and splattering mud everywhere—right on Billy Rockland's face, though he
must be standing a dozen feet away. The two smaller horses, mares
if the other's a stallion, do the same. Then, together, the three
horses return to ground, where they are stilled. The lead rider then
says from his perch on the stallion, "Ladies and gentlemen, cowboys and cowgirls," in a voice that's low and shrill, "why, today! You
will see before your very own eyes—Mexicans and Indians, cowboys expert at shooting, lassoing, and riding!" The lead rider dis-
mounts from the stallion, and a short, flighty man comes and
retrieves the animal from someplace back in the clouds of dust.
"And now, I introduce to you! The man whose show this is!"
Cheers. "William Cody! Or as you may know him—Buffalo Bill!"

Though he's attempting a better vantage, Billy Rockland still
can't see well, on account of the man's iron grip. The crowd around
him goes wild. People jeering, hooting, whistling as a backlit figure
emerges from the dust, a man dressed as the earlier man, though
in altogether more colorful garb—leather, red, yellow, turquoise
beads, turquoise jewelry, silver resplendent. Broad of shoulder,
lanky of leg. His walk is long and dragging, and it takes upwards of
four minutes for the man to amble as much as ten feet toward the
audience. It is, to Billy, almost comical, and he'd like to call out,
"Come on, hurry up!" In fact, he is about to, has dropped his lower
lip and placed his tongue to the top of his mouth, when off in the
distance he spots—that face. She is, as usual, smiling, so that, while
at first he's frozen with shock, very soon he's smiling back at her,
aglow. For what must be a moment but passes for ages, she holds,
statuesque, at a remove from those directly around her. Her hair, as
his, is fiery red and falls in ringlets around and over pasty skin. He
might even set off across the slag stage and introduce himself and
inquire of her what she thinks—"I'm thrilled," he'd say. "You?"
Instead, a hand's clamped around his neck, and a voice commands,
"Pay attention."

Clouds soon move in over the spectacle. The sky darkens, then
lightens, as if on cue. Buffalo Bill doffs his ten-gallon hat. His countenance, when Billy finally sees it, is veiled by an especially long and

red beard; the exposed part has leathery, divoted skin. His chest
swells, and so do his cheeks. He says, and the crowd quiets when he
does, "It was a long time ago altogether, an age of barbarism and
skip-shot individualism. Our country was young, and our ancestors
were ready to make it or be broken by what lay out there"—gesturing
with his long, long arms—"out west. For those of you who are new to
such a thing—today you will witness, with your citified eyes, what it
was like. Cowboys and Indians battling it out . . . you will meet
tough-gun Annie Oakley . . . and see, in all its gore, a buffalo hunt,
and . . . special for you folks here today . . . a reenactment of the
infamous Last Stand of General George Custer, in which," and at
this his head lowers, and he steps back, "I so happened to be a par-
ticipant." Pause. "Of course, I will be representing myself." Everyone
laughs. Billy looks on in amazement. "And now it is time to feast
your eyes on the first epoch, beginning with wild beasts and Indians."

Just now, as the dust settles somewhat, the Plains Indian dancers
come to the fore from the sideline, dancing and hip-swiveling. From
the yonder struts one white man, then another. The crowd remains
transfixed, quiet, so as to hear a lady, at some remove from the Rockland boy, cough. "Ooooh." "Aaaaahhhh." The drawn-out sounds of
women swooning. Amid the swoons and continued elongated jeers,
the stage once again clears, as fleetly as the sun slips behind a purple-
shadowed mountain, and out saunters—for this is a saunter, no mis-
taking it, and much practiced—a rather surprisingly stub-figured
young lady. Buffalo Bill emerges yet again and introduces her as
Annie Oakley, "Little Sure Shot." Taciturn as marksmen tend to be,
she says nothing—just aims, trigger-fingered, and shoots across a
great expanse of dust three tin cans in succession. To Billy's direct
right, a mother tells her son, "Now, dear, watch how she aims that."

Out into the slag rides a man with a white hat, and from the opposite direction a man with a black hat, both of them outfitted in black
velvet, upon which are attached little orbs of silver and bobbles made
of lace. Lacy, too, are the lassoes they begin to whirl high above their
heads as they trick-ride off into the distant dust. After a moment,
hundreds of riders enter from the left, while easily a hundred more

riders come in from the right—these last riders being shirtless, with hair long and resplendent in the wind, tied up and knotted with fabrics from vermilion to sun yellow. They hold long spears, to which are attached free-flowing feathers. Billy Rockland himself is loud as can be, full of little beeps and giggles, blips and guffaws. Shrieks and war cries hold steady across the midafternoon sky.

Very soon young Rockland has quieted, watching in utter silence as shirted and shirtless ride right at, and into, each other, spears or rifles positioned skyward. The horses range in color from cream white to shoe-polish black. As the horses rear back, legs kicking into the air, the muscles in their hind legs go taut, and riders shriek as some dismount, or are dismounted, and carry on the quarrel, fistfighting, if they can. They go at each other with knives, the blades of which have been dulled so as not to pierce actual skin. Dust is somehow kicked up, although the earth is muddied and as wet as the Nile. Billy has the idea to step out into it. He makes a jerk and then a thrust, his whole body drawn right into the fracas, out of excitement no less than fear. But a hand clamps right down on his shoulder and squeezes so tightly that Billy squeals, and the man with the black hat, not the one in the show but the one from the isle, lifts his capture up all hugger-mugger and begins to whisk him away. "Here we go now. That's enough fabrication to last you a lifetime," he says. And with that they're off.

Six

Ferris's Wheel casts its shadow even here, someplace not too distant from Public Comfort—the building, not the sentiment. Officer Debs rests for a brief moment before leaning over the woman, gripping her forearm rather forcibly, and saying, "You all right?" Shifty eyes darting to and fro. Music streams in from the nearby Electricity Building off in the distance. A small crowd has gathered.

"Ow," and Debs loosens his grip.

The woman has somehow twisted herself into a human pretzel. Her arms are up and folded awkwardly together. Her legs have been folded back and up along her spine. She should, with medical certainty, be in deep pain, yet the look upon her face says otherwise. Though one eye is open while the other's closed, there's a certain cherubic placidity in her creaseless cheeks. Her lips are touched together without being pursed; her skin is porcelain without having broken into a sweat.

They have cleared a ten-foot-by-ten-foot square around her so that air, should she desire it, will be accessible.

As the world around her comes back into focus, she notices another man whose breath is rank and whiskeyed. All he says is, "You brute."

"I'm just check—" Still, Debs lifts her. She lies there all a-grimace.

A woman up and fainting in the White City is a sight seldom seen, so, when Elizabeth Rockland collapsed, the crowd stirred about, unsure of what to do. Some just stood about, looking confusedly at one another or away at the far-off wheel, while others returned back inside to take in yet more art—Mozart's spinet, the king of Bavaria's furniture. Only after the guards had been summoned did the crowd wander back outside to see what might have happened.

"See, she's fine, you old ox," Chief Detective Simonds, of the Central Detective Detail, says, pushing aside the ruddy-faced Columbian Guard and taking his place right up in her face. They have been bickering since dawn about whether it's prudent to work nights while your family lies in wait, not attending the fair—whether on protest or because of the killer isn't clear. Debs being a solid go-getter, plus having little family to speak of, he takes the side of work over life. Whereas Simonds, having a new wife of late, would like a little free time to spend at home. Were it not for their polar outlooks, something might be resolved; as it is, nothing ever will be.

Debs's breath, Mrs. Rockland can't help but notice, smells frumpishly of the butcher's. He's 250 if he's a pound. His jowls are swollen as a puffer fish and all a-bulge.

It's time to move her. Guardedly, as you might relocate a fragile object from its mantel of long habitation, they move her upright, hoping that, once vertical, she may recall what it is she's trying to say. The reports were that this woman was mad, crazy, roving the grounds in a circular fashion while exclaiming the Devil's articulations. Yet, upon arrival, Chief Detective Simonds recognized this woman as the wife of one of the fair's few benefactors, Potter Palmer. Quickly it was brought to his attention, by Mrs. Palmer no less, that this woman was in fact a Rockland, and when Simonds glanced at her as though she were speaking in the tongue of a Laplander, the matter was dropped. Frequently Mrs. Rockland is mistaken for a Palmer, and at times they play it off, much to their own, if nobody else's, amusement. Yet not now, as Mrs. Rockland falls again and lies horizontal, listless and murmuring, "My husb—"

"Yes, yes," says Simonds. Quickly he turns to Debs. "Find—"

"Here he is! Gentlemen," an urgent Potter Palmer says, "kindly move aside."

By now the once-small crowd has been sowed to a good three dozen onlookers. People walking past stop to see what has happened. Women, children, top-hatted men stand in all kinds of positions—arms akimbo or floppy armed, half-standing, befuddled, wary. Quite a few of them are a-fright, for this is the heart of the White City, as far from the Midway Plaisance as water is from oil.

The crowd parts for William Rockland, yet he doesn't move closer. He stands there stone-faced, unsure of what exactly is happening and what exactly he should do. That is his wife, after all, lying on the ground, surrounded by strangers. Her body is bent together as if by a ghoul; her face is red as a beet; yet the rest of her pales to an almost greenish milky sheen. She could, he thinks, be dead. Such are his preoccupations that he doesn't scan around for his junior, doesn't even think to wonder what happened, doesn't do much of anything but gape. At last, Palmer gives him a nudge in the right direction.

"Where's Billy?"

SECURITY DEPARTMENT REPORT (cont.)

Number of reports of children lost *30*

Number of reports of children restored to parents *20*

Number of reports of "shadowy, suspicious" persons *539*

Seven

Past warehouses, tenant shacks, blacking factories, soap boilers, dyers, and tanning yards. Past gnarled trees and through alleyways strewn with all measure of paper-scabs, broken glass, ironscraps gone to rust, while the sky above holds a striking bruise purple. Through city marshlands, down streets without lantern, across railroad tracks, divots, and over the river in all its blue-green transparency. Past buildings as long as whole blocks and high as the heavens and equipped with chimneys set to smoking.

Finally here's a small anonymous building with a red door.

They start off one after the other—Skurlock the length of a grown giraffe in front of Billy, who's not sure why he's following this man but knows they will find something. He'd like at last to find something that holds his interest for more than an instant. He did try to give some protestation back at the Midway, but then he grew weary of it and stopped. A fatigue washed over him, and he could move no longer; now he's excited by the change of scenery—the sheer, yet brittle, newness of it excites him as the New World once did many an explorer. A single lantern, the only one on the block, hangs to the immediate right of the door, so that, as he enters, half of him is lit while the other half remains shadowed. The floor— wood panels by the sound of it—has many holes, so Skurlock instructs him to watch his step. They are in transit for ten whole minutes when they come to a blockade, and Skurlock, still wearing his threadbare greatcoat despite the coal-oven heat, does not know which way to turn. It is the kind of dark in which one holds a hand right up in front of one's face and still cannot see it. Music can suddenly be heard, at first at some remove but then right up and nestled in your ear. Laughter, too. On the far side of the cast-iron red door, the hushed murmur of people carrying on what passes these days for conversations, consisting more of silence and sudden volume than of anything substantial. There are shrieks of pleasure or its opposite, young Rockland isn't sure. Something bangs against the floor or a wall. A back-bellied, hippopotamus-throated groan is heard. Skurlock, standing there for a full minute, rasps on the door. The door opens.

Inside, everything is rose red or faintly pink—the draperies, the sofas, the women, the clothes—what little remain on the women— and the color of the women's cheeks. Once fully inside, Hannibal Skurlock, after an entire minute spent standing in one place, doffs his black hat again and holds it to his side. He turns to the kid and instructs him to do the same, even though Billy only wishes he were wearing a hat. Unaccustomed to the sudden exposure to light, Billy Rockland bumps into Skurlock, and then, as the man is cliff and plateau in one, he falls back giggling and beginning to blush. The womenfolk themselves, as though giggling, circle around the stranger and his young friend—his son, is what they figure, and one of them, with raven-colored hair and coarse cheekbones, inquires, "How old is he?" While another, a blonde, adds, "He looks just like you!" Everyone except Skurlock laughs at that one, for it's true, unbelievable as it may seem, that in every way, except perhaps phrenologically, Hannibal Skurlock and young Rockland do indeed look alike—identical, almost, if it weren't for the discrepancy in size.

Three more women, each with a bodice of an entire other color—red, green, and blue—enclose the two new strangers: "You are new in town, yes?" "We do not recognize you." "How exciting!" This last from a thin-chested redheaded woman—a girl, really, not much older than Billy, whose eyes are the color of chestnuts, and whose arms drape over Skurlock, and whose lips land like fallen leaves on the man's jawbone. Even Billy can hear her whisper, "You, my dear, are irresistible."

Then, from behind sheets the approximate color of the vascular organ, in waddles Madame du Convorce, her hair like a skunk's, a mix of black and white in all types of comical patterns. Her bosom is perky, despite her evident age, and almost as welcoming as her smile, as she announces, "We have white, black, yellow—any color you would like. We have old girls, and young, and even—for a price—a virgin, for your very own. . . ."

An old man wearing suspenders sits in full slump before a player piano that he's not playing.

She practically mows Skurlock down. Then steps aside and says, "Well then. It's . . . you."

Here's a silence. He stares at du Convorce without so much as a blink, then says, "A remembrance you might never have wanted to revisit, but oh, hell. I pray you have forgiven me."

"Not quite," she says dimly. "This business or pleasure?"

"Perhaps," he says, "a little bit of both."

"No matter." She shrugs. "And your friend?"

"He is my brother," says Skurlock. "Cute, isn't he?"

This being a brothel, inside it's rather dark, though not as dark as in the hallway, for there's a chandelier high above made of whiskey bottles, which sways without cessation—though it gives off little actual light. Still, he can see that what slight smile she came into this room wearing has now all but scattered.

The room smells of pudenda, jasmine, and fecal matter.

Madame du Convorce, slow to respond, says at last, "It has been awhile, hasn't it?" Silence, then, "You have been keeping busy, I understand."

Skurlock says with a nod, "Mm."

She refrains, but says, "One reads these things in the papers, but doesn't think about them until long after—until presented with it."

"Quite," says Skurlock. He offers the madame a sack, it seems, of ample coin.

She takes it but does not count the coins. Her teeth are as mahogany.

"Your friends," du Convorce says as she waddles away, "are in back." The room clears of women. "Waiting."

Billy Rockland sits back in a chair with a goat's head on each armrest and fabric resplendent with stones that glimmer. He is not sure how he got here from the gleaming White City and realizes, only now, that he has not seen his parents for quite some time and perhaps they might be fretting over his absence. But then it was Mother, wasn't it, who wanted more space, who wanted the company of her women friends and not that of the only child she has left her in this world?

"Hey, there," Skurlock says, and he taps the boy on the left shoulder. "Let's us go." Through a bookcase that opens upon touch and leads to a second passageway, this one lit by torch, they descend down and into a basement room where it is as cold as a meat freezer—which is what it is, a converted meat freezer. In lieu of still-bloody carcasses hanging on hooks are a few of the women from upstairs, half-clothed, their bodices ripped, skittering around as bubbly as all carbonation and as tart. Seated at an ovoid table are three men to whom Billy's soon introduced—Wade Graft, whose hair is one shade this side of crimson; Jimmer Fallon, whose cheeks are like a seal's, fatty, and who presently tips back a squat jug of absinthe and breathes out the libation, making chimpanzee sounds. Soon a third man hacks phlegm and says, "Good Lord, man—who's the kid?"

"Just some kid," says Skurlock.

Wade Graft, rising to greet Skurlock, says, "You're not going to the meeting?" Right now in front of the stockyards there's a gathering scheduled. Everyone is going, except Skurlock. That's either anger or disappointment in Graft's tone; either way, Skurlock will have none of it. He ignores Graft, but the third man, who's the relative size and shape of young Billy Rockland but who has a chalk white full-grown beard down half his chest, says, "We know what happened last time, Han."

"Wait," says Wade Graft. He purloins the absinthe and makes a go for Skurlock's boy, attempting to grab a tuft of hair.

Skurlock shields Billy and says, "We're tired."

"Have you," says Graft to Fallon, "heard the one about Wade's mother and the rhinoceros?"

"Why, no," a bemused Fallon says.

"It seems she had use for the second horn," and to Skurlock, "or was that the enema? I forget. It was only last night, but seems ages ago."

"It's your mother who prefers a good whipping," says Fallon. "Does he have a name?"

Skurlock, hand still on little Rockland's shoulder, grins while Billy says, "Billy."

After a silence, Fallon says, "Not like last time, Han." He peers around the room, and when he feels like it, he smiles. Billy walks on up to Fallon and asks, "What's that?" In reference to a piece of parchment upon which has been inscribed a picture—although what it is meant to depict, only its creator could know. Billy reaches out for it as Fallon snatches it away.

"It's mine," says Fallon. "Don't."

Wade Graft and the third man, absinthe shared freely between them, are engaged in a game of cards. They sit about and loaf, as bread in an underheated oven, talking at length about anything that pleases them. Jimmer Fallon, his cheeks ballooned out to Ceylon, has taken it upon himself to play his silver harp, which he carries in his vest pocket and kisses—for luck, naturally—before playing. Fallon says, "It's a pitiful lad come up to me and offer to tell me a joke for quite a bit of change. He was a sad fellow and without teeth. Do you know," glancing at the half-clothed womenfolk, "what we called them where I come from. Coonts. For they are as moist, and as slippery, as that most venerable," pause, "organ. As I say, he offered me a joke, and I, being myself, agreed and set about to wait for the punch line. Well, none came. The man, it seems, could not control his functions, and soon a most peculiar odor had crawled up my nose," he says. And promptly starts to blow at—or through—his instrument.

Wade Graft, with his meaty hands, bangs upon the poker table. Fallon, ever a shy soul, rises at once, to spritz Graft's face with libation. A fight promptly ensues—Fallon swings at Graft, Graft swinging back, but no one connects. Then, lunging across the table, Graft leaps for his foe's jugular. Billy, in the meantime, scans the shadow-stitched room for Skurlock and finds him seated upon a large chair with ivory posts. A woman with (he can see it even in the darkness, it's so bright) scarlet hair kneels in front of him as if praying. Skurlcok's own head is back, slack, and he appears as if in reverie. Billy Rockland looks for a moment, then looks away. Even once he's looked away, he can still see, crisp as daylight, the woman's head bobbing like a pump in a dynamo, so fast she almost blurs. Unable to help himself, Billy turns once again to watch. But she stops her bobbing and gazes directly at him, fixing her eyes upon him. Her face, even from this vantage, appears cratered, divot-pocked, and dry. She appears to have only one eye, black veins swirled in a red sea on account of her hair's phosphorescence, or Billy himself has drifted into reverie. He seats himself with his back bracing a wall as Fallon and Graft follow each other out the door and upstairs. Very soon the woman with the scarlet hair exits, followed by Skurlock, who doesn't bother to turn and catch Billy's eye before it shuts out the light of this world.

Eight

Out front, an oak tall as a skyscraper buckling in the wind. The squat hedge, once green as emeralds, has burnt to a dark russet color and gone wild and gangly as a starburst midburst. There's sun, but it comes and goes. Inside, the drapes have been pulled, so it's dark as Hades, or perhaps that's just the anxiety that's crept into the house.

Potter Palmer and William Rockland sitting in facing chairs downstairs in the unfinished study, Palmer with his legs crossed and hands in an arch upon his lap, "They've imported a sleuth from Boston, I hear, who studied under Professor James." To Palmer's surprise, Rockland has yet to show even one single sign of disquiet—he even looks sedated, with a face that resembles a mask and eyes that look without seeing. His hands are folded upon his lap; he appears to be praying. "I hear," says Palmer, "that it's a woman, no less. That's what they're saying. Bill?"

Just then, there's a sudden, pungent smell of java in the air, although the only thing in this house that's brewing is distress.

Rockland says, "I'm thirsty."

"You should eat," says Palmer. He uncrosses his legs and sits forward, making as if to stand, but doesn't. "May I fix you something—a sandwich, tea?"

"I am fine, thank you," Rockland chuckling. The thought of Potter Palmer—who has a servant for his wardrobe, for his hair, and to fix his breakfast, and yet another to drive his carriage to work, not to mention his personal assistant—fixing finger sandwiches and tea amuses William Rockland no end, so that very soon he has keeled over, gripping his stomach from excessive laughter.

Palmer does stand, and he paces. He lights a cigar, offers one to Rockland, which he refuses. Palmer says, "Here, I'll brew some tea," and repairs to the kitchen to set a pot aboil. When he returns, Rockland has one leg up and over the armrest, lounging, and swigs from a silver-plated flask. His eyes, when he turns to face Palmer, are red as beets, with veins running spindly over the cornea.

"I like what you're doing with the cornice," says Palmer, eyes taking inventory of Rockland's study. "Oh, and the molding on that chandelier—divine." Just before construction of the White City began, in 1891, William Rockland purchased this house at a modest price, the prices having dropped precipitously once Palmer led the charge away from Prairie Avenue, and set about to redesign the interior. Initially focusing on the upstairs bedrooms, bathrooms, and kitchen, leaving the study to be his "personal sanctuary," replete with a drafting table pilfered from the old Adler and Sullivan offices in the Rookery. At the time, Rockland hadn't yet been made a design partner. He'd started as an engineer in the employ of Burnham and Root, but his interests, once focused on calculating severe wind threats on masonry buildings, soon grew to include gables, mullions, and mansard roofs.

He fully immersed himself in the re-creation of his abode. It was his first real house, Billy had just started school, and William Senior still went flush in the face whenever his wife so much as smiled his way. Back then, too, it was still considered chic to live on Prairie Avenue. Marshall Field's and George Pullman's mansions, having been erected on bare prairie, were counted among its residences. Rockland would return from work and promptly retire to his study to draft. But once the planning and construction of the White City began in earnest, Rockland neglected his vision.

Another swig from his flask and Rockland saying, "The first time I met her, I never considered it would lead to this—a house, a child.

She was just a girl, a beautiful, strange girl with awkward mannerisms and crooked teeth, certainly not the person I thought I'd spend
the rest of my life with. A summer night, and Elizabeth knew better
than I. But, alas, I was a brute. Perhaps we were forced into it, the
marriage. I had feelings for her certainly, but love? It hadn't bloomed
yet. I don't know if she would have married me if it weren't for that
night, Tom," stealing a glance at Palmer. The man paces still; the
floor, on account of his bulk, creaks with every stride. The light
from the oil lantern in the front hallway cuts sidewise, so Palmer's
shadow grows longer the farther away he paces, appearing like a
shadow belonging to a Sasquatch and not a robber baron. Rockland
eyeballs the shadow, swigs, and then promptly spits up what he's just
swigged, on account of a guffaw. "Not my proudest moment, but
perhaps it has something to do with what has happened. Is it possible? That I did not love him enough."

Palmer, his pacing stopped now, responds, "The sleuth? I hear
she studied under William James, the one with the odd brother."

Rockland takes the time to rearrange himself in his chair, crossing and then uncrossing his legs. He breathes in a large gulp of air,
mussing his hair with a hand, which then finds its way over his face.
Another swig, and then he wonders aloud, "Where do you think he
is now, Tom?"

And when Palmer doesn't respond, again, "Tom?"

A nod, a swig, another guffaw.

"You should get some rest," Palmer says, "perhaps talk with your
wife."

Rockland's up and dancing around the study, whether with a
phantom or just himself isn't clear. His body moves as a drunk's,
awkwardly and without much grace, banging chairs, setting the chinaware in the cabinet across the room to rattle. Words dribble out of
his mouth, which Palmer can't discern on account of Rockland's
inebriated slur. Palmer is rather shocked, seeing that Rockland
hasn't been a drinker for as long as they've known each other; past
abuse of the bottle has been hinted at but not laid bare, so Palmer's
never known for certain. Shocked and frightened, for now Rockland charges at him full on, misses his target, and instead rams the

very edge of the fireplace, slitting his forehead. Blood squirts the near wall and splotches Rockland's steam-pressed shirt. Palmer offers help—a handkerchief to blot the blood. Rockland, though, shoves his friend away and says, "I'm fine," collapsing to the floor, his head in his knees and arms shielding himself.

Palmer stands there a full minute, then says, "Bill? Are you all right?" But keeps his distance. It must be difficult, Palmer knows, although he has not even a guess as to what it's like, losing a child; it must be worse than anything in Creation. He would like to console William, to offer whatever strength he can marshal—a calming embrace, an assurance that this will be over presently. After all, all Bertha has been talking about for the past few months is the prospect of having a Palmer junior. Now that this has happened, what will Bertha think? Will she still want a child? With the killer a-lurk, is it even a sound plan? Palmer being a realist, this is what he thinks about, not whether he'll be able to sleep again. With this in mind, he repairs upstairs to check on his wife and the grieving Elizabeth Rockland. William, by all appearances, is now asleep, slumped over on his side where floor meets wall. . . .

The teakettle whistling without remit.

"Hello?" The house, upon his wakening, feels abandoned; perhaps it is. Again, "Hello? Elizabeth, dear, are you home?" He hears nothing in reply, so he stands, thinking he'll scavenge, but as soon as he lifts himself, he keels over on account of his heavy head. At last, he stands and searches about downstairs for his wife, before treading upstairs. He pretends he knows what he'll say once he locates her; pretends, too, that he knows what to say to Billy once he's found—thinking that he, William, will be the one to find his son, not some sleuth. Upstairs, he checks every room, frantic, throwing open each door with a force that surprises him, and in Billy's room the door jams into the wall behind it, spearing the plaster. He realizes that he has nothing to say to his wife, nothing at all. William decides, then, that the best course of action to take is just that—action. He'll set off and search out Clemantis himself, if that's what it takes. He won't— he cannot—wait around for the official search to run its course.

Upstairs it's dark as night, but William stops in front of the Winslow Homer, a housewarming gift from the Palmers. It depicts, in swirling blacks and deep-set blues, a seascape in which a lone skiff, captained by a lone fisherman, embarks on a week's lonely voyage, set against all manner of wind and wave. Some waves loom the height of sky-scrapers and jut up into a sky that can't be distinguished from the sea. William stands there for eons, not so much staring at the painting (it's too dark for that) as letting what colors he can see blur and swirl in his mind till he's quite dizzy indeed.

She's in bed, the blankets pulled up almost to her eyes. Light streams in through the edges of the drawn curtains, then diffuses into blackest darkness, so all that's visible is a pale, white sliver of light dancing upon her forehead.

Awakened by his body pressed up against hers, she opens her mouth to speak, but the muscles don't work; she's dry, fatigued. She shakes—whether from cold or fright isn't certain.

"Sorry," says William. "Did I wake you?"

"Is it morning yet?" When he says nothing, she sits up in bed and says, "I'm not sure what you have planned for today, but would you please take Billy to school? I don't think I can muster the strength to get out of bed quite yet, dear." Eyes closed now, "I might have caught a cold."

There are many ways a husband can hold his wife, but at present William Rockland cannot for the life of him think of one. As a con-sequence, he just lies there embracing himself. Being a Rockland, he has the unfortunate ability to listen without quite hearing, so that words, no matter how loudly or clearly enunciated, drift in one ear and then right out the other. He knows what his wife just said, that she most certainly is delusional and might need to be taken to stay at Dr. Kellogg's sanitarium (he's threatened to take her there before, but never had the heart), that he at least should set her straight, remind her what's happened, that they've lost their only son. But here, in this day, in this age, in this house, denial runs deep. It's best, at times, to just push on to let things fall by the wayside and pretend they never happened.

"It would be a big help, dear."

He thinks to say, Do you not remember? Billy's gone. Instead, he says nothing.

A hand finds its way under the covers and along her torso in search of her own hand, to hold it. But he finds only fabric and more fabric, no flesh. She is still wearing her day dress, a heavy, black, funereal affair with a hoop midriff that balloons out almost to Kathmandu. He turns down the covers and begins to unclasp her dress's clasps, but she elbows him away and rolls herself onto her side and into a ball. He hovers over her, searching for an opening to hold her. Reaches out to her, to run a hand along the downy side of her face, to soothe her, to calm her. Perhaps, since words won't work, actions will; his touch becomes a declaration of continued love. But when his skin touches hers, he notices that hers seems liquefied, isn't malleable so much as a steady stream of clammy perspiration. Under her in bed is a puddle. Perhaps she has wet herself.

"Please don't keep Billy waiting, dear. Go now." He does, with a peck on her cheek.

Nine

$\mathcal{L}$ ondon's had its Jack the Ripper killings, but Chicago's victims are boys. After the first killing, no mother let her young son or daughter out of eyeshot for more than a moment. When schools opened, attendance was next to nil. Things have relaxed somewhat since then, because even with the killings, a fair's a fair and has its own magical, enigmatic allure. Attendance has risen, although it's hard to believe that, since opening, the White City's attracted nearly half the world's population. By pure statistics, it's no wonder that the White City has drawn a killer. Alongside the world's greatest achievements, there's evil, unchecked and in hiding.

Since she's been here every day she's wandered the city. Every day a different neighborhood; her shoes as a result have worn nearly through the sole, and her feet are incredibly blistered. Short of the killer walking up to her in broad daylight and introducing himself, she is well aware that this is not the way to go about searching for him, wandering aimlessly, as if propelled by a force larger than herself. Instead, she knows, one must have drive, one must have a *plan*, one must *know*. Having developed the morning's photographs, she exits the White City at 56th Street and walks west to Stony Island Avenue. She looks south toward the Midway, looks north toward the Loop. In all directions, smoke blackens the wakening city. After a few moments, she catches a covered phaeton, Loop-bound. They

pass neighborhoods with garbage piled along sidewalks and brimming from alleyways. Boys emerge from between the garbage
mounds, alerted by the thundering of the carriages' iron wheels on
the cobblestones. Farther north the streets empty, the sky darkens,
and in her fatigue Dr. Handley mistakes day for night. On account
of Mayor Harrison ordering business suspended citywide, the
Loop's vacant—not a soul in sight.

The phaeton lets her off at West Randolph, a strip of meatpacking warehouses just north of downtown. She walks west along the
avenue, stepping through pools of blood and over the occasional
street-side animal carcass. Even though it's not yet noon, the day
has already darkened to dusk. Packs of stray dogs cross the street,
bringing with them a cloud of buzzing flies. Even with the garbage, there's a pungent smell of jasmine in the air. A block and a half
west, the carcass of a horse lies in the street where it was trampled
by a passing coach, hours or days earlier.

"Miss," right behind her. She turns, but does not appear startled.

He is tall as a beanstalk, with cheeks as if sucked of life. Large
gopher's teeth going off in every direction imaginable. His breath is
so pungent it just about knocks her out. Bits of trash hang from his
garb, which is ill-fitting. If that's a smile across his face, she's chosen
the wrong profession and might be better served on the opposite
end of the couch, in psychoanalysis. With a gruffness that might
alarm any other soul, the man then jerks out both arms, offering
what's in the basket of his hands, which Dr. Handley at first assumes
is a pile of human waste. It is but a cat, black as night save for one
snow white stripe down its snout. Yellow, electric eyes. Whiskers
long as feathers. After a time, the man implores, "Take her, please.
She's hungry."

Just then, a phaeton charges right by them. Mud splatters up all
over Dr. Handley's dress and face and in her eyes. She doesn't wipe it
off. She only says, "Perhaps you should have taken better care of
her," and walks off across the street. She glances back over her
shoulder, thinking that perhaps she should have taken the trashman's cat, but it's too late, the trashman's gone. The Monadnock
looms like a phoenix into the heavens. It's not so much capturing

the killer as *understanding* the urge to murder. She must exhaust
every option; she must scavenge the city until every last dark corner
has been routed out; otherwise, she will have failed not only a grieving metropolis but an entire nation.

A flush of voices, first softer, then louder, all around her. Voices
behind her, in front, or to the side. She hears footsteps behind her.
Turns, but sees nothing. She feels as if she's being chased. Nervousness crawls along her skin, breaking her into a sweat. She doesn't
know what time it is—either she's been wandering the city for hours
or for but a few fleeting moments. In her pursuit of killers, time
escapes her. If she were to encounter the killer right here and right
now, would she be ready?

SALOON, the sign rickety and blowing in the wind.

It's a black cast-iron door opening into a room so smoky, it's like
swimming, entering. Dr. Handley sneezes, first just once but then
again and again and again. Three men are at the bar, one behind the
bar, one off to the rear, his black bowler pulled low, veiling his eyes,
and the third standing, but with one leg crossed over the other, so
he appears as a flamingo.

"Sir," the bartender says.

She can hardly breathe on account of the smoke, but still manages to say, "Could you point me to the W.C.?"

A long silence. "I'm sorry, ma'am, but this is a men's-only establishment." He has loose, flabby cheeks and eyes like marbles, piercing in a blank way. "I'm afraid you'll have to leave."

She might retrieve her government-issued identification card;
she might explain in her slight whisper that there will be a day when
women will be able to enter a local saloon and drink alongside men;
she might begin to recite James's *The Principles of Psychology,* the first
twenty pages of which she knows by heart; she might just lean over
the bar, grab the flabby-cheeked bartender by his lapels and lean
right up in his face, telling him, in a voice deeper than any she's
mustered before, that in fact she will stay and due to his rudeness
will drink for free, but she doesn't. Instead, she decides to leave; she
doesn't have the energy to stay. She'll return to her room at the
Palmer House. She'll close the curtains and sleep, and perhaps,

when she wakes, everything will be different; it will be like this never happened; there will be no killer, and she'll be here simply on vacation, a few days lollygagging in the big city.

Back at the Palmer House, Inspector Moreau's pacing in the lobby. He must have been waiting a long while, for when she enters, her face caked black with soot, he strides right up to her, grips her by her left elbow, and marches her across the lobby with the chandeliers as big as elephants and down a hallway with tessellated marble. Just outside the barbershop with the silver-dollar floor, he says, in a whisper, "He's taken another."

SECURITY DEPARTMENT REPORT (cont.)

Ten

It's not quite midnight, but it feels much later, as if morning has crept without so much as a whimper upon the night. William Rockland, though he knows this city as if by rote, feels lost. He wanders from Prairie Avenue south toward the White City, passing through empty streets and dim-lit alleys with smoke curling up into the starless sky. Soon, as if by divine intervention, he finds his way west to Ashland Avenue, where the stockyards start.

It's a meeting of sorts, dozens of men gathered around multiple campfires. Some hang from empty railroad cars, others pace about, kicking mud that's mixed with blood either animal or human or both, while others sit along the many bridges that crisscross the yards, with their feet dangling. Some bite into the carcasses of chickens that are being charred in the campfires, while others guzzle bottles that too appear charred, on account of the soot that's falling from a far-off chimney like snow, only black as ink. Their faces are masked by soot, so they appear as if in blackface. The feeling here, though, is far from minstrelsy. In fact, it's rather somber, despite the songs, many of them of a jubilant tempo, being sung fireside. Barrels are beat like drums, hands clap, and one fellow, with muttonchops so expansive they might as well be wings, plays a silver harp the sheen of which nearly blinds anyone who passes. William Rockland, as he shimmies between the muttonchop man and another, similarly bushy-faced fellow, spots his reflection in the harp and just about faints from fright—his face has swollen to the size, shape, and color of that new concoction, the basketball.

Above, that's either a shooting star or an ember gone astray.

Not looking, Rockland walks right into a tall and lanky man with a scar running from eyeball to ear, who says, "You better sit—here," offering a charred bottle. Rockland bats the bottle away, but the man, who despite his appearance proves more brawny than frail, forces the bottle in Rockland's mouth and halfway down his throat, till he's choking up a libation that's more poison than tonic. Soon, however, he feels a warmth skitter over his skin and seep down into his blood so that, before he knows it, he's tired. Almost keeling over, the brawny man places an arm around Rockland and more or less lifts him over to an upturned crate that's a foot too close to the campfire, since within minutes his face is seared.

Two similarly willowy men surround Rockland, speaking among themselves, "He's one of them, he is."

"Nice garb," as the second man fists Rockland's lapel and then releases it. "Expensive, to be sure." Rockland's lapel is made from silk imported from Ceylon—a gift, of course, from Potter Palmer. His watch is what's noticed next, and promptly snatched; the first man says, "Always wanted one of these, myself," both men cackling, which draws a crowd. Upwards of a half-dozen others now surrounding Rockland, who's still seated and by now has been deprived of half of his garments. They've left him only his pants and undershirt, which as soon as it's exposed is dusted with soot.

At first, Rockland's frightened. He's far from the sort of man who gets involved in a brawl, especially when he's outnumbered, but perhaps against his better judgment he's up and over the scar-faced man. By the look on his face, the man's more confused than surprised or startled—forehead scrunched together, eyes piercing, lips pursed. But when Rockland grabs the man by his own lapels and, to everyone's surprise, lifts him half a foot off the ground, the man appears petrified, if only momentarily. Rockland very nearly bellows, "Where's my son?"

"Sorry?" The men look on, confused.

"Take me to him," says Rockland. "I know he's here. Some-where."

Perhaps they'd know what he's talking about; they'd have heard the news, but what with them being laborers and working twelve-hour days in temperatures exceeding one hundred degrees in the summer and at a pay so low they can barely afford to eat, let alone provide for their families, many of them in foreign lands, they haven't heard anything about the missing Rockland boy. Many know of Clemantis, having heard the rumors—he's a monster; he's possessed by the Devil; he *is* the Devil; or, the running gag in the packinghouses, that Clemantis is, in fact, Hempstead Washburne, the Republican who lost to Carter Henry Harrison, a Democrat, in the April 1891 mayoral elections. A ridiculous notion, to be sure, but one that helps pass the time. All in all, though, everyone here thinks William Rockland a madman, perhaps an escaped lunatic who somehow got his hands on lavish threads. He's a street robber; he's a hooligan; he's a highwayman; he's a coiner; he's a footpad; he's a horse-stealer; he's a thief in need of being roughened up a bit. To this end, a man with what appears to be a glass eye, since one eye looks one way and the other another, approaches Rockland and without hesitation swings at him, connecting just under Rockland's left eye. Skin wells up into an apricot that's neither black nor blue, but some altogether new color. Blood spews from the torn skin. Rockland's dizzy, but doesn't fall. The one-eyed man comes at him again, yet upon approach Rockland falls and the man withdraws. What happens next passes as a blur—Rockland bumbling about, arms flailing, men charging, or perhaps he only hallucinates being charged, before dropping out cold. When he comes to, he's been all but abandoned. Over him, tall as the heavens, stands the initial wil-lowy man and a second fellow, this one squat and stocky as an ox, saying in a strapping brogue, "What's his story?"

He's taken across one yard, then another, into a shack no bigger than a closet at the Palmer House. It smells like a packinghouse, fungal and fecal. Other than the light from the squat, stocky man's cigar, all is shadow. Soon it is just Rockland and the squat, stocky man, who introduces himself as "J. T. Walsh, businessman by

trade," without offering a hand. His face, unlike the laborers', is free
of soot. In fact, it appears in the flickering light to be caked with
powder and slightly rouged. He has a handlebar mustachio, rosy
cheeks, a nose with the sheen and shape of an ivory button, and
teeth that glint even in the darkness. J. T. Walsh is a name Rockland
knows, but as for the man behind the name, Rockland knows next
to nothing other than what he's heard. Which is this, that J. T.—
short for Jonathan Timothy, they say—Walsh made his fortune from
the rails, sort of, importing and exporting everything from candles
to firearms to willing women and, it's been rumored, children. Of
course, none of this has been verified. In fact, Rockland's also heard
that J. T. Walsh, though his name does indeed exist in the city reg-
istry as that of the proprietor of certain property on West Randolph, is a fabrication, a mask for a well-known financier who
delights in living double lives. It's even said that the man behind the
mask is Potter Palmer, though, the first time he heard this, Rockland
shrugged it off, amused. And now here's J. T. Walsh right up and in
Rockland's face, saying, "You're that fellow lost his son, correct?"
Rockland doesn't nod, he squints. Smoke spirals up and around, so
only Walsh's teeth are visible. Walsh continues, "I have something of
a proposition for you, Mr. Rockland. I'm not saying I know who
took your son. I don't know who took your son, Mr. Rockland.
What I am saying is that I can find him. You want your son; I will
help you find him, but first there's something I need you to help me
with."

Rockland stops breathing for a moment. The other man's cigar
cinders, a husky orange orb in a gray swirl.

"Now," Walsh says, "I understand you are an acquaintance of
Potter Palmer."

MIDNIGHT MEETING BROKEN UP

Chicago Police, led by Sergeant William Banks, broke up a meeting of packinghouse laborers last night at the stockyards, just after midnight.

Sergeant Banks issued a statement saying, "We don't know what the purpose of the meeting was, but assumed it might be related to a future labor stike."

Mr. Armour, owner of multiple packinghouses, has not issued a statement.

No arrests were made.

Eleven

ust before sunrise, Dr. Handley and the inspector walking
briskly along the path circling the Fisheries Building. Passing
the building, they cross a footpath and enter the Wooded Island.
The wind's heavier, with gusts so arctic they crackle your skin. The
sky before them appears to be on fire, or electrified. Paths circle in
upon themselves, cutting suddenly left, swerving behind a menacing oak, so that the feeling of being on the isle is one of bewilder-
ment, being caught in a maze from which you can't escape. Past the
boat lodging and the Japanese Ho-o-o Den at the southernmost tip
of the island, on the far side of the Rose Garden, a small crowd of
Columbian Guards has gathered, along with a few up-all-night
stragglers just milling about. Despite the cold, the smell of roses
hangs pungent in the air, until the wind shifts so that all you can
smell is the Stock Pavilion, considerably farther south. As she
passes, Dr. Handley looks each in the eye, fixing their distinguish-
ing marks—mole to the left of nose, overlarge lips—in her mind, just
in case she'll need them later. Torches have been set up around the
scene of the crime, but with the sun just spiking the morning sky, a
bleary-eyed Columbian Guard snuffs them out.

Chief Detective Simonds, as they approach, steps out from
behind a wall of two Columbian Guards as big and hearty as Christ-
mas hams and says, without pause, "Here is where the boy was last

seen—by that man." He points, without looking, south, toward the Hunter's Cabin, where a squat man with floppy hair stands alongside his wife. It appears they're up past their bedtime, for the wife has taken to resting her head upon the man's shoulder even while fully upright. "Broad daylight, and here's the kicker—he's a Rockland."

A sigh from the inspector, if not the doctor.

"There is quite a lot of pressure, as you can imagine, to find the boy before he becomes another victim." Despite the arctic cold, Simonds has been perspiring for some time now, so that his woolen outerwear appears drenched, as if he'd just done a lap around the lagoon. "Mr. Rockland is rather vigilant, you might say, and when Mr. Rockland's vigilant, you can rest assured he will get what he is after. In this case, his boy. Are we in agreement here, Dr. Handley?"

She nods, without saying a word. A foot kicks at mud.

They travel farther inland, Dr. Handley towing her camera and its stand in a barrow behind her. On account of the increasingly rugged terrain, she soon has to leave behind the barrow and carry the camera as she normally might, slung over a shoulder.

The inspector, even though he knows this already, inquires, "What time of day was he taken?"

"Shortly before noon," the chief detective says. "The strange thing was this—we have reports of a tall, lanky, shadowy fellow wandering the isle, but nobody saw him and the boy together. It's as if they vanished into thin air. This when the isle was at its full capacity, with lunchtime loungers and curious wanderers packed on the isle like sardines in a tin. That will make your task all the more difficult, I'm afraid."

Right then, Dr. Handley retrieves from her trustworthy bag what appears to be a long and spindly apparatus, an instrument of some sort, perhaps a weapon or an oddly designed trowel. Inspector Moreau and Chief Detective Simonds regard each other, both hoping that this will prove to be a tool devised by the government in highest secrecy. Instead, it's but a cigar, which Dr. Handley places in her mouth and lights. A swirl of milky smoke engulfs her head.

"Were there," wonders Dr. Handley, "any belongings found—a cap, a wayward shoe?"

"Nothing," the chief detective says. "But you'll find over there," pointing toward a shrub that's been flattened, "the indentation of what we presume to be the boy's body—whether living or otherwise, we haven't been able to determine."

Dr. Handley approaches the spot in question. It is indeed a flattened shrub, in particular a chokeberry. She circumvents the area and leans in, having set her camera upon its legs. Her eyes scan for anything—a cap, a wayward shoe, even a freed strand of hair. A footprint. Fingerprints. She finds nothing, but isn't sure the indentation in the shrubbery was human-made, for it's too wide and uniform for that. "It's not the boy's, that's for certain," she says, whether to herself or the others isn't clear. "And I'm not convinced that this indentation was even made by a grown man, but if so, then either we have misconstrued our killer, or he's an altogether larger beast than we thought. Tall as the heavens, which, although this may render him rather easy to spot, won't make our task any easier. Were there any others?" She means witnesses. "I'd like to speak with them. Pardon."

The man is perhaps sixty, with muttonchops so frizzed they add an entire other dimension to his head. His bottom lip appears to have been cleaved, rather recently, for the scar has yet to heal fully. His wife stands a good half a foot taller than him, with sunken cheeks and wild eyes set deep in their sockets; either she's smiling, or she is one of the unfortunate few who look like they're smiling, no matter the occasion. The doctor advances toward them in a roundabout fashion, as is her custom in these situations, almost as if approaching a caged cat, so as not to alarm them or catch them entirely off guard; it's as if she's announcing who she is, so they might prepare themselves for her attack.

"Hello, I'm Elizabeth," she says, loud enough so they have no trouble hearing her. And she offers a hand in greeting. "I am fully aware of the late hour and the inconvenience this must have caused you, to say nothing of the cold, but anything you might be able to tell me will aid greatly in our rescue of the boy. You saw the boy. How old?"

"Young," the man says. Dr. Handley has always prided herself on constructing a whole person from just hearing a snippet of his voice, but tonight's witness, with his deep musty voice, runs in strict contradiction to his downier disposition. It mystifies her. She asks him to enumerate. "I don't know, nine maybe. Most certainly under ten. We have an eleven-year-old, ma'am, and this boy was altogether of a younger ilk than our boy."

"Do you mean he looked younger or acted younger?"

"Looked as well as acted. We'd seen him earlier, splashing about in a fountain and charging through crowds."

Here the witness demonstrates with flailing arms and lively steps something indicative of a jig, only without the leprechaunian enthusiasm. In fact, he never cracks a smile, although his wife appears to have been transported to the outer reaches of hilarity.

"When you saw him, was he alone or accompanied?"

"Not sure, ma'am. There were so many people about it was impossible to determine. Let me be clear on this: he did not seem frightened or lost, if that is what you're asking."

Dr. Handley touches the wife on the left shoulder, so she jumps, the wife, more startled than alarmed. She might have a fresh take on the matter, plus Dr. Handley would like a woman's naturally more detailed opinion, so she asks the wife, "What did he look like?"

"A spindly little boy, with hair the color of flames, but I don't think all that many freckles, oddly enough."

"No. I mean the kidnapper."

"Right," and then a long pause. The woman's smile dims. "All I can rightly say is that it was dark and I didn't get a good look at him, I'm sorry to say, other than this. He was huge—that I'm sure of. Bigger than any man I've seen before—wouldn't you say?" To her husband, who nods. "I knew, once I saw him, that he was up to no good. Oh." Dr. Handley allows the pause to thicken. "His walk, as I recall, was wabbly, and perhaps you might best serve your time by checking houses of the invalid around the city."

"And how would you characterize the relationship between the man and the boy?"

"Relationship? The man kidnapped him, ma'am."

"In truth," the wife says, "I'm not quite sure what my initial impression was, but I suspected they might have known each other.

He just went with the man, as if they knew each other. I'm sorry, I don't remember much, because I didn't think much of it. That actually might not have been the wisest thing to do, what with all that's been going on, but it was such a nice day out. I wish I could be of more help."

The husband saying, "May we leave now?"

"Yes, thank you," says Dr. Handley. And as they're off into the night, she thinks about a case she studied under the tutelage of Professor James. Professor James termed it "The Case of Jepthah Bigg, a Threatening Letter Writer." The place was London, the year 1836. The story this: Late in life, Bigg took to writing letters, first to men he met and then randomly, inventing names and sending letters to invented addresses, as well as to real women who caught his fancy. This was only a mild mania, the outgrowth of an obsessive personality. Soon, though, Bigg was writing only to one person, a certain Catherine Dyer. She was a widow, with one child. First she ignored the letters, but soon she grew enchanted with her secret admirer. The letters became more romantic, filled with poetry. Nobody would have noticed, or cared, until one day, a little under a year after Bigg sent his first letter, Catherine Dyer was found murdered, stabbed half-a-dozen times in the stomach. And when Scotland Yard discovered the letters, Jepthah Bigg was arrested and hung. A year later, thanks to the exhaustive work of a zealous inspector named Kenneth Gow, it was found that Jepthah Bigg could not have murdered Catherine Dyer, since he was in church at the time of the killing. A simple error perhaps, but not an unexpected one. Gow, having read the letters, just didn't believe that Bigg was capable of murder. It was a lesson, Professor James instructed, that things are not always what they may seem at first, a simple circumstance can be inherently complicated, and one finds her quarry where one least expects it. Perhaps, Dr. Handley thinks, the same applies here. Either the boy seen taken wasn't taken but went willingly, or the boy seen abducted on the Wooded Island isn't the missing boy, isn't a Rockland after all. Perhaps it is too late, and the boy is already dead. Perhaps another boy's already been abducted.

But before they go, "Oh, there was one thing." Dr. Handley

turns, her cigar no longer lit, now just a halfway-smoked stub. She's gazing off at the Electricity Building, not at the ever-smiling wife.

Wind shifts, the smell of the stockyards gone, if only momentarily.

"The man has a wooden leg, or looked as if he did."

The White City, all around her, appears to be aflame, such is the intensity of the reflection of the just-risen sun on the white buildings. She fears she will fail, fears she won't find the missing boy, fears she won't find the killer. There is, she fears, no way to avoid failure; whatever she does, however close she might, by chance or by luck, get to finding the boy and apprehending the killer, it will only end in disappointment. She resigns herself to this, one failure after another. Even with the celebrated case of Hudson Martin, she felt a failure—felt that perhaps it wasn't she who'd brought the case to its closure but some other, outside force. Father Handley, were he still alive, might concur.

Among everything, there was always the sense with him that she wasn't doing her all; that, because he'd failed, she would as well. Failure, in fact, has long plagued the Handley clan. Handley's Medicinal Miracle Tonic, for example. It had been an instant, scandalous success when it was first introduced in 1843, the first tonic in an age of tonics—part toothpaste, part underarm deodorant, part foot salve, all in one. And it made the modest Handleys obscenely wealthy. Grandfather Handley, no doubt unbeknownst to himself, had little idea what he was doing; he'd chanced upon the formula, in truth, but he'd ridden the success wave without taking the time to think about future pratfalls. When any sensible man would have passed on the family formula, Hiram Markson Handley, a newspaperman without the slightest hint of entrepreneurship, balked. So, when he died under a month later, he took the formula with him. The tonic soon dried up, leaving Hiram Junior with only his father's faded dream, a swelling debt, and incensed creditors. She'd been raised in privilege, no question, but of the worst kind—unearned. Once guilt beset him, there was little he could do aside from feeling the burden of the crown on his head. Of course, from all external viewpoints, the life and career of Elizabeth Handley, female sleuth, has been an out-and-out-success. But deep down she can't help but feel as though she's missed the final phaeton home. . . .

"Name's Tiggs, Theodate Tiggs." They're back at Public Comfort, Dr. Handley, Inspector Moreau, Chief Detective Simonds, and this man Tiggs, who hasn't slept, having taken the overnight train from Washington, D.C., but who's far from fatigued. Everybody else has made the trek to the far side of exhaustion. Bags as dark as Guinness sag under their eyes; cheeks are puffy and splotched crimson. Dr. Handley moves slowly, as if treading water. Perhaps on account of her state, or because she knows he's heard conflicting things about her. Tiggs eyeballs the doctor curiously, as if she's a mongoose in a zoo and not a seasoned sleuth. Neither Moreau nor Simonds says anything.

He's only somewhat tall, but his shoulders are as expansive as canyons, and his neck spindly and broad as a trunk. Standard black wool of the period. His collar perhaps a bit too tight. Shoes are scuffed. Nothing even approximating a smile, which would make sense were Dr. Handley to know that Tiggs here was in the employ of the republic. He's seated, with legs crossed, in a chair that might easily be mistaken for a throne, with arms the shape of a lion's upturned paws. And either there's a pistol in his breast pocket, or the man's torso is misshapen.

"I've heard so much about you. I've wanted to work with you for quite a while now," says Tiggs, "but there are some things we should clarify, before we get too involved in the hunt. I respect and appreciate what you do, Dr. Handley. In fact, I believe it's one of the truly forward-looking endeavors, this forensic business. And your being a woman—well, remarkable." That could be scorn, but against her better instincts, Dr. Handley doesn't think so. "That said, Doctor, you should know right up front that, when it comes to how the killer should be apprehended, our lines of thinking diverge. We have been tracking the killer for some time now," since he struck, as some believe, in Maryland, over a year ago. A rising politico by the name of Langdon, stabbed thrice in the gut in broad daylight; some had pegged him as a future president, but that was before Clemantis, or whoever, pegged him. It is a theory held by few, mostly elected officials who would rather believe that Clemantis the Husker did not come out of nowhere but rather has been slow to burn his way across the continental United States, moving ever-westward. Some believe that there are others, as yet unidentified, murdered upwards of five years ago by the same skilled, yet vicious, hand. Since coming to Chicago, Clemantis has chosen only boys, which fazes nobody but Dr. Handley, who finds the theory of pre-Chicago murders shamefully ridiculous, to say nothing of implausible. Still, the theory has many proponents, especially among newspapermen. Hence the government's interest. Tiggs, who once served in Garfield's Personal Security Unit, has been sent with certain objectives, most of which have to do not with the boys being murdered or their bereaved families, but with conspiracies. Why did Clemantis kill Langdon, and since he's made his way to Chicago, what politico will be next? "He's a threat, a menace, Dr. Handley, who should not be captured and understood, as I believe you would like, but regarded as a monster and routed out of his lair and justly hung for all to see. And to do this, we will employ force. That would be the sentence due him, not understanding," a near laugh, "Dr. Handley."

Though her back feels as if it will break if a faint gust of wind so much as whips at it and her legs might buckle without warning, though each and every bone in her body feels as if it might splinter any moment now, she manages to stand bolt upright at attention. Eventually she says, "I believe him to be a man of means with too much time on his hands. He is educated, perhaps in the medical profession. He has left little behind to lead us to him, which troubles me."

"With all due respect, the task force has yet to arrive, which gives you two days," says Tiggs. "I hope we can work together, but as I understand it, you like to work alone."

"It is not so much that I like to work alone," says Dr. Handley, "as I have yet to find someone capable of keeping up with me."

"Fair enough. But do keep in mind that we *will* intervene when the time's right."

Without saying anything else, Dr. Handley eyes Moreau, then

promptly takes her leave. Moreau follows, but not before he has a few words with Tiggs.

Outside Public Comfort, Handley's off into the morning, with Inspector Moreau jogging after her. "Please, stop. Dr. Handley!" She does, but doesn't turn. The inspector catches up with her and stands right behind her, very nearly heaving, so close that she can feel his breath on the back of her neck. The sensation is clammy; she's not sure if it's stimulating or repulsive. Outside it's freezing, the clouds of their breath the only moving thing in the White City at this hour. Silence, too, save for the distant grumbling of a dynamo.

"Dr. Handley, there is something I've been meaning to speak with you about." The inspector bites his lower lip. "Something," he says, "of concern to me."

"Speak your mind, Inspector," she replies. "I trust you will."

"Well, I wonder if we're going about it in the wrong way," after catching his breath.

"The wrong way, Inspector?"

"Yes, well, perhaps that's not quite putting it right. I mean, there are some among us—not I, Dr. Handley, I can assure you—who believe that, to put it politely, you are mucking up. Now please don't—"

But she interrupts him: "There are?" And now turns, although the look upon her face is a look not of concern or alarm but curiosity. Her forehead wrinkles, and her jaw slackens, as if by anesthesia. That others might not understand her has occurred to her, of course. It ran rampant throughout her mind the first time she met the inspector and the chief detective, as well as earlier tonight, with Mr. Tiggs. Nobody understands, but no matter. However, before she could obsess over it, she forgot it and began to think of herself— as is her nature—with some remove, as if speaking of herself in the third person. Dr. Handley will go on, thinks Dr. Handley, in spite of all obstacles. That she is the only female involved in the search for the killer they call Clemantis she doesn't mind, but others it both- ers—acutely.

"I have placed my trust in you, Dr. Handley," says the inspector while the doctor retrieves an already-smoked cigar from her dress and places it in her mouth, almost swallowing it whole without lighting it. "What else am I going to place my trust in? I am not of much help, I'm afraid. And Simonds? He is an idiot. So, when they told me a psychologist from Boston was en route, I was overjoyed, to put it mildly. Everybody else was, too. Perhaps, we thought, even if he can't catch the killer, perhaps he will be able to explain everything to us. There is much to explain. Dr. Handley, our expectations rose so high that only disappointment could follow. When Simonds reported that our psychologist was *female*, Dr. Handley, I'm not sure if we were surprised so much as terrified."

As Moreau speaks, Dr. Handley, her eyes averted up and on the starless sky, chews on the cigar as if somewhere in its rolled leaves it contains a magical elixir. Then, with an authority customarily reserved for politicians, Dr. Handley spits the cigar in an arc up and over the inspector's head. The wind dies down, then a moment later swirls back up to a hurricane's speed. Dr. Handley's hair whips across her face; she makes no effort to remove it.

"Inspector," she says, "I'm curious—do you think violence is fundamentally a funny thing?" She doesn't expect an answer; indeed, there isn't one. The inspector's brow waffles. "Because I do. Funny not in a humorous way, that is. Funny as in weird. Killing." He has a skilled way with knives, has a knowledgeable grasp of anatomy, but is utterly, shamelessly insane. As time passes, the murders become more and more gruesome, indicating, perhaps that the killer is either becoming more comfortable with his killing or increasingly careless. "I mean, simply, why does one kill? Is it euphoria one experiences? Something that lessens the dread the killer, much like the rest of us, experiences on a daily basis. Can he not effectively contain his dread? Or is it merely a task, like taking out the trash? Is our killer conscious of killing? That is what we must find out before we find our man—or woman, Inspector."

He looks confused, as well he should. Clemantis a woman? The mere suggestion, he thinks, is ridiculous, so he cackles and says, "A woman? Really, Dr. Handley, get a hold of yourself."

At first, she herself didn't believe it possible. A woman, much like Dr. Handley, like any woman, capable of these crimes, capable of doing this to boys. Not on this earth. But then it occurred to her—anything's possible. Everyone, no matter their disposition, is capable of evil. But how can a woman, capable of birthing a boy, murder one with the ruthlessness that's descended upon the White City like a black veil? There must be shame involved, and fear, panic, paranoia. Much wrath, but little stealth. The killer—he or she—has done little to cover his or her tracks. Each corpse has been found easily, without searching. It's almost as if the killer has been taunting the authorities. And that's how Dr. Handley came up with her theory that the White City killer just might be a she. Women, though fickle, are far more cunning and ruthless than men. Dr. Handley knows that Clemantis, despite his or her surface negligence, is nothing if not cunning.

"Just a hunch?" the inspector wonders. "Perhaps, Dr. Handley, you shouldn't follow your hunches so um—sporadically. I presume you know where that can lead you, or us."

Silence. Dr. Handley says, "And what is the government's involvement, Inspector?"

"This is bigger than all of us, Elizabeth." It is the first time she has been addressed by her given name since her arrival on the shores of Lake Michigan, and she's not certain how she feels about it. Startled on one level, charmed on another, and dismayed insofar as she feels a bit threatened—as if, just by saying her name, Inspector Moreau has pierced the fragile bubble of her personal space.

"We are meant to be a team. I will come with."

Without rebuttal, she's off. Walking at a breakneck speed along the path that curves south of Public Comfort, headed for the terminus, just west of the stockyards. Inspector Moreau, breathless, charges after her, wondering, "Where are we going?"

Just then, as she passes the Minnesota state building, Dr. Handley halts, snaps her head around, and says, "I suggest you keep up if you want to come with." Before Moreau can catch his breath, she starts back up, passing Michigan and Colorado and California, the second-largest state building, and the largest, Illinois, with its intricate spires. She doesn't stop again until they're in front of the Women's Building, at which point she paces, as if demarking territory, away from the building and toward the lagoon. If only the inspector could hear over his own huffing, he'd hear her counting off each step. Once she's reached the very edge of the lagoon, she stops but doesn't turn, just looks first left, then right, then appears to inspect the place where water meets soil.

"This is where the mother fainted," she says, "which means this is more or less the exact point where the missing boy ran off. And that"—pointing north, toward the Palace of Fine Arts—"is where the father said they were earlier, yes? So does it not seem logical that the boy would go south?" At this her gaze turns southward, directed at Transportation. "But if I were a boy, is that were I'd go?" And now toward the southeast and the massive Manufactures and Liberal Arts Building rising above the Wooded Island. "Now that makes more sense, but I'm not sure whether that would be the target or only a way station of sorts, a nice place to pass the time before moving on to other things. Which leaves us with—Electricity? It is entirely possible, but for a boy of eight not exactly plausible. Therefore, guns." Krupp's Gun Exhibit, east of South Pond, on the far side of the elevated railroad. "Boys must have their guns above all else, Inspector."

"Certainly, but how do you figure that is where the boy was headed?"

"I'm just thinking out loud, Inspector. Please don't mind me." And with that, Dr. Handley starts off again ringing the lagoon, headed still for Terminal Station. Still at a breakneck speed, but she is trying to slow her gait so that the inspector may catch up. So far, they haven't passed another living soul. It is strange but oddly comforting, the silence and the emptiness of the White City before it opens. Not that she'd notice, since whenever she's off wandering the White City, even if it's jammed with fair-goers, she hardly notices anyone, or rather she notices only parts of fair-goers: eyes, hairstyles, men with uneven arms, anyone with a limp. Inspector Moreau, whose stride is no longer than he's tall, struggles to keep pace. As she walks—and this is only walking and not jogging or trotting or galloping—Dr. Handley mumbles to herself, although on account of the wind the words are carried off toward the west, so all the inspector hears is a muted grumbling, which itself might be the wind. As they pass between Transportation and Mines, the wind picks up, blowing right at them with a gale's vigor.

Just outside Hayward Restaurant they're surrounded, as if the wind just transported them to an entirely other place, by a throng of fair-goers scurrying past quick as lightning and just as transitory—men, women, and children whistling and spitting out cashews, and scowling, either on account of the brisk air or because the day's first train has arrived but the gates have yet to open. One irate man has taken to thrashing another, smaller man, right in front of the conductor, who's too busy turning away elderly ladies with crooked legs and twisted backs. Others join in, and soon a riot of sorts breaks out, everybody charging everybody else, pummeling, striking, wrestling, anger spilling out as from a well, without recourse. Inspector Moreau stops to aid a young mother shielding her young daughter from a brute with streaming whiskers and sausage arms, but Dr. Handley maintains her course, slipping past the beefy pugilists as a phantom might, without being seen by human eye.

The wind's stronger, kicking up scraps of paper.

She's past the Chocolate Menier and the Band Stand when the throng thins and she realizes she's lost Moreau. No matter, she forges on, past South Canal and the obelisk, past the Stock Pavilion and under the elevated railroad, past what will become the Agricultural Implements display in an hour or so and to South Pond, a place entirely devoid of people. Sweat dribbles from her brow, but she doesn't feel even a bit fatigued; it's as if she's been running a marathon and yet has the energy to run another one, straightaway. When she catches her breath, she realizes she's ambled into a garden in miniature. Azaleas, rhododendron, day lilies, each still in bloom despite the unseasonably arctic October chill. A man, a hobo by appearance, stands there with his arms outstretched, as though he were crucified rather than urinating, as he is. A guitar's slung over his shoulder. The hobo is tall and rangy, with hair puffed out and up. In his low voice thick as molasses, he is heard to be singing—a song whose melody Dr. Handley might know but the lyrics of which may as well be in Laplanders' tongue: "There's a

place in . . ." As if stricken by lightning, suddenly Dr. Handley feels
the ground beneath her swell and undulate and her body slacken,
and she places her hands over her kneecaps for support. Her lungs
seem to have flooded, for as the morning has worn on and the electric flares have gradually flickered out and the sun come up, the air
has become as thick as oatmeal, without being quite so tasty.

The hobo notices Dr. Handley and hisses.

Dr. Handley says, "You shouldn't be here. The White City is
closed."

In a voice that's lost all hint of song, the hobo calls out, "Just
doing my civic duty here, sir."

Sir? Dr. Handley very nearly laughs. She steps toward the man.
Though scarcely a seasoned tackler, she's prepared herself, in her
mind, to stymie his escape, should one be attempted. He could be
anyone, an escaped prisoner, a disappeared businessman, perhaps
even the killer, or just an ordinary hobo—whichever, her guard's up.
She might look willowy and feeble, but she's solid as a boulder, if
nowhere near as broad. Clip his ankles, then bring him to the earth.
Dr. Handley, though she'd be the last to admit it, is seasoned in the
art of intimidation, which must be called upon in a time like this.
Ruffians, loafers, bummers, rapscallions, bullies, robbers, riffraff—
they are, deep down, soft as a schoolboy, their tough-guy exterior
little more than a shell that can be removed easily, if you know how
to manipulate the situation. To this end, Dr. Handley, dizzy and
fatigued still, steps right up to the hobo and ogles him, her face
devoid of expression but her eyes piercing, inquisitive. "I think you
should leave now."

Having finished his business and retrieved his guitar, the hobo
says, "How's that?"

Just for an instant, Dr. Handley considers what would happen if
this hobo were indeed her quarry. She's been preparing for a
moment like this, but now that it's here, she's stricken with doubt. Is
she ready? Will he deceive her? Will he capture her? Will she be the
first woman he's murdered? She's not sure she, herself, could escape
that—could escape, period. Not sure she would have the gumption,
the will. Would he torture her before killing her, or kill her without

torment? Would he ravish her, or does his hunger for blood have little to do with lust? Fearless, Dr. Handley grips the hobo by a wrist and begins to lead him away, saying, "This way now," and to her surprise, and perhaps even to his, he goes without dispute, muttering his song. He throws an arm up and across her shoulder, his guitar whacking the small of her back. On account of her dress, she hardly feels it, but she smells the whiskey rising like a turgid perfume from his every pore. She wheezes, for lack of breathable air, and leads him out of the miniature garden, pointing him off toward Terminal Station. She knows he won't get far, likely will get nowhere at all, so that when after fifty feet of stumbling he tumbles to the ground, she's not surprised and continues on.

Throughout Chicago of late there have been countless vanishings, many of them untraceable save by wiring faraway cities with a description and a plea or visiting the morgue every few days, hoping the disappeared body doesn't turn up. And if the disappeared were a Polish girl or a Negro laborer, they could be counted gone for good. Without money, and lots of it, no patrolman's going to get a search on. Were the boy not a Rockland, Dr. Handley knows, she wouldn't even be here. Lord knows there have been incalculable vanishings since the exposition opened, on the first of May. A Mysterious Disappearances Department has even been set up, under Chief Detective Simonds's watch. So far, none have been investigated, all catalogued. Disappeared women are presumed ravished, men robbed. Corpses wash up along the shores of the Chicago River on an almost daily basis, or are simply dumped in the area known as the Cheyenne, on Clark Street between Polk and Taylor. And what is she to do with all of it? Her mind's nowhere near at ease. How should she process this? She's in no condition to be searching all day, all night, without sleep, with little food. And why did Washington send their man Tiggs? She doesn't even know whom she's searching for, a killer or a disappeared boy. Presently, as the wind whips up. The doctor shivers.

The miniature garden leads into a field, the mud here coagulated, ruddy, despite the proximity to the White City. This might be the stockyards, or part of the Ethnographical Exhibit. She's boxed in by

the Anthropological and Forestry and Dairy Buildings, but to her
surprise doesn't feel claustrophobic at all. No, this can't be the
stockyards, for they are on the far side of the Intramural. Smells at
this point are no longer so much of hyacinth as of an underarm fun-
gus. A few last stars are still visible, yet only when she squints, as she
does presently. She's not certain if she's reached a dead end or
merely an impasse of sorts, but she's determined to search on. She
heads toward the lake, away from the stockyards. She has a fairly
dependable visual memory, but can't remember how to get to
Krupp's Gun Exhibit from here, whether it's north or south, so she
removes a map of the White City from a pocket and inspects it in
the faint moonlight. It's just north of the Leather Exhibit by the
south loop of the Intramural. Map back in pocket, she passes by the
Ruins of the Yucatán and between Dairy and the Ethnographical
Exhibit, or where it used to be, as laborers have worked half the
night to strike it in case of rain or sleet. There are a few mallard
ducks and one swan circling South Pond. Dr. Handley wishes she
had another cigar. A sudden sound, of shoes pressing down against
pebbles, startles her. She turns but sees nothing, just the shadowy
White City. Before her is the Convent La Rabida, and to her right,
farther away, lies Krupp's Guns. She passes over pebbles and mud
and short, ankle-high prairie grass. On account of the earliness of
the hour, and the doctor's fatigue on account of not being able to
sleep again, everything begins to blur, and she feels her body about
to pass on into a world of sleep, but still her eyes, being suspicious
and curious to know what might lurk in the unlikeliest of places,
involuntarily glimpse over the earth, which has turned this close to
the water to sand.

Then another sound, a sobbing.

That's when she sees it, a cadaver. It is buried in the last patch of
prairie grass before everything turns to sand, just inside the Stock
Pavilion. Her eyes cast along the pasty white skin, which has already
set to clot, like cottage cheese, only faded to an off-green that
verges on purple. It is the corpse of a young boy, although in
appearance, if not in age, the boy hulks overbig and could easily be
mistaken for a full-grown man. Dr. Handley hunkers over and

inspects. Could this be the disappeared boy? She hasn't yet seen a photograph of him; it occurs to her that she hasn't even been given a description. Only a few first hairs stick out from the chest skin, which, as Dr. Handley gets closer, darkens to a ruby red; it has, in part, been flayed. She knows not to molest the evidence but can't help herself; the cadaver's skin is cold to the touch but astonishingly soft. The corpse has also been stripped, whole, of garb. A rat has gnawed at the left ear, which as if by voodoo has already set to heal and is a dark, charred-wood color. One eye is open; the other has been excised. Then, again, there's the sobbing. Dr. Handley turns at once and spots a boy, a living boy.

Wind's in off the lake, brisk.

He's in shadows; otherwise, Dr. Handley might be able to ascertain the young boy's countenance. Back on his haunches, holding his head as if shielding it from all the world's murder and mayhem, the boy has eyes that glow, though they appear unseeing. The boy, it seems, is not so much hunkered over as he is short as a runt and as lanky. Against the scrim of shadows, at first sight, the boy's skin appears white, but then, as if magically, becomes a darker, more substantial color altogether: soot black, without being inky. Though reason might suggest otherwise, Dr. Handley feels in her gut that this is the disappeared Rockland. The cadaver is but an anonymous vanishing. She takes a cursory step toward the living child, but stops. The boy shoots back a good three feet, saying nothing. Dr. Handley offers a noncommittal hand. The boy fails to take it. The doctor, down on all fours now, level with the living boy, says, "Right, well, we can just stay here and wait, if that's what you want, but you'll catch your death." She thrusts out her arms and encloses the young boy, scooping him up. And then they walk off with the wind.

Twelve

Skurlock and Billy walking side by side down a shadow-stitched alleyway. That's the lake up ahead, blue as the Mediterranean but nowhere near as docile. Wind dodges, swirls, and switches, coming first from one direction, then its complete opposite, shape-shifting as a wayward spirit, or a boy who cannot make up his mind and even if he could would prefer not to.

"Where," he wonders, "are we going? I'm tired."

It's just before dawn, Tuesday, and it seems to Billy that sleep has yet to leave him. He can't remember whether a real or phantom hand woke him from his slumber and lifted him up and out before anyone else awoke. Is this but a dream, or does it only seem like one? "Don't worry about it," Skurlock says, tugging at the kid's hand more forcibly than before. A chase could have commenced, on account of the abruptness with which Skurlock and the kid vacated the lair of the Walsh Gang. "We'll have fun today."

"All right," says Billy.

Wind's stronger than before, and Skurlock wants to know, "Cold?"

The kid shakes his head no, but then says, "Yes."

"We'll be there soon," says Skurlock. His boots tap, tap on the brick, and one ankle cracks with every other step.

They walk in silence for a long while, and then Billy, whispering, wants Skurlock to know, "You're funny."

Looking sheepish, he says, "What do you mean?"

First sunlight slants down, bleached, blurring the edge of every-thing either sees. Billy feels as if they're being followed, although by whom he hasn't a clue. It's a strange experience, and occasionally he'll turn, sparked by fright, only to find out it's nothing. No one is following.

"What I said," Billy says. He giggles.

Laughter comes from high above. From a rooftop, it seems, or the heavens. Without warning, Skurlock grips Billy by the shoulder and forces him to a halt. They both stand there listening, silent, glancing straight ahead.

Up ahead, there are three shadowy figures bent over a fourth, deflated man.

Dead? "What is it?" Billy wants to know.

"Shh," Skurlock says, pressing a finger over his lips. He takes the kid's hand and squeezes. He's about to turn the other way and make a run for it. Instead, his hand slides up the right side of young Rock-land's face and musses the boy's already mussed-up hair. Billy coughs.

Abruptly, brusquely, one of the three standing men turns and spots Skurlock and the kid, calls out, "Heya!"

They're caught. Hesitantly they approach, Skurlock walking in front of his friend now—whether to buckler or seclude him, Billy hasn't a clue. Their hands are still interlocked. Tight.

One of the standing men, on closer inspection, has a peg leg and is supervising the other two. Nobody says anything. Eyes meet, but do not hold.

On the ground lies a Negro, his head dripping blood, bashed to a pulp, twisted, oblong. It is scarcely recognizable as a human head, if even as a gourd. His arms are twisted around unbelievably, and a white bone perforates his dark thigh. Young Billy's seen a Negro before, with Father at the yards, but never this close and personal. Then, again, is a dead Negro a Negro still? Is Billy Billy still, after espying Death?

Skurlock, fearless, wants to know, "What happened here?"

Peg Leg, choking back a grimace, offers, "None of your busi-ness. Get it?"

"But it is," says Skurlock, "precisely my business."

Peg Leg's face hardens. He looks somewhat confused, incredulous, says, "I trust not."

Right away the two other standing men stop kicking the Negro and turn their attentions to Skurlock and the kid. One of them lets it be known, "Scram." It is a nasalized, little-kid's voice but menacing still.

Billy, from behind, begins to convulse.

The man with the peg leg says, "What do we have here, a troublemaker?"

Silence. Then Skurlock, fearless, retrieves a firearm from an inside pocket of his coat and aims it at Peg Leg.

Peg Leg, guffawing, says, "Sorry?" Presently, he cackles.

Skurlock pans the firearm to the head of one of the big men and fires—a loud, echoic thunderclap. The big man, his neck snapped, kicked back, topples, as gravity sees fit. The other big man sprints off, Skurlock aiming the gun back at Peg Leg, who stutters, quietly, but says nothing of substance.

Skurlock says, "Go!" And Peg Leg goes.

The Negro, once they get to him, has ceased to breathe the air of this life. Billy stays back, while Skurlock checks the dead man's pockets for identification, money, anything. He finds nothing. You can still hear the shot, thunderous, murderous. Two corpses, one black, one white, each spewing black-red blood. Skurlock waves Billy over. Eventually Billy comes. His eyes—he can't help it—remain closed, clamped down, never again to open. Skurlock commands, "Open your eyes," and Billy's eyes, as if of their own volition, open wide. "See," says Skurlock. Billy can't move—he's frozen—but nevertheless he looks.

"This is how Death appears," says Skurlock. "Take a long look, and never forget it."

Up and in the dead Negro's left armpit, a rat gnaws at its first meal of the day.

Billy says, "Where are we going?"

Skurlock is about to say something, but then does not. He shrugs.

They set off at once, Skurlock checking around and over his shoulder repeatedly, so that, soon enough, Billy's nervous. What, he wonders, could Skurlock be on the lookout for? They pass down alleyways and skirt streets in favor of the cloak of a tree-shadowed park. Skurlock hasn't entertained the possibility that someone, some-where, might want the young boy returned, unharmed. Instead, he's worried that they're being tailed. Perhaps Graft has let Walsh know, and Walsh has sent out a posse. If that is the case, no stroke of luck, no last-ditch evasion, no threadbare disguise will render them safe. So wide-reaching is Walsh's clutch on the city and its inhabi-tants, he'll easily ferret even Hannibal Skurlock out. They walk in silence, and after a long while Skurlock puts an arm around the kid, says, "You did good."

Before them now beckons a soup kitchen. They enter and stand in line, surrounded by men with scars that cross their faces or ring their necks.

After a bit, "Han?"

"Yes, what is it?"

"Were you, um, born here?" He blinks. "Do you have a mom and a pa? Do you," and here Billy looks down at his feet, "have a boy of your own?"

Skurlock doesn't answer at first. With food in hand, he leads Billy toward the rear by the kitchen, so that, were anyone to walk in, there'd be an easy out—out back and into the alley. For a mo-ment, Skurlock neither touches nor contemplates touching his eggs. Billy, however, scarfs his meatloaf. He burps. This incites Skurlock to finish his eggs in one grand, theatrical slurp. Then, finally, with yolk stretching from his teeth to his lips, he says, "Do you really want to know?"

Before Billy nods, Skurlock's already started his tale . . . a cool, balmy night when he first arrived here on the Chicago Union. A man whose nose appeared either sliced off or so small it may as well have been sliced off told him, "Go to the yards," and so that's where he went, the stockyards. Upon arrival, Skurlock met a man called J. T. Walsh. Short, with a nose as big as a baby's fist. Skurlock was emaci-ated, wearing tattered clothes. At once, Walsh took Skurlock in his carriage to what appeared to be an abandoned building on West Randolph, across the street from a saloon marked only SALOON. Inside and down stairs that creaked underfoot as an oak in a gale and then down a long and winding passageway obstructed with cobwebs and certain crustaceans so briny that Skurlock kidded himself into smelling the sea. That's where Skurlock met the men Billy met last night, Graft and Fallon. At first, Walsh provided Skurlock and Graft and Fallon with work around the clock. Loading trucks. Slicing carcasses throughout the night and without break in meat freezers as large and in their way as grand as ballrooms. Outside was hot as an oven, but the cool of the meatpacking houses made life bearable. Hannibal Skurlock had never killed a man, then, but Graft, whom Skurlock talked to more than Fallon, had, once. Now, Walsh kept a boardinghouse, on West North, for his men. Graft's was the only vacant room so that's where Skurlock bedded down. Days passed, then months, during which time Skurlock and Graft became something of brothers.

"For the first time," Skurlock tells Billy, "I felt truly—" Safe? Loved? He says nothing, since right there, just outside the soup kitchen, he spots the unmistakable fire red flop-haired head of none other than Wade Graft. Presently, he scoops Billy up into his arms. Before Billy can tell what's happening, they're out the back door, back into the blustery wind.

SECURITY DEPARTMENT REPORT (cont.)

Number of attempts to gain admission with fraudulent passes *33*

Number of reports of attempts to pass counterfeit coin *10*

Number of reports of ex-convicts on grounds *135*

Thirteen

They're in without a word, first Potter Palmer and then Rockland. It's half past ten, Tuesday morning. A room high above the White City. Walls are a dark cocoa color; windows are covered by an inch of dust and rattle, on account of the wind, which seeps in, so that even inside it's wintry. Palmer greets everybody enthusiastically, talking a full minute to each, longer to Sergeant William Banks of the Chicago Police Force, while Rockland, without so much as a nod, takes a seat, saying nothing. Vacant face, with darting eyes. Sergeant Banks, once Palmer's finished speaking to him, sits directly opposite Rockland and smiles an instantly distrustful smile and says, "Now Mr. Rockland, we're not sure if Billy's in the hands of that rogue the Husker or if he's just, um, lost, but you can rest your faith on the Chicago police. We're hot on Clemantis's trail. Not that I would have thought for a moment you'd doubt us, sir, but under the circumstances"—here Banks glances at Palmer, who nods— "we want you to know what we know as we know it. Now, as you may have heard, Mr. Rockland, we have a specialist on the case. She'll be here presently. She has uncovered quite a bit that will lead us right to the killer, I'm certain. As well, Mr. Tiggs"—the man seated to Banks's left—"has joined us from Washington. You see, Mr. Rockland, even Uncle Sam is working with us on this one. Mr. Rockland, are you all right?"

William Rockland's skin has clammed up and appears slick, as if
with oil and not human perspiration. He glances around the room
nervously, tapping his feet, his hands shaky, and his voice quavers
when he says, more to the table at which he's seated than to anyone
in the room, "Oh yes, very much so." In truth, before him, wherever
he looks, he sees the white-powder countenance of that rogue. He
still hears the voice, "I trust you want your son back. Think of this
not as something you have to do but as something you *want* to do,
Mr. Rockland." He's surrounded by men who can help him, were he
to alert them. Should he?

"Not money, Mr. Rockland. I have plenty of that. I want the contract for the Cosmopolitan. I am, as they say, expanding my interests
into construction, and when I heard that the son of Palmer's chief
architect was missing, I thought, well, here's my opportunity. Let's
not disappoint each other." Not that William Rockland hasn't been
asked, when working with Potter Palmer, to cut corners, to overlook
certain city regulations, to disregard under-the-table payments. He
trusts that, were he to tell Potter Palmer, Palmer would hire Walsh.
He also knows that there's the slightest chance that Palmer would
tell Banks. Were this to happen, everything would be botched: Walsh
would become incensed, and as for Billy, he'd likely never be found—
so Rockland sits in a muddle, sad, bewildered, confused.

Palmer, being Palmer, grasps Rockland's hands, leans close, and
says, "Bill?" Upon contact, Rockland jerks back, almost teeters over
his chair, but maintains his balance, managing half a grin. "It will all
work out."

Sergeant Banks, with hands that gesticulate wildly, says, "I can
spare fifty, the best guys I got. Send them out, tear this town apart, if
you want. But for right now, all we can do? We have to wait. Mr.
Rockland, may I be frank? Because, well, the thing is? I've done this
many times before, and it's the same every time. Mr. Rockland?
Three times out of five, no, four, you have to believe me, they come
back. You never know, never can tell. And I know, believe me, this is
not easy for me. I've been there before." His gaze drifts from Rockland to Palmer and back again. "Mr. Rockland, I'm going to suggest
something that you might not want to hear. We're trying. We're

doing our best on this, but we need something from you. Patience, Mr. Rockland. Can you do that?"

Rockland avoids eye contact. He stares at the table, folding his hands one over the other.

Sergeant Banks himself folds his hands together, saying, "Now, Mr. Rockland, is there any reason Billy might have disappeared of his own volition yesterday? How has life been at home?"

When there is no response, Potter Palmer introduces Roy Boyd and Alex O'Malley, of Allan Pinkerton's Detective Agency, who are seated on the far side of Mr. Tiggs. Both are men of sturdy demeanor and with beards that trail the jaw line and form a V at the cheek, both wear ragged purple vests, both are simpering, and both, as Siamese twins, move as if in synchronicity, only reversed—Roy leaning forward while O'Malley leans back, O'Malley saying, "We have reason to believe that your son might have been abducted by the rogue Clemantis."

That this contradicts what Sergeant Banks was saying doesn't seem to affect William Rockland. In fact, Rockland deadeyes the table, saying nothing, Pinkerton Boyd saying, "The Husker, as he is known."

At this, Mr. Rockland nods. He hangs a finger off his lip. Finally he says, "I read the dailies."

"We believe," says Pinkerton O'Malley, "he may be in the Middle West. Now, as you have read, he is a most vicious person and must be apprehended at once. We will need all the help we can get."

And shoots a look at Potter Palmer, who nods.

Pinkerton Boyd saying, "He is, as the phrenologists tell us, a 'copycat' murderer. That is to say, he is not an original man; he seeks his inspiration for his killings—twelve to date—from the renowned London doctor Jack the Ripper."

"He may even be the same man."

It is Dr. Elizabeth Handley, the sleuth Potter Palmer was telling Rockland about. Rockland watches the doctor enter and seat herself to his immediate right, apologizing to the room for her tardiness and making eye contact with everyone in the room save Mr. Tiggs, Rockland notices, and to Potter Palmer saying, "Hello, Tom."

"Hello," says Potter Palmer.

Dr. Handley reminds William Rockland of his own Elizabeth, and not just because they share the same given name. Both women also share the same bodies, and both move their bodies in a similar fashion, as if they're not comfortable in their skin and might knock into something at any given moment. After introducing herself to William Rockland, Dr. Handley says, "There is so much we don't know."

"Only," Pinkerton Boyd says, "instead of women of the night, our killer preys on young boys."

"Which is why we believe he may have abducted your son," says Dr. Handley. William Rockland just listens. "It cannot be a coincidence that Billy disappeared on his own, and now. And what he does with them is, well, an altogether different kind of game."

"We believe," says Pinkerton O'Malley, "that Clemantis is not a stationary killer. That is, he is here for the exposition, but he won't be here that much longer, we're afraid."

"He does get around," says Pinkerton Boyd. "Why, between Boston and New Haven, Clemantis was in California."

"How he got there, and so quickly," Pinkerton O'Malley very nearly chuckling, "is something of a mystery."

"In any case," Dr. Handley says, "I should inform you of what might happen. That is, in the worst-case scenario." She sits forward in her chair and cups together both of her hands and presses, till the skin is translucent and bones stick far out. "The first victim was found" . . . a lump of flesh, or lack thereof, in a deep wood with blood gushing out in tides and crests; the second, a minister's son, had had his throat gashed from ear to ear; the third had been shot with a flintlock, then hung from a dead branch—the boy was so young and weightless, he could be hung from a dead branch without snapping it; there were two, both sons of night inspectors, who had been divested of their genitalia; the next was missing each finger—from the knuckle on up; the sixth boy, a mute, had had his eyes pecked out, whether by Clemantis or crows could not be ascertained; then, there were four who had been lifted, as it were, of their noses, as well as one ear each; the penultimate boy, who at first did not seem violated at all, had skin that had turned to a spectral green of the sea, yet, when they examined his mouth, they found him toothless, his gums as if pared clear off; the last boy, the son of a renowned newspaperman, had been stuck with a knife so many times he appeared almost to have disappeared. "In each case, the Gimbernat's ligament was severed." A pause. "Oddly enough."

William Rockland, at this, gags and by accident bites his own tongue and wheezes, as if being strangled. Once he has regained his breath he declares, "Dear God."

"Of course," says Dr. Handley, "and then there are the ramifications of such crimes, specifically on the families of the victims, in particular the mothers." At this, she looks Mr. Rockland dead in the eye and winces. Being certified just last year as a doctor of psychology and having duly studied with the estimable Professor James in Boston, Elizabeth Handley has a magnetism about her, or perhaps that's just her height, for she's a surprisingly tall woman— taller even than Mr. Rockland—yet her face is that of a porcelain doll, deadly serene in an eerie way. She neither smiles nor frowns. Expressionless, she continues, "It is an ugly sight, what this beast does to these boys. I have been helping the families of the victims cope for quite some time now, and, still, I do not sway altogether gently with it. There are things, yet, that I have to comprehend. Why, for instance, does he leave his trail of terror open to so many different interpretations, if at heart each crime seems committed for a specific reason? Which we know, first, because there have been a few letters. Or where, finally, might his allegiances lie—with the Old South? There is so much we do not know, Mr. Rockland. That is my primary concern."

In a voice scarcely above a whisper, Pinkerton O'Malley includes, "The man most certainly is completely mad."

"But that," appends Dr. Handley, "is precisely our conundrum. For it appears that Clemantis is in possession of all his mental faculties."

Potter Palmer cues in with a nod.

Here's Mr. Tiggs out of nowhere, "We must, as well, be particularly careful, for the Husker, we believe, is a Negro." He is speaking, each knows, with the consent of President Benjamin Harrison, but it's clear to everyone at once that not even the government knows what to make of the killer. "In fact," he continues, "the United States government is under the suspicion that Clemantis the Husker may be two or eight or twelve men, working for certain forces both known and unknown, native or alien, who would like to see the waterloo, if you will, of our republic." He pauses, as if speaking to a full convention hall, with his eyebrows raised and lips furled. "This is to say, we believe this abduction to be politically motivated."

A long silence, during which sounds from the world outside begin to saturate in and buzz around—laughter far off in the distance; the calming susurrus of wind; a few early drops of rain, noisily spattering the panes; the jingle, jangle of the Midway, jeers and salvos and a few faint bars of a song you've never heard before but recognize at once and without delay. And here's the tolling of the morning's first launch.

"Please excuse me," William Rockland announces. Before he exits, he glances at Dr. Handley and says, "It's very much appreciated, but I'm afraid I should attend to my wife." That's not what's on his mind, of course. What's on his mind is the Cosmopolitan. And Walsh. What he'll say to Potter Palmer has passed through his mind a thousand times, but now he's not certain he should say anything at all. Was it a bluff, a smarmy, questionably savvy business move on Walsh's part? Or does Walsh or someone Walsh knows in fact have Billy? Is Walsh Clemantis, or an acquaintance of the man? He is, after all, a businessman of sorts, and that is how the dailies have described the Husker—as a businessman with an ax to grind. Most probably, Walsh is an impostor, and his demands are a bluff. For the first time, then, William Rockland thinks of telling someone—perhaps Dr. Handley, if he could only get her alone. He feels comfortable with her, feels familiar.

"Mr. Rockland," she calls after him out in the hallway. "A word if you will."

He halts and fixes his eyes on her.

"I'm not sure how you'd feel about this, but I wanted to run it by you on the off chance that you might think it a good idea, as I think it's a good idea, considering the circumstances," says Dr. Handley. Rockland says nothing, so she continues, "I would like to speak with your wife, if that's all right with you." His eyes are as an eagles', scrutinizing her, but still he says nothing, so the doctor feels compelled to abridge her proposal. "I think it might benefit her, if I may say so, to speak with someone."

After a time, Rockland says, "Fine. Come by this afternoon."

Just then, she offers a hand, but William Rockland has already turned and walked off, downstairs and out into the White City. Outside there's drizzle, but the sun's piercing, so he shades his eyes with his hand and scuttles off into the crowd, past the Esquimaux Village and out onto 56th Street. He looks over his shoulder periodically, checking to see if he's being followed. Every eye he meets causes him to become suspicious, but as far as he can tell, nobody's trailing him.

On Stony Island Avenue, he flags a phaeton and heads home.

POLICE NOTICE
TO THE OCCUPIER

On the morning of Monday, October 8, a young boy disappeared while visiting the White City with his family. Should you know of any person to whom suspicion is attached, you are earnestly requested to report at once to the nearest Police Station.

Chicago Police
9 October 1893

Fourteen

Blood floods West Randolph, a major thoroughfare north of the Loop, making passage difficult. Outside the slaughter-houses, carcasses have been amassed in street-side piles or what might pass as pyramids. The sign reads, WALSH MEAT, and inside, its owner, J. T. Walsh, is seated in full repose at a large ovoid table, encircled as ever by his thuggish men, each as tall as a mountain and wide as a caribou and each smelling of gruel. His cheeks being rosy, it's apparent that he's sopped, even at this early hour; but the company he keeps mistakes this for mere frivolity. Dressed in his velveteen smoking jacket, with nothing underneath, he's buttressed by two vast ladies, one blond and the other raven haired, each attired only in silken bodices and the finest jewelry and each, too, giggling as irascible Walsh slips his mitts into their nether-growth and says thunderously, "Boys." His voice being singsongy, yet mawkish, the feeling's one of unease—and trepidation. The thugs, being thugs, and with limited vocabulary, retreat now off to another room without a word, leaving only Fallon and Graft. After this, Walsh says, "Sit."

They do, but say nothing.

Before long, the two sirens are excused. The men's eyes trail after, lingering.

Without hesitation, Walsh wants Graft and Fallon to know,

"Whatsoever your inclinations in the matter of flesh, we have business to discuss."

Graft nods, while Fallon drapes one leg over the other. Neither, as yet, has so much as blinked.

There's music, a waltz, in the far-off, lying low but dynamic, before it fades.

"These, men," Walsh says as he pitches his whole torso forward and onto the table, "are not happy times. People, as you well know, are starving. Families go on, unfed. Women with their breasts tapped dry cannot provide for their offspring. Elder mothers and fathers, those who did not go naturally, wither. Men, these are trying times. We cannot take this ever so lightly. There are measures that can be taken, and people to carry them out. But no one steps forward, as yet, and we are left with amateurism. Do you reckon it so?"

They are about to nod yes. But Walsh continues, "Four score years ago and all that bullshit, but the bitch of the thing is this, gentlemen. We, sirs, are being plundered for our souls. The Negro, who but twenty odd years ago was enslaved, today is hired by Mr. Pullman and his cohorts at rates less than those of our pigmentation. While, by the by, our country folk arrive here dehydrated and malnourished and can't for the life of them find employment. We are not European, and do not cosset ourselves as a European would. On these shores, lies are passed unwittingly from generation to generation . . . It is a travesty, men."

"It is, sir," says Graft.

"There comes a time in one's life when forces beyond one's comprehension conspire to set things aright, even if that involves going the whole hog against the grain of our republic," says Walsh. He pauses—for effect.

Fallon, between his heavy lids, eyes Graft. Graft does not return the gaze. Neither one speaks.

"Hence the Socialist Labor party. But that goes only so far, as you may well know. What I'm after is results. That is why I am asking for your help. You will be given the product, and are to deliver it to Electricity. It is a symbol of everything that is wrong with the republic. I trust," eyeing Fallon, "you know how to detonate dynamite. But we do this at night, so nobody's hurt. Do we speak the same language?"

They nod. "We do, sir," Graft says.

"For now," says Walsh, "we eat." He reveals a long, sinewy sausage, the smell of which, being beyond pungent, immediately cinders one's sense of smell, or perhaps someone has just impregnated the air with a meaty tang. "Later, we'll get down to business." He stands and walks on, having masticated an enormous chunk of meat that squishes in the wetness of his mouth. He is known as a glutton and revels in being gluttonous publicly. Graft and Fallon follow Walsh into a second back room, this one replete with two encompassing hearths, each burning, and large, coal black cauldrons presided over by men who each show various states of facial growth and who are wearing identical spotless paste white toques. One stands pressed up against a countertop and is putting all of his substantial weight into flattening dough; sweat beads up across his forehead and drips down into the dough and, as oil, is massaged liberally into the mixture.

"I believe," Walsh says from behind a marbled carcass that hangs from two iron prongs threatening as fangs, "that the blood of animals invigorates the soul and just might expand one's mental facilities. In truth, this will alter the course of humanity as much as any kinetoscope."

Everyone's put to work—grilling *payard*, game hens, simmering soups and roiling pastas, spicy Oriental noodles, flavored stock, everything rubbed over with a tart-smelling secret lotion.

"That, sir," says Fallon, "smells as the insides of a woman's undergarments." He pinches his nose for emphasis.

J. T. Walsh, chuckling, holds aloft a bottle of Scotch and announces to the room, "You best behave yourselves, as Mrs. Walsh will arrive presently and I don't want her to see how my educative measures have backfired on me."

A lone laugh. Then from Fallon, "You, sir, are married?"

"Fifteen years, man." Next come the crawfish hors d'oeuvres, accompanied by red and white wines flowing, unfettered, from copper spouts meant to depict the snouts of dolphins. Once everyone is heartily sopped, into a final back room they all go—Walsh followed by Graft followed by Fallon, then Leston Biggs, Daley Anderson, Jackson McCloud, Franklin Spitzer. Everyone, at their leisure, picks a place to sit, and sits.

Conversations cease, then restart afresh.

"That is not the problem, as I see it," Leston Biggs, who's so tall and skeletal he teeters, even sitting, says to Daley Anderson, a man of more girth than height. "The problem is that the institution of slavery—"

"That is a problem only for Negroes." Biggs, being a Negro, very nearly shudders at this. He'd like to hit Daley Anderson but knows that Anderson is Anderson, stubborn as an ox, and cannot be swayed without an ordeal.

Walsh says, "The Industrial Age is simply a reinvention of the institution of slavery. It does not suit our enlightened age well that our diverse and free republic should participate still in vanquishment of the flesh. It is ignorance, pure and simple."

"Your kind must get over it," Daley Anderson says loudly so that everyone hears, "and join in, and help build the boats, and help lay the rail. Violence is only the means, not the end."

"We do so," Walsh says, "not by choice, but because there is nothing else for us to do. Give us better employment, and we will take it with great—and due—thanks and prosper."

Daley Anderson is about to speak again, but Biggs says, "Do you forget: we are subjugated and cannot move about at will. We are marketable commodities and risk death at the hands of white men now with greater trepidation. Whereas before it was a loss of property, now," and with this, his voice wavers, "it is not a loss to a white man whether a Negro lives or dies. Alas, man, it is but a sport."

Fallon out of nowhere says, "But Mr. Lincoln was quite fond of your people."

Walsh, it is rather clear, isn't listening, and he says to Anderson with finality, "A white man is a great loss to the economy, while, were a Negro disposed of, there's always another. It is a heinous view, and I do not share it."

"You traffic in ken, man, but your people eat entrails," says Anderson savagely. "Tell me, how did you come so far?"

"I only share compassion," Walsh says, "not charity and certainly not pity."

There is a long silence, during which the other men in the room, save Walsh, set about to play hundred-point billiards. Walsh takes Graft by the wrist and leads him off to a corner.

Fallon, though he hasn't been summoned, follows.

40 LADIES FROM 40 NATIONS

World's Congress of Beauty

INTERNATIONAL DRESS & COSTUME EXHIBIT

Fifteen

There's something eerily comforting about an empty house.

She voyages from room to room, drawing the curtains. They are already drawn, but she opens and closes them again. It is early afternoon, Tuesday, the sun outside piercingly brilliant. Despite this, she feels as though she could sleep and never stop. Each moment stretches out so that it feels as though just scrunching a fist lasts a thousand hours. Her body feels slack as porridge. She examines the porcelain finery in the dining and living rooms, which she insisted on keeping here during the renovations. She returns to the master bedroom but does not lie down upon the bed. She will have to remember, before laying her head on the goose-feather pillow one final time, that, all in all, hers has been a worthy, robust, zealous life—a life she would live no way other than the precise way in which she has lived it, were she given a second chance. She watches the horizon of the bed for a very long while before circling it and sitting at the very edge. She will have to remind herself that—above all—she has been loved and has loved heartily in return. She glances at herself in the mirror to the side of the Colonial armoire in the hallway just outside the bedroom, which is visible despite the room's darkness. In the mirror opposite the bed, she doesn't see her own face but the face she had in her childhood. A face terribly unrecognizable yet instantly familiar. All at once, she falls back into the bed. Oh, she has forgotten to draw the curtains in this room. She cannot move. The curtains are drawn, there's no light in this room, but still there's a piercing light boring holes through her eyelids. She lies, massive, weak. The darkness swirls around and descends upon her. She glances about and notices a book on the side table. Billy's gone. She would like to flip through the book—*The Tomboy Who Was Changed into a Real Boy*, one of Billy's favorites—but hasn't the strength. She knows he's gone but still can't bear to think it.

"Dear." Rockland rushes into the house. Upon entry, he knows something is amiss. It's a quarter past two o'clock, the afternoon's dazzling—if wintry—but here the curtains are drawn, it's stiflingly warm, and the whole house smells sharply of camphor. Perhaps, he thinks, something has caught fire. He sprints from room to room searching out the potential inferno. The wind, still strapping, batters the windows. He can't see even a foot in front of him, so he knocks into chairs, tables, slips on a rug. Everything—floor, wall, ceiling—shakes as William Senior, having failed to find the source of the rancid burning smell, climbs the stairs and searches upstairs with increasing fanaticism—for he realizes, just now, that, if there is a blaze, it's sure to have taken his wife. Without ado he's in the bedroom, breathless, standing in the doorway, calling out, "Elizabeth!"

She is where he left her, in a ball in bed, buried in blankets.

He throws himself upon her and shimmies up and down, warming her. Still, there is no movement, and he's not certain she's breathing. He flips her, attempts to lift her, turn her slantwise to free her breathing passage, but she's heavier than he remembers her being, and she doesn't budge. After a while, he strips himself of his clothing and joins his wife under the covers and wraps himself around her, holding her till she wakes.

Her skin's like a seal's—cold, slick, dank.

Women's bodies have always confused him. He's not sure he understands their intricacies, the way they unfold languidly over time and not in one sudden, fleeting tumescence. The curves bewilder him; the softness around the hips frightens him; the few hairs on his wife's hips deter him. He's not confident in his abilities as a man to please a woman. For one thing, he's not very experienced; he and his wife procreate but rarely and when they do, briefly. In truth, he can count the number of times on two hands, and since William Rockland, unlike many of his compatriots, is not the sort of man prone to visit ladies of the night (it has happened once, but he's not even sure he remembers it happening), he's only familiar with the supine Biblical position. Still, his mind wanders, as now, into the Devil's territory. For a moment he feels the urge to enter his sleeping wife in a way he has not before, and would not, were she awake. To this end, he runs a hand along the slope of her back from her shoulder on down to the furrow at the small of her back, where he lets it rest. A fingernail grates along her spine, a palm presses deeply into a shoulder blade, but she does not flinch. Should he proceed? It would be strange, perhaps even a violation of the code of man and wife. At present, however, he is moved more by impulse than by reason, and with little excitement he lets his hand trail farther south to her fundament.

Suddenly, "Bill?" Her breath is mossy, but he doesn't mind. In fact, it excites him.

"We're late," says William. "We have to go."

She turns over onto her side, so she's facing him. Her face appears as if smashed together between two beams; pillow wrinkles run rivulets along her cheeks and jaws, around the eyes, and to the chin. Phlegm has dripped out of her nostrils and has dried upon her upper lip, so it appears, in the shadows, that she might have a mustache. Her lips are so desiccated, they're crinkled and appear to be on the verge of falling off entirely. When she speaks, he's assaulted by her fungal breath, but he doesn't pull back; he remains up and in her face, about to kiss her.

"Where are we going?"

Then he does—kisses her fully on the lips, and when she does not return the kiss, he plants another, and another—the last with his tongue slipped between her lips. The inside of her mouth is warm and wet and alive; he's as excited as he's ever been, sexually, but perhaps because she's not returning his affections, or perhaps because he just now remembered why she's so run-down, he pulls back, sits up, covers himself with a pillow, and says only, "I'm sorry."

At this, she herself pulls back and covers herself with blankets, saying, "Why am I naked?"

"I don't know, dear," says William. "That is how I found you."

"I'm hungry," she says. "Feed me."

"Soon," he says. "Come, we must go to the Palmers now, Elizabeth." He isn't sure what he's doing, lying to her or simply urging her out of bed and back into the day, back into the world of the living. "They'll feed us."

Surprisingly, as if she hasn't spent the past day and a half in bed, but instead has been out and about with Bertha Palmer, enjoying the wonders of the White City, drinking carbonated soda in the slanting sunlight, Mother Rockland rises from the bed, lights a lantern, and proceeds to dress as if it's a new morning and not late afternoon. Once she's prepared her face—rouged her cheeks, darkened her eyes, and painted her lips—she says, "Let's go." That might even be a smile creeping across her face.

Sixteen

They traverse alleyways, cross byways and abandoned, junk-filled fields, and pass through a wooden door, as that to a shack, only this is a barn surrounded by city. Inside they find a place where they can hide, maybe rest. It's dark, but not warm. The barn, it seems, was abandoned long ago and never razed. A good three inches of dust rise as they come to their landing—by a wall that faces the city street. There is a peephole through which Skurlock can monitor shadows' progress, should there be any. Skurlock kneels down, then at last sits, coiling his legs together. A gust of wind creeps in through the slits in the barn's walls, causing them to shiver.

They're hiding, Billy knows, but from what? "Who is it, Han?"

"Don't know."

"Are they going to hurt us?"

Nothing. But when Billy's face takes on the appearance of a gourd, Skurlock says, "No, they won't."

"How do you know?"

"They might hurt me, but they'll leave you be," says Skurlock.

Billy says, "I don't want them to hurt you."

"Neither do I," says Skurlock.

"Why are they going to hurt you? What did you do, Han?"

"I don't rightly know." He scowls. "Nothing." Then, after a time,

Skurlock says, "Malice is but a cloak you pick up one afternoon and wear with pride. You can take it off whenever you want."

"I'm tired," says Billy. It is true: his eyes have shut to a sliver and are crimson red.

Skurlock glances at the kid and says, "No one will find you down here. You're quite safe here with me."

Billy, however, does not look it. His forehead has just folded, it seems, in and upon itself, like the forehead of an octogenarian in winter frost. Again, he says, "I'm tired."

"Here," says Skurlock. He takes a hand to Billy's face and with slight force brings the boy's whole head down and into his lap. A moment later, young Rockland is heard to snore. As soon as it begins, the snoring ceases, and Billy jerks up, says, "I can't sleep!" It seems, by the glaze of his eyes, that he is on the verge of tears, so Skurlock, ever mindful to check the world outside the slit in the maple, inquires, "Want me to tell you a story?" Billy, delirious, though that is yet a relative term, for the lids of his eyes have all but shut out life, replies with an audible, screechy "Yes!" "Shh!" Skurlock affixes a hand over the young boy's mouth and ear so as to impede the inflow of oxygen, just for an instant. Then a dart of the eyes, so that Billy knows this is not farce. Coughing once Skurlock's removed his hand, young Rockland breathes out a word that may or may not be, "Sorry," yet Skurlock can't tell. "Okay," he says, and as Billy places his head back into the older man's lap, he sets off on his tale.

"Let me think, then," says Skurlock. He shifts his whole body, so as to become more comfortable and, perhaps, fall asleep. "Oh, yes," without noticing that his audience is already one glint this side of sleep. "There once, and you should know this was when I was about your age, perhaps a year or three older, was a man—our neighbor, actually. And although we—that is, my mum and pop—didn't talk to him much, save as a matter of commerce, like, well, anyway . . . I'm not sure I remember what he looked like, but he always frightened me, for, thought I, he was a character out of a storybook, and not life. This would not interest you save for how he passed from this world." At which point, all at once, there's a laugh. "My mum was the first to notice it, and she complained to my pop. There was a peculiar smell, she said; she couldn't quite place it. He didn't do anything, having made up his mind long ago that mothers live in accordance with an entire other notion of reality, one prone to fantasy. In any case, a few days passed, and then my pop began to suspect that Mum was right all along. There was, in truth, a peculiar, rancid smell, and when, after some rudimentary detecting, Pop ascertained that the smell was coming from our strange neighbor's, we all went to investigate. Why they brought me along, I don't know. Perhaps they just forgot. We banged upon the neighbor's door, yet received no response. My pop quickly grew frustrated and retired home and returned after a minute with a sledgehammer. Mum was not quite sure a busted door was protocol, yet she didn't stop him. He hammered in the door, and we were bombarded with stench. Take the worst you ever smelled and times that by a hundred, and that might only begin to describe that smell. Mum even almost fainted. Soon, we entered our neighbor's residence, yet you could not be sure. Affixed to the four walls and the floor and the ceiling were images, reproduced from books, of men and women in all states of dress and especially undress, copulating. In the photo reproductions there were chains and saws and clasps, the kind they use in medical schools." He pauses. "Does this excite you any? Have your parents told you how you, well, came to be in this world? Do you touch yourself?" There is no response, so Skurlock continues, "And after gaining our bearings we went in, Pop leading the way and my mother right behind him. We found our neighbor, as if by chance, by stepping on him. He was, and had been for a while yet, quite deceased. Attached to his head was a wire mechanism of his own devising, to which he had affixed yet more images of the carnal act. Now, the wire headgear had caught to a long nail hanging from the ceiling, and the man, not having successfully extricated himself from his gear, had hanged himself—dead, to be sure, yet all that flesh in a state of utter euphoria, to say nothing of rigidity. It would, I fathom, be quite a nice way to go." He stops, for here young Rockland has fallen under. Skurlock checks the world outside. They are, for the while at least, safe. Before shutting his own lids upon the light of the world, he searches through a pocket, locates the glass jar, no bigger than the size of his thumb, he keeps in his breast pockets, on account of his restless heart. He opens it—doing so makes his hand shake—inserts a finger, and places a drop of the jar's contents on the tip of his tongue. All at once, everything fades to blackness.

SECURITY DEPARTMENT REPORT (cont.)

Number of reports of known killers of men and boys
in attendance at the Exposition .... *o*

Seventeen

Dr. Handley sitting across from the boy in a chair with a leg that's been kicked off and recently reattached and a back that reclines more than it supports. It is Tuesday evening, just before dinner, so the doctor asks if the boy would like to eat, but he says nothing. The boy, his body twisted at an awkward angle, knees just about to buckle, still wears a frightened face. Dr. Handley peppers her speech with pauses that are meant to pacify. In her lap's a leaflet upon which, should she choose, she'll write, but from the sound it makes when her fingers tap it, it might as well be a drum. Though her skin registers little sensation, there's a smile, wide as a sunrise, creasing her face.

"What," she begins, "is your name?"

The boy, who wouldn't know a smile if it nipped him on the bum, says after a long pause, "Nix."

"Do you live nearby?" When that finds no response, the doctor inquires, "Where do you go to school?"

The boy nods, and the doctor inquires further, "Were you lost? What were you looking for—your mother? A father?"

Nix nods again, but says, "No."

Dr. Handley doesn't know what to say, so she says, "Are you hungry?"

"No, but thank you."

At last, she leans in and brushes the boy's hand, as if to assure him that all will be okay. Suddenly, Nix jumps back in his chair, almost tipping it. Dr. Handley, being trained in these matters, withdraws her kindness and says, "It's all right, it's okay," over and over. The young boy moans, at first, and later wails. Finally, he's calmer, although his shoulders, standing straight up, still shake, as do both of his hands.

A Columbian Guard, his walk more waddle than anything else, enters with a meal of sorts, consisting only of mashed potatoes and a slab of beef. The thinking was that the boy would be hungry, for it's likely he hasn't eaten in many hours, if not in days. The skin on his body hangs, stretched way out, almost entirely off his bones.

His is a quick and complete retreat. His body coils in on itself, as if for safety.

Directly behind the boy there's a clock, and right at this inopportune moment it shoots its ding out into the room.

Dr. Handley now recoils, startled, saying, "Oh, my."

Nix laughs. It is like thunder, loud and echoic.

Some might consider this progress, yet Dr. Handley is not certain. She falters on, inquiring, "Are you an only child, Mr. Nix?"

The question is meant to open the pathways, not close them. Nix's eyes, all of two slivers, well up and turn glassy. Either those are tears streaking the boy's face, or they are shadows. The boy places his head at a side-turned angle that looks as though it might break his neck by its sheer horizontality, then he cranes it downward, where it flops into the bowl his hands form.

"My father," Nix starts. But then he's silent.

Dr. Handley, though she knows Professor James would suggest otherwise, presses forth. Though young Nix has said all of a half-dozen words and betrayed every communicative facial expression, eventually the boy, rocking in his chair so that it almost keels over, says, "My father killed my mother, and now I don't know where he is."

Often, trust and time are needed to elicit such catastrophic information, so at first, in truth, Dr. Handley's somewhat suspicious. She's not certain she should take what the boy says as definitive fact. Perhaps he's trying to get a rise from her, or test her in some way. It is a common psychological manipulation, Dr. Handley knows. Nevertheless, it's common for a reason, because it works so well.

She can't believe what she's just heard, for sure, but the fact is that, just a moment after the boy's said it, his face, once expressionless, breaks into a playful smile, the doctor asking, her own face mimicking his, "And how did he do this, Mr. Nix?"

"He slashed her throat with a paring knife."

"He did?"

"Yes."

Dr. Handley shifts in her chair. "Was it an accident, or did your father murder your mother?"

"Oh, it was murder, ma'am," the boy says. He's no longer smiling, but neither is he simpering. "I was there—my father killed my mother with me right there, watching."

Should she play this out with him? She says, "That must have been a difficult experience." Though she'd like with all her heart to believe him, she doesn't. His eyes are too wide and probing, as if he says what he says and then waits for a reaction. It is a common trait among liars, cheats, and thieves. But boys found under the corpse of another boy in the White City? Dr. Handley wouldn't have thought so. Since she's been here, though, she's learned quickly to live her life under the assumption that stranger things have happened, and will again. "Why didn't you stop him?"

"You don't know my father, ma'am."

"He is a big man?" She is enjoying this perversely, so for just an instant she allows a smile to pass over her face.

"Very," says Nix, "although in truth I am not certain in what department you would like to know if my father was big."

A loud, sustained cackle from Dr. Handley. The door opens, and in marches Theodate Tiggs, who it seems has been just on the far side of the door. Eavesdropping, Dr. Handley suspects, in case anything about the Husker's mentioned. Nix himself cackles, only his cackle sounds more like a chicken cackling than like anything else either Tiggs or Handley has heard. Tiggs's face, once he enters the interview room, turns rigid. His forehead wrinkles together tightly, and his lips purse in what's either worry or worry's distant cousin, disquiet.

"Is it a party?" wonders Tiggs. "I'm sorry, but I don't think I received the invitation."

With Nix still cackling, Dr. Handley soon calms herself and says, "Yes, but the invitations haven't come back from the printer's," at which she cackles again, nearly as loud as Nix. She feels idiotic and ignorant all at once—idiotic for letting the boy continue and ignorant for not following her earlier instinct. Given the circumstances, she decides she might catch a little fun once it rolls around, and since fun's foreign territory to Dr. Handley, most especially of late, it hits her as a drink hits a recovering alcoholic, with vigor, so that, as she cackles, half of Dr. Handley's body's thrown forward and the whole of her appears to be in midconvulsion.

Tiggs says sternly, "I need to speak with you, Doctor, if you don't mind."

Out in the hall, Dr. Handley says, "Make it quick."

"Dear girl," says Tiggs, "even you would not have predicted what our murderer has done with this last one"—that is, the cadaver.

She is, it's true, at a loss. Having already studied the world's sleaziest murders—among them the Highland mob doing in James I; the scalping of Jane McCrea; Mate Bram; the 23d Street Murder, that of financier Benjamin Nathan; right on up to this very year's Lizzie Borden fiasco. Even so, she has yet to witness anything quite like this, including, as well, the maraudings of the London Doctor. There have been severed body parts; there has been blood, rivers of it worthy of the Tigris, yet slower moving, in addition to putrefactions not even a Puritanical minister in the midst of sermonizing could have dreamed up. Yet it is the age of these cadavers that leaves one so squeamish. Here's a life, lost. Dr. Handley not only cannot, but won't, let her mind imagine what might have been.

"What," she asks of Tiggs, "could it be?"

After a long while, their faces pale as phantoms', Chief Detective Oliver Simonds and two Columbian Guards emerge from the examining room down the hall where the cadaver's being inspected, and they march right on past without a word. Mr. Tiggs, training his eyes on the young doctor with frightening concentration, says, "All the signature marks have been left on this last one, I'm afraid, but there are two new"—a pause—"phenomena."

Dr. Handley coughs, as if on cue, then nods for Tiggs to continue.

"The anus has been extracted. Expertly."

Coldly, as if that is the only way to deal with matters like these, Dr. Handley asks, "And the second?"

Tiggs appears to be wincing, but since he cloaks his emotions with such bravado, Dr. Handley has no idea what he's thinking. He says, "The scrotum has been squashed to a mulch."

The doctor, nodding, looks down at the floor as if to consider her own feet. At last, she glances back at Tiggs, and though he has started to walk clear away, she says, "So he might be schooled, a surgeon perhaps and not a simpleton as the dailies have supposed."

"That is true," Tiggs says without turning around, without making eye contact of any sort. "It appears that your killer has learned a thing or two since we last heard from him."

Dr. Handley's saying, "Assuming the killer killed the boy we found with Mr. Nix, why didn't the killer kill Mr. Nix? Certainly his life must have been in danger, and if he was there for the killing, perhaps he knows what our killer looks like. I mean, simply, how can this be explained? How?"

"I'm not certain, Doctor."

"We must be certain."

They are sitting in a conference room that is or seems to be identical to the room in which Dr. Handley interviewed young Mr. Nix a moment ago. Perhaps because of this the doctor comes across as distracted. In fact, she isn't listening at all. Only when Inspector Moreau suggests the killer might himself be a Negro does she come to attention.

Confused, she'd like to know, "And how do you explain that?"

"Because," says Inspector Moreau, "how else do you explain not murdering or at the very least molesting our young Negro boy, unless the killer himself is a Negro? They tend to stay together."

Under different circumstances, Dr. Handley would refute this, would perhaps even charge Inspector Moreau with being uninformed in matters of race. Negroes do not befriend other Negroes simply because their skin is the same color. Or do they? The more Dr. Handley thinks about it, the less certain she is. She says, "It's possible, isn't it, that the killer simply didn't see the boy."

"Or perhaps," says Inspector Moreau, "he simply did not have time to finish off two boys, or perhaps he didn't want to."

"Oh, he'd want to." It is Chief Detective Simonds, who's accompanying the Pinkertons so that they might meet young Mr. Nix. He appears to have just eaten, for he holds his belly and moves and speaks with noticeable languor.

"If, that is, he's a he." It just slips out. Dr. Handley didn't mean to say it, not to Chief Detective Simonds or the Pinkertons, because that would entail more explanation and that's the last thing Handley feels she can do at present—explain.

But already it's too late, and Sergeant Banks has said, "I'm sorry, what did you say?"

"It is possible," says Dr. Handley. She should explain her theory. She should explain that, though largely undocumented, murderesses are equally as likely to be found dagger in hand, having these days the added cloak of anonymity, as well as her speculation that crime, when committed, is mostly done by a male wearing dark, anonymous garb. She should explain that it is indeed possible, if unlikely, that the murderess was a respected, well-liked, out-and-about member of the community who, having been serenaded so long with the samba of the Lord, felt herself, and let herself, navigate to the other side. That is at least possible, is it not? Dr. Handley knows it must be. She knows, even, given the way the world works sometimes, taking you wholly unawares, that she herself could be possessed by such evil. This being a most trying time for family and friends alike, she hopes word does not get out that they do not know yet whether they are looking for a male or female.

Chief Detective Simonds would like to know, "What's next, Doctor?"

"Well, with this latest information, my profile will surely change," says Dr. Handley. "Perhaps the boy did see the killer, but even if he did, I am not of the mind that he'll tell us. He's something of a trickster, and I feel that the memory is buried, so as not to devastate Mr. Nix more. That said," she continues, "though more narrow, our search is now thwarted by the possibility that, as a professional, our subject will be increasingly difficult to find."

Pinkerton Roy Boyd says, quiet so only Pinkerton Alex O'Malley hears, "You never know, do you, with a Negro?"

O'Malley doesn't laugh, but Boyd does. Heartily.

"They are, aren't they, quite the beastly race." It is Potter Palmer. Granted, he's far from serious, a fact that is lost on both Pinkertons, who are not familiar with Mr. Palmer's championing—at the prompting of his wife—of the cause of racial equality.

"We have," says Potter Palmer, "a complication. Which is that we may very well have a strike on our hands before too long. It is a matter that has not been thwarted despite my better efforts."

Chief Detective Simonds considers the complication, then asks, "Will the results be those of the Riot of 'Eighty-six?"—that is, the Haymarket.

"Worse, I'm afraid." Everyone looks to Potter Palmer to continue, which he does. "It seems that Wayne Cindolerna," the union leader, "was found to be involved with a certain meat-packer's daughter, who—the meat-packer—was not happy, to say the least. An altercation ensued, as tends to happen, and Mr. Cindolerna is not altogether still with us, though you can see him, if it pleases you, even if he can't see—or hear—you." In response, the union has threatened a citywide strike.

"Won't that cripple the republic's economy, Mr. Palmer? American securities, because of the exportation of American gold, will liquefy; European investors, lured to and dazzled by the exposition, will sell American securities, which in due time will lead to multiple disasters around the globe—won't it, Mr. Palmer?"

"It will."

"Then I suggest we step up the search for the killer, as now he'll have a darker cloak with which to hide himself."

"Hello," Potter Palmer says to the doctor. He offers a hand. "There is so much I'd love to ask you. I'd love to mine your brain, Doctor. I have read so many wonderful things about you. You will find our Billy, won't you?" But before she can answer, "I trust you will."

"I have a lot of work to do," she says. "I'll be going," and with that she goes.

Potter Palmer, his smile as wide as the Sahara without being as dry, claps together his hands and wonders, "His name is Nix, you say? Take me to him, please." It was an impulse response, one he didn't discuss with his wife but one he was willing to bet his soul would have a positive outcome for all involved. For so long now, that's all she's talked about, having a child.

Entering the room to meet Nix, Potter Palmer nearly chirps, such is his giddiness. The boy, unresponsive, looks dead ahead without seeing, yet, once Potter Palmer enters, there's a chill in the air. Palmer sits directly across from Nix. They are scarcely three feet away from each other, yet at the same time entire worlds apart—one, one of the richest men in the republic, while the other's but a fatherless boy.

On account of the fat walrus man whose body reminds Nix of a rotund clown's, or of Mr. Kringle's, and whose whiskers, when he so much as breathes, don't shift, and whose eyes he can hardly see in this dim light, Nix laughs out loud. He covers his face in his hands, leaving a slit for a vista.

Palmer, not so much taken aback as delighted imagining just what he might do as a father—take the kid on midafternoon strolls, go sailing—laughs.

The boy stares at his own hands.

The light in this room is dim, being mostly gas lanterns and deep-drawn shadows, yet there's a certain brightness to the ambience that's unmistakable. Potter Palmer feels an immediate sense of closeness with young Mr. Nix. He, Palmer, should tell the boy that in all honesty he, Potter Palmer, has never wished to be a father, and frankly never had the time, and never thought he'd make a good one, not on account of an inability in paternal matters, just a lack of desire for them. He should tell young Mr. Nix that now he is no longer quite so certain. He should say that perhaps because of the kidnapping and the aftereffects the kidnapping has had on the Rocklands, those he's witnessed firsthand, he'd like, just once, to set everything right. If he were a father, everything would be. He wants to be a father; he feels he's ready. But he says, "I think you'll enjoy the house."

&ighteen

Those could be the stomps of searching feet, solid, fast, coming down on the gangplank overhead. First light breaks early and hard, this Wednesday, cutting in through the peephole in the wall. Their exit, while rushed, is slow, contingent upon the ebbing of sleep. They awake around the same time, except that young Billy prefers to return to dream and Skurlock, jerking upright, exhaling a cloud of breath that smells of three-day-old cabbage, elects to get a move on and to this end says, "Let's go."

Billy wants to know where, but he's still halfway asleep, so every word's garbled.

Where they're headed, however, not even Skurlock quite knows. What he does know is that, soon enough, whoever's after them will be able to find them all the easier on account of the daylight. Best go to the exposition and blend into the throng and seek the pleasures everyone seeks.

Billy, as yet, isn't ready to get a move on, so he says, "Leave me alone, Han."

But Skurlock will have none of it and lunges in and grasps both of the kid's forearms, tugs.

"I'm tired."

"Don't care," says Skurlock. "We must get out of here right this minute," and the tall man stands, stretches, refits his head with his black hat, straightens his trousers, kicks the soot from his boots, for they slept in a cavern of coal and appear to this world as Negroes. "Come on," and he leans in once again and grips the boy's arms, so hard that the boy hoots. His face already crimson, he lifts Billy from his slumber and into a wall. He places his left knee in the kid's crotch and presses with all his weight, such that the boy's hoot is now a howl, a yelp, and Skurlock's screaming, "Come on, you little fucking tyke, we're leaving. *Now!*"

They go. Down passageways so steep their feet skid on the wood, under trellises crowded with cobwebs, up stairs so rickety that one step breaks as Skurlock ascends, and finally across a wide, open room, the walls of which are gold, the ceiling a pictograph of a clement day in the Italian countryside, the colors once vibrant, now darkened by time, the flooring a marble dulled to concrete with occasional floorboards overlaid. Skurlock almost trips.

They're outside now, in the sunlight and the wind, which seems stronger even than last night.

Both of their faces are sooty, itchy, but only the boy has taken to scratching it. The effect is that, once Skurlock has taken his hand-kerchief and wiped Billy's face of soot, there linger red scratch marks, the skin around them swollen so that he looks as if he's been pressed up against a wall of bars.

The sky above is blue as azure and cloudless, save for one lone bird.

All at once, Skurlock hears the searching steps behind them coming closer, louder in volume. Where to go? Back to the White City? That might be too predictable. He knows this place beyond city limits where they could go, where the world as you know it appears to fall from the earth, apart from gravity. Pullman Village, it's called. It's a veritable Utopia, Skurlock's heard. He has a friend who told him about the place and said, if you ever need safe harbor, this is it. Only problem is, to get there you have to travel through the White City.

Where West Randolph meets State Street, they turn right, walk-ing abreast of each other, headed toward the Alley El and then the fair. They pass Palmer's magnificent store, the sun in the curved windows blinding. Despite the early hour, all of downtown's packed, people out enjoying the sun and laughing. That there's a killer a-lurk seems to be as far from everyone's mind as Mount Olympus. Skurlock doesn't really pause to wonder why so many people might be headed north, away from the exposition. A bespectacled man in black-on-white offers young Billy a bag of peanuts, and since Billy's too shy to respond, Skurlock accepts for him.

He checks left and then over each of his shoulders for a sign of his shadow. He has a hunch who it might be—Graft, sent by Walsh. Who else? Fathers instruct their families in the new art of window-watching. They pass men walking abreast of each other, sharing libation, headed toward the Midway, their eyes aflame with images of the Little Egypt girl and her swiveling hips. And policemen, too, out in spades—so many that it's nauseating.

Skurlock watches his own feet, so as not to meet anyone's eyes.

Just then, he tramples right into an elderly woman with a pearl-inlay brooch, and somehow, perhaps on account of his swift gait, the woman's brooch becomes loose and falls. Since it's a family heir-loom, as soon as she notices it's gone, she screams, thinking she's been robbed. Too, their eyes have locked, and the elderly woman has without uncertainty recorded the mien of Hannibal Skurlock, down to the birthmark to the right of his left eyebrow. Skurlock takes the kid by the arm, and they're off so fleetly that Billy has plumed out horizontal to the ground, nearly two feet in the air.

Down the block and around a corner, where they join in line for a tram. They're muddied, from their shoes on up to their knees, on account of the dew-dappled slag of downtown Chicago. State and Madison, where the cable line loop runs off to the west side before heading south. Everything is mud and yet more mud, a yawning trench four feet deep that runs the streets and under the raised gangplanks, past Prairie Avenue and alongside the gardens that adorn the mansions of South Michigan Avenue. The running gag about town at present is of a man encountered in downtown slag with only his head and shoulders showing. "Might I help you, sir?" "No, thanks," the man replies. "I have a steed under me."

The line to board the tram is long, so they wait. They disturb the air with their hands. There are moms and pops milling about, but still Skurlock's fixated on the children; some of them are younger than Billy Rockland, others not, yet all have skin that pales to an alabaster, as in a Caravaggio, only without the sullenness.

Sunlight stings young Billy's eyes, so he squints. Skurlock takes the boy's left hand in his own and jabs himself in the side.

"Here," he says. "Poke me—harder."

Before Billy knows what's happening, Skurlock's saying, "Come on, punch me as hard as you can!"

Billy might, but Skurlock's tugged him to the front of the line, where a man who's more granite than flesh blocks their passage. Skurlock affects a shove. The granite man doesn't budge. Skurlock's about to clock the beast when the beast clocks Skurlock— softly, considering the man's size—and he falls back, just missing the kid. Billy laughs and makes a run for it. This time, when Skurlock approaches the boy and takes the boy's lapel in his oversize hand and forcibly relocates the boy from his current positioning, it's different. There's something darker about the look on Skurlock's mien, and it's not just the caked-on mud. It's in the eyes—a glimmer of rage. With a motion that's anything but smooth, Skurlock steps up to the boy and sways there, as though possessed of an overflow of spirit. All at once, everything goes as if muffled, like it's ricocheting underwater.

Bells toll off in the distance. There are, as yet, no fair-bound trams.

The man's eyes could well be glowing, they're so bright. With the sun coming down on all sides and perhaps because of the man's face being mud-caked and far from recognizable, Billy mistakes Skurlock for his father. He is, in fact, a complete stranger, and it strikes young Rockland that he is out of his wits for having gone with this guy in the first place. Billy glances across the faces of those around him, yet each face he meets is a strange face. No one would come to his rescue, would they, if he were in danger. He begins to think he just might be. Skurlock, before everyone, caresses the rear of Billy's head as a father would a son, perhaps, but there's something about

Skurlock's leer that's unsettling. From the top of the child's head, he travels down the neck. Under his shirt and down, farther yet, to unexplored territory, Skurlock's hand probes.

Billy's not sure what to do. Skurlock's big, while Billy's yet a boy. He could make a run for it, but isn't sure yet if he wants to. He could scream, but doesn't. It's almost nice, and for a brief moment, until he looks up and gauges the expression on Skurlock's face, he closes his eyes and respires, as he might in a bath. Skurlock's face, when Billy spots it, is twisted into a wad, and it appears as though the big man's in pain, not pleasure. Sweat beads from every pore and dribbles down his cheek and over the side of his jaw. The skin, despite the mud, is so pale it's ghostly. Before long, Skurlock, smiling, says, "What sight would you like to see at the fair today, my dear?"

Billy stares straight on, says, "The wheel."

Nineteen

ednesday noon. He's down the marble balustrade that's aswirl with grays and a color one shade this side of white, at the bottom of which he's approached by an ever-smiling gnome of a man, who asks, in an accent Nix can't place but would like to, "Did you pass the night well, sir?" Sir? It must be a dream, from which presently Nix will wake, that has transported him to this castle, this better life. When, however, the gnome leans over to pat down the boy's upturned hair and then detach from behind the boy's left ear a doubloon, as a gag, the feeling's as real as anything. The boy nods, but says nothing. The gnome presents Nix with the doubloon, at which point Nix smiles widely and moves his lips, though no words escape, only chirping sounds. Hand in hand, they descend the last flight of stairs together, the ceiling above them opening to reveal a room so large it's nearly endless—stocked with wonders he's never before beheld, with antiques aplenty, with chairs from the French Revolution, tables, armoires from Louis the XV, a gilt harpsichord, potted plants large as trees, paneled walls gilded where paintings aren't hung, and a fresco on the ceiling that's intended to look like the latter-day work of Michelangelo.

"Feel right at home, dear," a minty voice calls out. "How was your sleep?"

She is taller than he'd expected, also frumpier. Even so, she moves as a ballerina, with a certain marked grace, only she's wearing a black wool dress with iron casing that juts straight out and jiggles whenever she moves. Her face, which holds layers upon layers of white powder, is serene without being staid. She's kneeled down, her face right up in his own, and because of the consummate effort it takes for her to maneuver in her dress, her brow and cheeks are sopped, are rosy red and darkening, even through the chalk. When her new son says nothing, she says, "Hungry?"

Behind him stands the Negro gnome, who affixes a piece of fabric around the boy's neck, before tightening it till Nix gags.

"There," says Bertha Palmer. "Don't you look handsome. We'll eat."

She takes young Nix by the hand and leads him across the entire galaxy, it seems, down a hallway into a smaller yet no-less-wondrous room. In the center stands a wood-block table with seating for two, mother and son.

Just now, Nix notices his garb—its smooth, silken feel that's cold to the touch without being discomforting, its layer-upon-layer thickness, as befits a prince, so that, should harm encroach, he will be amply padded and not shiver. He's been dressed, at some point between sleep and waking, in a suit and shorts and even socks, which he's heard of but never donned. The Negro gnome aids him as he sits in his chair, locating him up flush against the table's edge, almost so close he can't breathe. A napkin, folded in the form of a swan, is undone and placed around his neck and tied so as to conceal the virgin clothing underneath. Even his skin feels silken, this noontime. Sunlight slants in through a skylight high above them, placed in the direct center of the ceiling, though whether for appearance or function Nix has no idea. There's a small doorway at the far end of the room, which must lead to the kitchen, for from there waft smells of boiling meat, simmering vegetables, and from which two other servants, Negroes both, come bearing this noon's foodstuffs.

"I prefer," says Bertha Palmer, "to dine in the room where the help dines." Her hands fluttering here and then there, as a maestro's. "But today is a special day!" Her smile cracks in half. Nix blinks.

"Soup." The gnome sets down a steaming bowl.

"Not Thomas, I'm afraid," says Mrs. Palmer. As her soup's set down, she's sure to touch the gnome's hand in gratitude, smiling at her new son all the while. "Alas, Thomas prefers this room."

Oh! She means his new father, not Nix. Perhaps it is only a coincidence they share the same first name, or perhaps not.

After a while, she says, "Eat." He does, although the only method he can devise with which to eat the soup is to pick up the bowl and sip, so he watches her. She draws up a silver spoon with which to scoop the liquid, then blowing on it, all at once, then sipping, as one swills one's own spittle. He follows her lead, but whereas her movements were graceful, his are ungainly, and soup spills out the side of the spoon and onto the napkin he's wearing as a bib.

"I know," says Bertha Palmer, "that you're still not used to this, that this indeed must be a shock, but I hope that you find it possible to adjust, if only for a little while, to our lifestyle, which now is your lifestyle as well. If you prefer Thomas to Thom, that is fine. Otherwise, it's Thom, or Tommy, from here on out. All right?"

Without blinking and without saying a word, he stares at the swirls his spoon makes in the soup as it's set down. Finally, he looks up, fixing her eyes with his before he glances away. What is this, some joke? He cannot seem to remember what has happened to him in his life of late, other than what happened last night. Shivering there in the coldest cold for all that eternity. There is a mystique in regard to meat that's infectious, that begs you pay attention no matter your present stage of hunger or satiation. In reference to the plate of boiled gristle that's soon set down before him, Bertha Palmer would like to know, "You do like meat, yes?" The flesh glistens vein-splotched and darkened to a deep purple. "This is so scrumptious—you'll love it!" Nix nods and digs in, using fingers instead of fork, masticating the meat with his own teeth. Raw flesh smacking around, being buttered by saliva, has not sounded to Bertha Palmer as an orchestra in search of a symphony until now. She, who eats only of the legumes and the not-red globes that pass for tomatoes this season, says, "Please do feel right at home, if that's not what you're already doing."

She watches him eat in wonder, in awe, delighting in his mere presence. The child she's never had, but all these years has desired more than anything, now sits across from her, flesh and bones. Were they to tell her to let him eat alone, she'd do it, if that'd mean he'd grow more comfortable, quicker. But for the remainder of the meal, she allows herself to watch, rapturously, while her boy stabs at his gristle. When the boy's finished, she says, "Jencks will take you to Thomas now."

Mrs. Palmer stands over him now, smiling. Her smile's so infectious, he can't not smile in due course. She kisses him gently, maternally on a cheek, then says, "Have fun!"

Fun it is, for soon he and the gnome are off, headed for the exposition. The ride down is, surprisingly, very fun indeed, on account of the gnome's abilities in the black arts, passing coinage from nothingness to being, summoning as from pure air a carrier pigeon to flutter, then fly. What is that atop your head, a squash? No, it's but a cucumber, whereupon to the boy's amazement out is removed an elongated cucumber, his eyes searching without encountering, wondering without saying, "How did you do that?"

They take a boat down, which for young Nix is but a wonder in itself. Wind and the occasional cry of a gull and the churning, droning pull of the engine. The city behind them is a blur. He feels sick, on account of the shapes about him shifting without warning and the world itself rotating faster and faster and everything as if dancing, only without the music. He presses his head into Jencks's arm, searching for a solidity with which to steady himself. Finding none, he tries the leg, which is hard as a rock and similarly a-jangle. One minute he's so fidgety he can't sit still, while the next it's as if his head falls of its own volition down and into Jencks's lap, where it remains. Before he'd like to be, he's sleeping.

Awakened by Jencks's sinewy hand through his hair, "Where are we?" He doesn't remember the White City. The buildings are gargantuan, but he remembers only a boisterous Cairo street that smelled of bodily secretions, not flowers, as the White City smells. People here, too, move without jerking about or muttering or bumping you, and their teeth are pearly, and their smiles, it's apparent, have been perfected. Just walking about, eyes glazing everyplace, is enough to make one weary, and, soon enough, young Nix again feels faint, like he might collapse if the wind changes.

Jencks, however, is a fireball of energy and says with glee, "That is termed the Peristyle."

He follows Jencks's outstretched finger and spots it—a wall of white columns stacked with yet more white that stretches out to the farthest reaches of the horizon, and at the center a large archway through which you must pass if you're to enter the dreamland within. Atop the colonnade stand horses poised for battle. A few erect men brave the winds, savage this time of year. As one especially arctic gust whips up, Nix shivers. It is Jencks's job to come prepared, so he places over the boy a blanket made of wool that itches yet does what it's meant to, warms, and Jencks's hands, which are warm as loaves freshly out of an oven, seize the icicles that pass as the boy's fingers. They are the same height, give or take, and viewed from a distance, passing through the Peristyle, they could easily be mistaken for brothers.

PEERLESS PRODIGIES
of
PHYSICAL PHENOMENA

AND GREAT PRESENTATION OF
MARVELOUS LIVING HUMAN CURIOSITIES

THE WORLD'S LARGEST, GRANDEST, BEST
AMUSEMENT INSTITUTION

Twenty

Here they are, where they first met. Today, the Wooded Island's chockablock with fair-goers, many of them walking briskly through, on account of the wind, which, since noon, has become as nippy as any February's. Skurlock manages to find a place that's shrouded, if not entirely private. With a suddenness that's alarming and anything but called for, he places an arm around the boy, as if to shield him from whatever storm might lie in wait. He squeezes the boy rather hard, so that he squeals. Despite his being a boy, the squeal's loud as a hundred men, and as a consequence, Skurlock places both hands over the boy's mouth, until his eyes pop out and his skin goes crimson. He leans in and begins to speak, then stops. Instead, he unmuffles the boy. Billy says, after he's caught his own breath, "I thought we were here for the wheel."

"We are," says Skurlock.

PALMER TO EXPAND HIS HOUSE

The financier Thomas "Potter" Palmer has announced plans to purchase another hotel, to rival his celebrated Palmer House.

"We would like to offer as many people as possible the class and comfort now known to a select few," stated Mr. Palmer.

Interest has been expressed in the World's Fair Inn, in Englewood. However, the Inn's chief proprietor, Dr. Henry H. Holmes, could not be immediately reached, and Palmer's secretary denied it. Since the start of the Exposition, Englewood, because of its proximity to the White City, has thrived and would be an appropriate locale for the next P. Palmer project.

Potter Palmer was one of the chief fund-raisers for the Fair and routinely contributes to the betterment of the City of Chicago.

Twenty-One

The room they're in, with wood-paneled walls so dark they're as if covered by soot, is lofty and houses a breeze almost as brisk as the breeze outside. Nix voyages from room to room, inspecting the paintings, all of them depicting various lone vessels surrounded by waves as big as the Pyramids and a sky that's darkened to the color of a raven. As if to propagate the painting's darkened sky, the shades have been drawn, to keep out the crepuscular sun. One lone lamp, its oil kept in an emerald-and-azure-swirl crystal basin, has been lit—though it sheds little light on the room.

"Hello again, Mr. Nix," a sprightly voice says.

Jencks, as if to push, moves the boy in first. He moves in fits and starts, wary; after all, it's not every day you have a new father.

"Interesting name you have, Thom," says Potter Palmer. "May I call you Thom?"

The boy nods, catching his new father's eye before turning away with panic. A rotund Columbian Guard brings the boy a refreshment. In the glass, bubbles rise to the top of the liquid with ferocity.

"Carbonated soda," Palmer says tenderly. "I think you might like it."

Nix sips, then sets down the glass. His mouth bubbles.

"What," Palmer wants to know, "would you like to see today, Thom?"

After a while, the boy says, "What are my choices?"

It's the first full sentence Potter Palmer's heard his new son say, and he's caught off guard and laughs, from surprise. An education at Eton and then Harvard might, after all, be in the making. This pleases Palmer no end, so he inquires chirpily, "Do you like it?"

Nix sips, saying, "Yes."

"Are you happy, comfortable? Would you like—anything?"

"No."

"Oh," faltering, "this is Detective . . . just—you can call him Simonds, Thom."

"Hello," Nix says to Chief Detective Simonds.

"Hello." Chief Detective Simonds's smile makes his face appear as oatmeal, so Nix laughs heartily, as does Potter Palmer.

"Perhaps," he says, "we should go someplace. Yes, but where?"

Chief Detective Simonds's face is blank, if not vapid. And Nix has lifted his glass up and is inspecting the bubbles in the lantern's light.

"Hm," says Palmer. "Well . . ." In truth, he doesn't know what to say.

Chief Detective Simonds says, "There is so much, but it's getting late, so maybe we should get a move on before it's too dark."

The boy finishes his drink in one gulp, then says, "Let's go, Father."

In truth, Palmer would like to scream. He was just, for the first time in his life, called Father. Although he's imagined the moment on numerous occasions, he's still taken aback; frightened more than surprised, for it's been said, and there's no turning back. Palmer thinks, too, of the Rockland boy and for a brief moment feels awful. That his happiness comes at the expense of William Rockland's bothers Palmer horribly, but he also knows he can't let Nix suspect this, even for an instant. Spotting his new son eying a Winslow Homer seascape, he says, "Do you like the sea?"

Nix, as if taken aback, nods but says nothing.

"Have you ever seen the sea?"

"No." It's almost a whisper.

"Shall we see more?" says Palmer. "I mean paintings."

And they're off to the Palace of Fine Arts, which would normally be closed at this hour, but it's kept open for Palmer and his new son. They pass through the guarding lions and drift about in witness to wonders culled from the globe over. Palmer, with Jencks trailing a few feet behind, rattles off a litany of names—painters, Nix assumes. Aube. Gelert. Lenback. After a while, Nix's mind wanders, and the paintings, which are interspersed throughout 140 rooms, soon begin to look very much alike. Soon only the glassed-in animals interest him and, at that, only mildly. Velvet curtains of various blues and purples are draped from the ceilings, darkening the room. The air is smoky, stuffy. There are so many artifacts, from headdresses to pictorial countrysides with rolling hills, that Nix has no idea what's real and what are but the lynchpins of a dream.

Up the grand stairs till they stand under the dome, which is gilded in part and otherwise multicolored. They are walking two and one, with Jencks trailing behind. Palmer, at times, holding Nix's hand, until after a long while they come to a rest and Nix breaks the hold. Pointing upward at what passes as the heavens, he explains, "It's like a Greek dome, or is meant to be. See?"

"What's that?"

"Oh, it's a large vaulted—do you know what a sphere is?" Before the boy can respond, Palmer has continued. "You know, a ball? Something you play with, or toss about. Well, a dome is a sphere split."

"No," Nix says. "That, right there." Pointing not up but out at the windows, three in all, which offer a magisterial view of the North Pond and beyond that the other buildings of the White City. There's the Illinois Building, and through the gape in the trees, the Wooded Island. "And that," Palmer instructs, "is the Grand Basin. Perhaps you'd like—" He stops himself short, for Nix has just pressed a nose up against the glass. He doesn't think to take the boy's hand and say, "Oh, don't—the glass might break, and you'll fall." He doesn't think to instruct the boy on the properties of falling bodies. He would, if only he could, teach his son physics and the beauty of falling in love. However, life being as it is, all business, all Palmer could teach the boy are transactions and interactions and the occasional infraction, leaving explanations of the curvature of the globe or Diesel's engine,

or the way Ferris's Wheel can revolve without rolling away, to someone else. It's capitalism, after all, which propels the republic, not
the gyrations of a bisected sphere and not the osmosis of solid into
liquid, of which man-made engines know little.

From outside there's music—a light, wispy violin—and the
sounds of shouting, of people caught up in the excitement of the
moment. Palmer, alongside young Thom, now presses his face up
against the glass, and together they watch from above as below people snake around the beaux-arts buildings and gather for a time
between two weeping willows and a magisterial, though leafless,
oak, before heading home for the evening. They watch in silence.
The only sound surrounding them is the few people who remain
talking quietly, few knowing what has transpired: one father's lost a
son while another's gained one. Is this how the world works, in sym-
metry? Replacing what has been plundered. Palmer takes his son's
hand in his own and squeezes.

After a while, a man dressed all in black, with a monocle the size
of a bottle with the mouth chopped off, is upon them. The man's
eyes are of two distinct colors, one chestnut and the other gray.
Palmer recognizes his face but can't place it. Beside him stands
Jencks, as he was before, neither smiling nor cleaved by a frown.
Palmer knows already what has happened. There is a certain scent
to this man that is familiar, an enviable smell of soothing lavender.
Palmer affects a blank face and nods solemnly. He stations a hand
each over his son's ears.

"They've found another one."

Through the window you can see the Wooded Island, yet you
can only guess at the wonders, green and overgrown, that may lurk
there.

STRIKE IMMINENT

A Citywide labor strike might be scheduled for sometime this week, possibly later today, say sources close to Mr. Armour.

However, the Police Force is already overextended on account of the search for the rogue Clemantis, the Husker. "We have put a full push on," says Chief Detective Oliver Simonds. Consequently, the Pinkerton Agency has been employed to aid in the search.

Twenty-Two

Screams. Shrieks. Wails. Whimpers. Everyone stands back. This is the Midway, just northwest of the Hagenbeck Animal Show, so it's entirely plausible that it might be a night-prowler, a possum or a raccoon, drawn to the gated lions and tigers. On closer inspection, however, it proves to be worse. It's a shadowed shape, no bigger than a pillow and twisted all helter-skelter, as if it had been run through a thrasher and mottled much later with blood; in other words, it's a body. Celebration instantly turns to dread when the man who found it steps forward, hands in his frock coat, telling of the find—how he literally stepped on the body, kicking it out of the way, thinking it was a deceased varmint. As Chief Detective Oliver Simonds tries to organize Columbian Guards, the man apologizes for not knowing what it was. His cheeks are flushed crimson, and his body shakes. It might be the wind that's rid his body of blood; it's probably the horror.

THIRD BODY FOUND. Everybody knows who's culpable. It's a name the papers toss around as confetti, at first innocent-sounding, smelling of fragrant bouquets left tableside all night long, its vowels showy as its floral cousin. It sticks in the mind with ease and little discrimination, lodging there, expanding—Clemantis—multiplying—Clemantis—then exploding, until you're terrified and spend every waking moment dwelling there with him, following him, imagining scenarios while walking down the street.

The sun hasn't set, so the sky appears as if smeared with oranges and frighteningly luminescent purples.

Columbian Guards mutter as they file past the crowd, mobilizing to clear the onlookers. Some leave, while others lurk, intent on witnessing the consequences of evil firsthand.

Today's Columbian Guards are Jon C. Trumpet, from south of the Mason-Dixon; Jacob Devins, a Puritan; and Matthew Pawson, a father of three. These are regular, everyday men who rarely before were given to wonder but now ponder the deeper, darker forces of this world. Nothing could have prepared any of them for the task ahead. They have been warned by Chief Detective Simonds that even in the darkest narrative there are occasions for shock; that this find could very well be *your* son or daughter; that years spent in study of crimes of this caliber will not prepare you for the actual, brute experience—the smell, which oddly is of iron; the appearance, the misshapen head; the torso, which, as expected, is skinless. It's a sight no man should see. Each guard shudders. When they signed up to become Columbian Guards, it seemed an honor. This was supposed to be a celebratory task, after all—the razzle-dazzle of technology, perhaps a go-round on Ferris's Wheel, art from the continent, buildings so austere and majestic you can't help but gape and swallow your every word, exotic food and strange, just-invented implements—not a lesson in the evilest vice.

Dr. Handley, without anyone knowing it, has been pacing throughout the crowd, observing from afar.

"I hardly know what that is," says Tiggs, behind her. His brow, despite the chill, is sopped with perspiration. His hands have been bleached to a pale white; were the light different, they might even appear translucent.

"A corpse, Mr. Tiggs," Dr. Handley responds. "Nothing more."

Tiggs, arms folded over his chest as armor, avoids eye contact with Dr. Handley. It is an awkward moment for both of them. His mouth drops open, then closes. What could be said? He fidgets. He paces. He can't seem to settle on one thought. He squishes his face till it's a prune, and he finally mutters, "That is what I'm afraid of."

"It's not something we need to get everyone worked up over, however," Dr. Handley says.

Chief Detective Simonds, approaching them, says, "I have men to spare should we need them."

"But that will only make matters worse," Dr. Handley says with a curtness that sends a shiver along both men's spines. "That will only draw attention to our search and bump up the challenge. We might not be able to meet it."

"Surely," says Tiggs, "you will meet it, Doctor."

"My men are ready when you are," Chief Detective Simonds says to Tiggs. He nods in Handley's direction. "But that would mean taking an altogether different route. It would mean shutting down transport to the fair, if not the fair entirely. And combing the city, block by block, leaving nothing uninspected. I believe that is the proper course to take at this point in time."

Dr. Handley, watching the Columbian Guards' faces shift from horrified to panicked (will their child be next?), says bluntly to Tiggs, "On the contrary, what we need is stealth. I have been tracking this man"—or woman, she thinks—"from the very start. We know some of his moves and would like to continue on as we have been, without anyone getting in our way. It is absolutely imperative that we work at this on our own, without impediments."

Chief Detective Simonds with hands in pockets, "There will be more if we don't act on everything we can act on and use everything within our grasp."

"That," says Tiggs, "seems to be the only option we have now at present, yes."

"Dr. Handley," says Simonds, "you will go about your business as you have been these past few days, and we will proceed along our course as well, and hopefully someone will capture him before he kills again. This is an order," but Dr. Handley isn't listening.

A Columbian Guard named Debs has appeared out of the shadows. "Sir," he says, panicked. Only Handley hears. Did Debs only imagine it? He must have. Two guards have hunkered down over the corpse and are talking, only in what language Debs isn't certain. He moves back, as if by intervention, over to them and hunkers down again. The corpse, the young boy, *moved*—a slight jerk of its left shoulder, where the skin has been flayed. When Debs leans down over the body, he notices straightaway that its eyes sparkle, even through the blood. It's almost imperceptible, but its lips, or what's left of them, move about as if in a chattering fever. Debs leans closer still and tries to discern what, if anything, the child is saying. With everyone still looking on devoid, for the most part, of emotion, he reaches out to touch the child, so that he might succor the corpse back to the land of the living. Just then, there's a hand on his shoulder. He turns. It's Dr. Handley, her face quashed together in a look of massive confusion. "What's going on?"

"He lives."

Dr. Handley herself kneels down. With stern eyes, she observes the living corpse. Its lips are missing, and its teeth, if that's what they are, have been removed save one, which is a stump of red goop. Dr. Handley says nothing, only listens and waits for the boy to speak again. Wind rushes in off the lake, mussing her hair. Try as she might, she can't keep it out of her eyes. Perhaps because she can't spare the energy, she lets it fall over the boy, blanketing him. A long time passes. When he speaks, it's as if he's speaking underwater, his mouth being clogged with blood, saliva, and air. Before he breathes his last, Dr. Handley makes out one lone word, "Mother." Whether it's a question or statement, Dr. Handley isn't certain.

Though he makes no move to find out for himself, Tiggs wants to know, "What did he say?"

Dr. Handley, though she hears him, doesn't answer. She leans over the body, her face right up to its face. Its breath, though faint, still warms her cheek. Its skin, though chilled, steams in the evening's cooling air. Surrounded, and with everyone watching her every movement, she cups its head in her hands and leans closer still, so her lips graze what's left of its lips. To those watching, Tiggs included, it appears the good doctor is attempting to breathe life back into the boy. What transpires between the doctor and the corpse is more an asphyxiation than a resuscitation—Dr. Handley places her mouth over the child's head and sucks it of its last breath.

She's not the kind of doctor to resuscitate it. Still, she feels at fault. She's just killed a boy. Though the boy was on his last breath anyway, and his resuscitation would be but a ruse, still, the doctor feels herself culpable for his death. Clemantis did not kill this one; Handley did. Once she realizes this, she panics. Her face, to anyone except the man who stands before her, smacks of guilt. Her skin's blotchy, and dark circles ring her eyes. She must flee, fast.

As a Hagenbeck lion roars, a voice right behind her calls out, "Dr. Handley, might I have a word?"

It is Inspector Moreau, twittering his eagle-beak nose.

Dr. Handley says nothing, only nods. Just then, she notices a piece of parchment paper, more yellow than white, affixed by a rusted nail to what was once a sweater, and is now a darkened, blood-soaked film. She repositions herself as to veil the corpse. Nobody, she figures, sees what she removes. It is a letter written in a disordered hand. Doctor, it says, as if it's written directly to her. (It is.) *Meet me at Gray's Tavern, Sixty-third Street off Wallace. Eight o'clock. Don't be late, I'll be in back.* It is signed only "*S*." Once she's read it, Dr. Handley slips it in the same pocket from which she presently removes a previously smoked cigar. She stands and faces the inspector.

"Yes, Inspector," she says. "What is it?"

The inspector leads the doctor off away from the scene of the crime and over to a tall oak, its leaves still implausibly vibrant, green as apples. Just to their left, there's a carriage, the sides of which say in large white lettering, MORGUE.

"What is that?"

"What is what, Inspector?"

"You just placed something in your pocket," he says after a moment. "Is it evidence?"

"A handkerchief. It is not your concern."

He might, under other circumstances, be waylaid by her almost clinical abruptness, but in truth he's rather excited by his news. A promising lead hasn't presented itself since they've been on the Husker's trail. But earlier this evening, Moreau was approached, while dining at the Palmer House, by a woman with sunset mahogany hair wearing a sunset mahogany velvet dress that sloped down and trailed along the marble floor. She was a graceful sight, to say the least. Moreau was taken by surprise and almost choked on a broccoli spear. Before he could invite her to join him, she left, trailing the ever-inviting scent of Woodbury's. Moreau, as if entranced, followed. She was waiting in the corner, just outside the barbershop. He did not know what she wanted, but Moreau being separated from his wife for months, his imagination raced; whatever it was she wanted, he'd make sure he could provide it. What she wanted, however, was simply to inform him that she knew the true identity of Clemantis. He wasn't thinking straight, so he failed to press her, to figure out if she was telling the truth, if she might, in fact, possess the missing piece of the puzzle.

Handley now lights the cigar and says, "What is his identity then, Inspector?"

"She will take us to him, Doctor."

"She will—take us?" Handley steps toward Moreau. He's engulfed by a puff of smoke. She says, "That, Inspector, is your version of police work?"

Here Moreau pauses and strokes his chin as only those from the Northern Provinces can do without being snickered at, as if in remembrance. "I understand," he says, "but she was very adamant, very persuasive. For some strange reason, I felt I trusted her."

"I am sure you did," says Handley. "I suggest you follow up and keep me informed." She walks off into the dusk with her hand raised up in what might be intended as a wave and trailing a lace of smoke over and behind her. She's not sure what time it is but figures it's fast approaching eight o'clock. Gray's Tavern, if she understands Chicago geography right, lies some distance to the west. She will flag a phaeton, or walk.

Inspector Moreau, for his part, is more baffled than anything else. For a full moment, he waits, confused as to what he should do. He could meet the woman himself, but he was hoping and expecting that Handley would come with him. After all, now that he has had a moment to think about it, perhaps it was too abrupt; perhaps he was misled by her presence; perhaps it is but a trap, and Moreau a nincompoop. But he figures that it is too late, that he has gotten himself in too deep, so he runs off. Tiggs but not Simonds, who's still busy organizing the Columbian Guards, watches as Moreau runs off. His run is more of a waddle than anything else, his legs as if uneven so that his whole body's off balance. Since penguins waddle, Tiggs finds this rather comical and laughs and doesn't stop laughing until Simonds approaches him and watches Moreau run, saying under his breath, "Canadians . . ."

The body, meanwhile, has been covered with a sheaf of canvass and removed, as instructed, from its former locale. Placed on a gurney and taken—as though it's a fair-goer in need of shade, otherwise she might faint—to a food court located by the rail. Once there, it is set upon a table, uncovered, and inspected by Josiah Bates—a short, buttress-bodied mortician whose face is half-paralyzed on account of a run-in with a grizzly in childhood. He wears a dark mourning coat, the darkness of which is punctuated by a solitary, bright pink carnation. There's a kerchief round his neck, on account of his being frigid by nature. As is common among men in his profession, he hardly sweats at all and talks little. He prefers to work in complete solitude. To accommodate him, the area has been cleared out save for Theodate Tiggs, who stays. A slight odor lingers in the room. Tiggs places a handkerchief over his mouth and nose. Josiah Bates, however, immerses himself in the work at hand—in touch, feel, smell.

The dead boy faces down, his arms placed alongside with upturned palms. Bates hasn't need to gaze into the boy's eyes. The corpse is so compacted that it could easily fit into a picnic basket and be borne about, weighing, as it does, slightly more than air. Tiggs doesn't watch but rather attempts a half-completed crossword. There is a science to death, a singular way of reckoning that verges on the perfect. Bates, as is his pleasure, notes the way the skin hardens where it was peeled off. There's a dark crescent shape in the middle of the upper extremity, minus skin. The shoulders are pressed together and might be broken. The lower extremity, from the pelvis on down to the foot, is largely untouched, though halfway crusted with blood. The hands are likewise untouched and appear as fine and pale as alabaster. There are no scars, no dirt under the fingertips. He checks the boy's rectum for sign of penetration—there is none—and then he turns the boy over and inspects his front side. There is neither abrasion nor mark of teeth, but there are markings running up from the boy's penis to his heart. The result could be either the boy's being dragged through rocks and pebbles or being sliced with a jagged *pesh kabz*. Bates pushes down on the boy's stomach, to see if any liquid comes up through the throat and mouth. With a wheeze that draws Tiggs's attention for a moment, he sticks two fingers down the boy's throat and pries open his jaw. Leaning in, hovering over the corpse, he feels around the boy's mouth with one hand, while the other lifts up the boy's head. One of the boy's eyes, which till now had been closed, opens and stares directly at Josiah Bates, as if pleading, *Please don't let anyone please do that to me again*. Next, Bates checks the incision just below the abdomen. He places one finger in, then another. It is as he suspected: the Gimbernat's ligament is missing. Clemantis has somehow—expertly—removed it with hardly a scar. Located backward and outward from the spine of the *os pubis*, the Gimbernat's ligament is scarcely over half an inch in length and takes the form of an easily lost triangle; its excision generally requires years of training to so much as locate it. Bates only knows to look because it is turning into the killer's signature. It is the focus on the Gimbernat's ligament that has boggled everyone, including Josiah Bates, who now slides his fingers in again, to insure that the ligament is indeed missing. It is. As he inserts his fingers yet again, suddenly, abruptly, so much so that Bates turns round and in doing so almost sprains his neck, the door swings open, and Tiggs stomps out in search of a sausage and a pint. It's work, honest and taxing, that leaves a man famished and with little else on his mind.

BODY FOUND

Yesterday, another body was found in the White City. The identity of the deceased has not yet been released.

The body was found in the cellar of a building very near the White City. It seemed to have been placed thus, with the arms stretched up and out and the legs at severe angles. The skin had been flayed, entirely. It is not certain whether the corpse is male or female, on account of its genitals being removed. The manner of the removal was that of an expert, or one very nearly trained expertly. Blood was not extracted from any vein, for it had long ago been drained by a force pump. Neither could the corpse's identity be determined from facial characteristics, as the nose had been filed down to bone and the eyes removed. After a lengthy examination, the county coroner determined that the cause of death was a forceful blow to the head with a blunt object, likely a hammer of some sort. A memorial service will be held tomorrow morning in Choral Hall.

Twenty-Three

Earliest evening, Wednesday. They cross the people-clogged avenues in single file, Fallon followed by Graft, who's soused and singing in a falsetto that's appallingly high timbred, to say nothing of embarrassing, a song Fallon hasn't heard before, which begins, "There's a place in France." The plan, straight from Walsh, is twofold: to plant sticks of dynamite, seven per corner, by the Electricity Building in the hopes the detonation might call attention to the laborers' cause; and should they, in the course of their travels, happen upon the wayward rogue Hannibal Skurlock, they are to apprehend him and bring him back, living, so that Walsh can deal with him. "He pilfered my purse, and nobody does that without paying for it," Walsh had said. Because Skurlock is a large man, tall but with the brawn of a much shorter, stockier man, Walsh sent along a third man, Franklin Stubbs, to insure that Skurlock's apprehended without much of an ordeal.

"We have to—" The look Stubbs gives Fallon says, What? "*Stop* him."

Stop Graft, that is. To add to this, Graft was outfitted with the day's purse, a robust ten dollars, and somehow, without Stubbs or Fallon knowing it, spent it on drink and the day's paper, so that they are now virtually broke. To get to the White City, then, they're forced to take foot, not steamer. Fallon confiscates the *Times-*

Herald, yet, before tossing it to the wayside, he notices the day's headline and glances over at Stubbs, who doesn't glance back. BOY MISSING, it says. For the life of him, Fallon can't help thinking that the etching looks like the kid Skurlock brought by yesterday. Then again, Fallon is of the mind that all boys, being boys, look alike. Franklin Stubbs, being a man of few words, nearly frightens Fallon when he says, "And what should we do with him?"

"Who?" Fallon's not sure if Stubbs means Graft or Skurlock.

In the far-off revolves the wheel. It's a miraculous sight, sneaking up off the horizon and looming large and indestructible as any mountain. They have come a long way and are tired and annoyed and would like to repair to the nearest opium den, without finding Skurlock, spending the rest of their lives in blissful nothingness. Wind, blustering off the lake, tussles their hair and cools their skin, which is dribbled with sweat. The streets here are rather empty, but when, as now, they pass a Columbian Guard, they tip their hats, grimace, and say, in choir, "Evening, sir."

As soon as they've rounded a corner and passed half a city block, insuring that the guard's gone, Jimmer Fallon directs Graft straight into the avenue. Straightaway, Graft falls to his face and passes out of this world and into another; a moment later, he returns to consciousness, only to find that he has been abandoned to an oncoming horse and buggy, and if he is to avoid being trampled, he must do so immediately.

Stubbs inquires of Fallon, "You say you know where he is?"

"I do indeed, yes," but just then, Graft, having righted himself in time, charges at full gallop straight at Fallon. He is more angry about being abandoned than about being placed directly in Death's path. But here's Stubbs to Fallon's aid, shoving Wade Graft with the strength of a dozen men clear into a lamppost, which, upon contact, is extinguished.

They walk on. The sky's flushed a bruised, pulpy red, on account of the recently set sun, which hovers over the water as the wheel hovers, no longer moving, over the Midway. The White City won't close for another half an hour, but families have begun the long trek home. The streets are clogged, so that walking the early-evening streets has become a duel for space—a duel that on account of the sun's intrusive luminescence must be carried out blindly.

"Impressive, isn't it?" says Stubbs, regarding the postmeridian light, as Wade Graft knocks into him and almost punches him in the gut.

"Oh, jeez," Fallon says when Graft thuds him with a clenched fist.

That sets him off. With one hurried, rigid jab, Fallon levels Graft, who lies there, body twisted, moaning. Fallon then leaps atop Graft and swings at him, until Graft's head squashed and flopping about—begins to leak thick-flowing blood. While Stubbs, who's built rather like a squashed pumpkin, but more muscular, and whose legs, though squat, are the thickness of pythons, approaches Graft from the rear side, and with all his weight suitably behind him, he kicks Graft in the shin, in the stomach, and in the groin. Graft's body lies there without moving, curled up in a fetal position, coughing up jet streams of blood. Blood squirts from his nostrils and spritzes Fallon, who is pummeling as Stubbs kicks. Soon three whole teeth are dislodged from the man's mouth and catapulted up and into the air, one just missing Fallon's eye. This guy is finished, thinks Fallon. He stops, stands, and walks off, touching a finger to his nose to wipe off the snot. Stubbs leaps in the air, high, so, when his foot comes down on the man's face, it does so with all his weight and scrapes a sliver of skin clear off. Stubbs then stands and catches up with Fallon. They walk in silence, side by side, their shadows fading in the crepuscular light.

Politely, "Shall we?"

"Actually, I know the place." Fallon catches his breath, and together they're off, Fallon obtaining from his pocket a tin that he opens and from which he secures a pinch of tobacco. Stubbs walks on, almost skipping, so excited is he to reach their destination. Excited, too, because from the beginning he's had qualms about Walsh's plan; he's certain that what they had been charged to do was beyond, far beyond the realm of morality, to say nothing of sanity. It is a random, senseless act, he thinks. Skurlock was a friend of sorts. As a boy, he had seen his own father carted off to prison, and this he feared for himself, if not his friend. Graft, however, is an entirely other story; his incarceration would certainly be welcomed. Stubbs and Fallon quicken their pace, checking over their shoulders to see whether Graft has noticed, which he hasn't. In fact, as they turn the corner, headed toward the darkening horizon, Graft hasn't even moved.

"Here we are," Fallon says at last. It is a grand structure on a quiet street with trees, many of which, on account of a virus brought over not too long ago from Europe, are leafless. It's very near the White City, yet an entirely other world of solitude. The entrance is through a loose-swinging iron gate and down a brick-laid path. The path then runs past poplars and willows, stray cacti, and a dirty-water wading pool, which houses goldfish imported from the Far East and as big, if not as succulent, as roasts. The ground has gone barren, and what few leaves remain on the trees have been glazed over by a light coat of frost. It is now very cold and dark. A lone man whistling a tune of his own imagining walks down the avenue, setting each lantern ablaze.

The house is gangantuan. Easily half a Taj Mahal, with granite slabs the size of carriages and dark-wood, varnished windows, from which not even a sliver of light emanates, it looks like something out of a storybook—to be encountered during the part of the narrative when the count, his spoils plundered, holes himself up inside a castle and waits upon Death, or the county magistrate, whoever's fleeter, to knock and demand entrance. This is a neighborhood of summer homes, places that lie dormant half the year. The windows are boarded, and the furniture inside is cloaked to ward off dust. Stubbs follows Fallon off the brick-laid path and over to what appears to have been, in more clement weather, a vegetable garden. Around the side of the house and back is a ramshackle structure, which is composed of planks of wood. With its gravity-betraying, asymmetrical architecture, it appears as David to the other's Goliath.

Fallon leads the way in through a door, which falls clear off its hinges the instant it's opened. No sooner are they in than they almost step into a hole in the flooring. The inside is no more promising than out; yet there's a certain warmth for Fallon. For Stubbs, however, the feeling is of an enlarged outhouse, which, having been used by a hundred men in rapid succession, rebuffs the nose and sets the eyes to watering and calls back from memory the gruel that passed as this morning's breakfast. Lights have dimmed, even since Fallon and Stubbs came in, yet absolute darkness hasn't encroached just yet. It's supper time, but neither man has thought to eat. There's a cough coming from right behind Stubbs. He turns and is startled to find nothing. Now, to Fallon's right, there's a crash, which causes him to turn, his heart having come to an abrupt halt, but it is only a rodent scampering away. Relieved, Fallon looks to Stubbs, but Stubbs has wandered off, down a hallway with inward-slanting walls and a ceiling that becomes lower the farther in you walk. Fallon follows.

The hallway opens into a darkened, cedar-walled room devoid of furniture, save for a sofa upon which reclines a younger gentleman with the coarse, sunken skin of someone easily four times his age. He's so tall that his feet dangle off the down-sloping end. A hand's extended up and over the opposite sloping end. Stubbs leads Fallon in, and together they sit, cross-legged, next to each other, facing the first man. His eyes, even in the dim light, burn a radiant yellow. Skin's a gray-greenish color. From the man's mouth extends a pipe that's a dulled turquoise, with glimmers here and there. It is the only color in the room. Fallon looks at Stubbs, but Stubbs watches the man on the sofa. He appears dead and might as well be for he hasn't moved since they entered. Then, suddenly, his head flops to one side. He'd fall clear off the sofa if it weren't for that second man's shoulder. But not just a second man—three, eight, twenty men, and the occasional woman, splayed about. Legs are intertwined, some garbed in woolen finery, others in rags. Fingers poke at another's eyes, body upon body.

With one swift, nearly invisible motion, a Chinese fellow emerges from behind a brocade curtain, carrying a chipped lacquer box. He sets it down as he kneels, saying nothing, hardly even glancing at Fallon or Stubbs. When he eyeballs Stubbs, he holds the stare with an intensity that sends shivers up Stubbs's spine. Stubbs looks immediately away, out of nervousness. By now, the Chinese man has opened the lacquer box, from which he culls a large, soft, black ovoid mass. He places it gently on a separate lacquer tray with two knives, a wire spindle, matches, and a glass lamp. From a hole in the floor, right in front of Fallon and Stubbs, he withdraws a pipe, perhaps two feet long, made of dark wood, with a stone basin and a brass saddle. The Chinese man divides the soft ovoid mass into equal parts. He lights the glass lamp, placing one of the divided soft masses at the end of the wire spindle, holding it over the lamp's flame, so that the mass forms a perfect dark hazel cone he transfers to the mouth of the pipe's stone basin. Fallon takes the pipe but passes it to Stubbs. With the Chinese man holding the stone basin over the glass lamp at such an angle that the flame hits the drug's sweet spot, Stubbs places his mouth around the pipe and inhales till his skin has been sucked so taut around his bones that he appears as a skeleton, the opium bubbling far below.

WANTED

Twenty-Four

Gray's Tavern sits midpoint on a street some blocks west of the Midway, between an abandoned field on one side and a pharmacy on the other. Across the street hulks the massive World's Fair Inn, which, with its gaslit lamps all ablaze, appears to be a burning citadel, not a top-notch hotel bustling with fair-goers. It takes up nearly the whole city block, and in comparison to it Gray's is but a munchkin, albeit a cantankerous one. Tonight it's chock-full of people, men mostly, who'd rather hawk their offspring than go a day without a drink.

Inside Gray's is mostly that—gray. Walls, tin ceiling, even the floor, which is covered by sawdust.

"Excuse me. Pardon." She parts the evening crowd, which hovers around the three overturned doors that serve as a bar. Men with arms around each other, singing. Mugs are raised above their heads, and ale flows freely as from a geyser, spritzing everyone. She covers her face with her hands so she can see well enough to maneuver through the bar. Gray's, although she's been here only moments, reminds her of her days at McClean, the asylum outside Boston. Here, as there, life's lived under the spirit of Bacchus. Merriment spreads as an influenza; compulsions surge and hastily subside. One minute everyone's drinking, dancing, singing; the next a brawl breaks out. She's not certain exactly whom she's looking for, so she

171

scans the faces of drinking men, searching for anyone who might
set off an internal alarm. It could be anything—a hand gesture, a
wink, someone's general demeanor. So far, everybody's far too jolly,
but she circles the bar. It's entirely possible that the killer and the
person who left the note on the corpse are two distinct people, or a
duo working together. A man with half a beard raises another man
so small and hairless he appears to be a boy onto his shoulders.
They proceed to dance around, blocking the doctor's passage. She
skirts around them and ducks a flying elbow, then a suddenly raised
knee. A mug sent flying across the room nearly beheads her. A few
men grope at her, but most mistake her for a man, overly curva-
ceous but a man nonetheless, so by and large she's left alone. She's
just about to give up and return to the Palmer House for a much-
needed nap when she spots a door. She decides to check before
leaving. In stark contrast to the front room, the room in back is
empty save for a few miniature tables and two booths along the back
wall, at which people huddle, whispering.

"Sit," a voice behind her says.

Spontaneous decision-making has never been Dr. Handley's
forte, but despite logic and against better judgment, she considers
her options and takes a seat at the booth in back. Directly opposite
her slides a cloaked figure. Is this, at last, it? Or is it but an impostor,
someone suspiciously fond of playing practical jokes? Does she,
without knowing it, have a stalker—someone who'd wish her harm
and has lured her here with that in mind? Or are there in fact two
killers—a behind-the-scenes man and the man who totes the knife?
At this point, anything's possible, and Dr. Handley, whether from
exhaustion or acquiescence, has resigned herself to the belief that
whatever's known about the Chicago killer should be reexamined
promptly. There's more to this series of killings than meets the eye.
She knows what she needs to do, and if this is the killer or even if it's
not, she has to find out, not so much in order to apprehend him as to
understand where the urge to kill comes from and how it plays out
in his psyche. If it's possible to stop once one's killed, would he want
to? Or is the urge, as she's thought on and off for some time now,
akin to an addiction, something that grips at the throat and won't let

go. Whatever, the doctor's deductive reasoning won't help her now. She's sitting across from either the Devil himself or just another bumpkin. Hanging over the table, there's a lantern that flickers, shadowing everything, in particular the figure seated opposite her.

"I wasn't certain you'd come, and to be honest I was a bit apprehensive about asking you here," the cloaked figure says. The whisper, Handley notices, has turned into a hiss. "I suppose you are wondering what I have to say." The voice betrays either sex—it is a high-pitched warble one minute and the next a basso so profundo it rattles the half-finished stein the cloaked figure sips from sporadically. The assumption, when she first sat down, was that the cloaked figure was a male, on account of his posture. The voice, however, begs Handley to think he might be a she. Dr. Handley wonders if there are others lying in wait to pounce once the cloaked figure's given the signal. She checks once over each shoulder but sees nothing. Though in her mind she's always anticipated that this moment would happen, she finds that, now that it's here, it's not as she imagined. She's very nearly frazzled, seated up almost on the table. She'd like to light a cigar to calm her nerves but thinks better of it. Too much smoke, and the doctor's vision might be compromised. An attacker could appear, and she wouldn't see him coming. "I am an acquaintance of the man the papers call the Husker, or rather I was."

"All right," says Dr. Handley, relieved that the cloaked figure does not claim to be Clemantis. There is so much she can say, although she can't formulate any of it into words. "I suspect," she says at last, "you want to tell me of his whereabouts."

"I might." The hiss turns back into a whisper. "But what I really want is to tell you the story. I've waited a while, and I think it will help you to know this man."

"What I want to know," says Dr. Handley, "—that's another matter."

Just then, a woman with wild hair set back in a bun and skin that hangs from her jaw sets down a plate of mutton chops with fat that glistens in the lantern light and potatoes that are more creamy than mashed and vegetables that look like mangled twigs; the cloaked figure promptly leans over the food, as if veiling it from Dr. Handley. Sounds of gristle being masticated provide an oddly comforting relief from the silence. From the front room come sounds of glasses breaking on men's heads, people cursing—sounds like a fight. Briefly, Handley feels at ease.

"For a brief while, I was the Husker's captive." Here the Survivor's head lifts; Dr. Handley can almost see what's being veiled. The voice softens, so Dr. Handley's pressed to lean in closer still. "It was more than eight years ago, but some mornings I wake up thinking I am still his captive. Much has changed. In fact, everything, at least since my escape."

A cloaked hand emerges and sweeps across the table, settling upon the empty plate. A finger's exposed— a finger that appears to be ground down to bone, spindly and disfigured. The Survivor scrapes the plate of gristle, then licks that finger, Dr. Handley leaning back to conceal her revulsion. When the Survivor speaks again, she's pressed to lean forward against her inclination. She knows what's happening: the Survivor's exerting a frankly embarrassing masculine type of placement control over the conversation.

"My mother passed away giving birth to me, so I was raised by my aunt." Here the Survivor removes a cigarette from his cloak and dangles it from his mouth, waiting for Dr. Handley to light it. After a long while, she does. "The man you seek owned the town's only pharmacy. He was known by everyone and liked. Very charming, the sort of man who'd take dinner to old ladies just because the feeling stirred his gut. He became enamored of my aunt. My aunt appreciated his kindnesses, but as they became more frequent, she could not stand his personage. And then, abruptly, my aunt married the local cobbler, whom she'd known since childhood and who for the past few years had been living in Boston. The man didn't stop coming around. In fact, as all spurned lovers do, he began to scheme. Within months, my aunt's new husband turned up deceased—a heart attack, it was ruled, but I had my suspicions. His demeanor gradually changed."

Here the Survivor exhales a cloud of smoke, momentarily compromising Handley's vision. She feels vulnerable, but it's a stirring, exciting sort of vulnerability. It is the closest Handley's felt to a man in a very long while. She'd like to touch the Survivor. Though she knows this is impractical, if not implausible, the thought crosses her mind to reach across to him as he speaks. She's not certain she would; in fact, she knows she wouldn't. Still, for a brief moment, she envisions it happening—closes her eyes and attempts to will the touch, imagining she has the wherewithal to go through with her desire, and not let it simmer.

The Survivor, as if batting a fly, seizes Handley by the wrists, holding her there. She looks about, panicked, then focuses on him once again. "Needless to say, the man stopped coming by. I was glad for it, but then one day, when I returned from the store, he was there. I froze with fright, attempted to run, but he had me by the shoulders." Here's a silence, interminably long. All around them, the whispering from neighboring tables grows louder. Dr. Handley watches as the Survivor licks his lips, leaving a glistening trail of saliva that dries instantly. "He brought me, in clear daylight, to his home. In the basement, there was a hidden room, in the center of which was a table with two place settings and a candle already lit. It was then he handed me the purple elixir. Everything was blurry—an effect, I'm certain, of the elixir." With the victim unconscious, he prepared the operation room, which was located in a secondary, soundproof cellar, through a trapdoor and down a short flight of stairs he'd constructed, entirely by night, with extrawide berth. "He strapped me to the table. Just as I slipped from consciousness, I felt the pain." He'd been to medical school for a brief while when younger but had never finished and thought it was time to reacquaint himself with the practice of medicine, since life as a pharmacist, which he fell into as if by default, bored him greatly and shamed him, in a way. Medicine he'd practice, but it was to be a new kind of medicine, one based on understanding what the body goes through while experiencing different types of pain. There would be no anesthesia, just raw dissection. He knew of no doctor the world over blazing this trail. The subterranean operation room, then, would be a new frontier and he its pioneering practitioner. "Pain such as I had never experienced. I couldn't tell where on my body it was coming from, or determine its cause. For a very long while, I didn't see the man. I thought I could smell him, but soon his smell was overtaken by another, much more fetid odor, as if my bowels had been ripped out and placed upon a plate. Everything was numb." He fastened the boy to the operating table, stripped him of his clothing, and then, with a steady hand, made the first incision. The boy did not flinch; his breathing remained even. The lancet cut cleanly. Blood sprayed everywhere—on the floor, on him. He managed to keep his calm as he tied off the arteries—a simple oversight. "There was something about the way he looked at me—I knew, even in my drugged state, that I would not die." Quickly, he removed the testes from their sac and placed them in the jar. "When I attempted to move, I discovered I couldn't—not on account of the shackles but because, when my mind went to tell my body what to do, it wouldn't." He was tempted, admittedly, to mutilate the boy's genitals. He stuck a finger into the gaping scrotum and then licked it, tasting the boy's essence. After a moment's indecision, he decided to stitch up his prize. "At last, when I could finally see him, he was neither smiling nor frowning. His eyes appeared as if burnt in umber, even in the dim lighting. His lips parted but nothing came out, then his jaw appeared to move but, still, I heard nothing. I was very much aware of my body but could neither feel it nor understand it. It was as if I was hovering over it, watching the proceedings from afar. Then he smiled. I will never forget that smile—a purely innocent, faraway smile, not the suave smile he often smiled at me during his visits. His teeth, I noticed, were stained with blood. And after all that," the Survivor says, like everything, without affect, "he just left me there."

Dr. Handley's not at all surprised. If this person did in fact undergo what he says he did, and for some reason, against her better judgment, she believes him, then there would be essentially two paths one could take: that of the emotional, or its opposite—calculated remove.

"I don't think I moved for a week, possibly longer. The room smelled of chemicals. I tended to fade in and out of consciousness. Eventually, I realized the daylight. It was coming from up the stairs. I felt the wind rustling through the stuffy room. The door must have been opened since he left, but I hadn't noticed. When I attempted to move, my body faltered. I pictured myself moving, but nothing happened. I am not sure how, but I remember the struggle, each step as if it were a million, the passage to the stairs spanned as if it were the Abyss. By the time I emerged, he'd long ago left town."

Here the Survivor unveils himself. Under the cloak, he appears as a she. Long ringlets the color of maple wood burst out in all directions, and the skin is like porcelain, white as snow. The face, in fact, has been disfigured—the cheeks are caved in, there is a scar across the top of the mouth where the skin had been peeled back, and the eyes appear misaligned, with one higher than the other. For a full minute, the Survivor allows Dr. Handley to admire him. His head's averted to avoid eye contact. He knows what she is thinking; everyone thinks the same, once he's unveiled himself. Dr. Handley does not turn away. She yearns to delve deeper into the tale, to press him. This is you now, changed? Is it possible to change so completely? Why did you feel that you had to do it, or did you choose to? What haunts your dreams? Instead, she's dead silent. She just watches the Survivor.

After a long silence, the Survivor says, "Do you believe in God?"

"I do not," the doctor says.

"I believe logic states that, if you prove something's opposite, that something in turn must be true." Here the Suvivor runs a gangly hand through his hair, so it flows everywhere. "Once I experienced evil, I knew good to be true. I have spent the last eight years trying to locate this man. When first I read about the Husker killings, I'm not certain why, but I just knew it was he. He's here, and you would like to find him, yes?" A pause. "I will tell you where—across the street. The World's Fair Inn, it happens, is his hotel." Without saying another word, the Survivor stands, veiling himself once more. He then follows the back wall to a hidden back door he seems to have known about. When the door opens, wind whips in, frigid and daunting. Dr. Handley follows him out back into an alleyway. Trash is piled high up against the buildings, as if barricading them from the alley's travelers. Out here, the wind's so cold it brittles skin upon contact and just about bowls Handley over. Her coat is nowhere near warm enough, her feet have frozen clear through her shoes, her nostrils have clogged, and she's about to pass under, since it's been nearly a day since she's eaten anything of substance. She's not certain where or how far the Survivor will lead her, but she's not worried; she has come to trust her guide. She follows him around front. As they pass in front of the tavern, the Survivor halts in his tracks, pointing across the street at a hulking structure that sits on a full city block and appears as a castle of darkness, each window cloaked so nobody can see in, nobody out. As if lured, Handley crosses the street, drawn by the sight of a man spying out from an upstairs window. When he notices that she sees, the curtain falls.

Twenty-Five

erris's Wheel, as geomancy sees fit, spans 250 feet in diameter and spears the sky with that plus 14 additional feet. Into the earth it sinks 40 feet, so that its total capacity, 2,060 fair-goers, divided up into thirty-six cars, each holding 60, and each 26 feet by 13, does not cause it to buckle and topple over, killing everyone. Built in Detroit by Bridge and Iron, the wheel weighs nearly three million pounds and is powered, when on, by two thousand-pound steam engines and braked, six times per rev, by Westinghouse pneumatics. The price? Two revs for just half a dollar. Even Skurlock could afford that luxury. Evening encroaching, and they're about 200 feet away, even if it seems miles, Skurlock carrying the Rockland boy atop his shoulders, Billy wearing the man's black hat, which covers his whole head, and batting at the man's hatless head, so that every few moments he must instruct the kid, "Stop."

"But, Han, it's not working," says Billy. He doffs the black hat and tosses it wayside. It spirals in the air and holds upon a billow of air until flopping to earth. "Why isn't it working?"

"I don't know." Skurlock shrugs. "It's late, Billy."

Silence. The gentle susurrus of lake-borne wind. "Why don't you know? You should know."

A first snowflake, as big as a puppy, falls upon the crown of Skurlock's head before melting. He's sopped. Soon it is snowing rather hard, and Billy says, as he whacks his steed upside the head, "Put me down."

Skurlock obeys. Released, the boy runs in ever-tightening circles in the tendrils of snow until, carefree as a sprite, he's spinning, his arms spread-eagled and hair flopping in the wind, matted down by clumps of snow. On account of the world around him spinning faster and without yield, he collapses. He lies still, with his face pressed into a mound of snow. Skurlock, watching, becomes more and more aware of how cold the boy must be. His urge, were he to follow it, would have him sprint to the boy's rescue, flopping upon him and warming him. Instead, he merely watches. Soon, in fact, he begins to like just watching. Until Billy, thrashing about in the snow, calls out, frantic, "Han!"

Skurlock sprints over to Billy. He can't seem to stop thrashing about and screaming, so Skurlock takes the boy by the wrists and grips hard till Billy's no longer thrashing, only screaming. Nervous, Skurlock looks around to see if anyone's watching. What would this look like, a grown man upon a boy in the dead of night when the Husker's still a-lurk? He'd be hung, most certainly. Thankfully, he sees no one, neither humans nor vermin. Only snow and, far-off, a few first lights blinking in the White City. Soon the boy ceases his screaming and turns, looking up at Skurlock, icicles of snow upon his face. As his nose shrivels, he says, "I'm cold."

At once, he can't stop. He covers the boy's body with his own body and presses his face close. His lips settle upon the boy's, seeking the only warmth he knows. Billy squirms under him, thrashing about. Very soon Skurlock has stopped and sits up. Their legs are still interlocked. He can't bear to look at the boy, so he doesn't. He places his head in his hands and weeps for an instant. It is so cold and windy, his tears freeze in his eyes. Blinking very nearly hurts. Finally, he looks upon the boy, who is sitting upright in the snow, confused. His eyes, Skurlock notices, are neither open nor closed.

Skurlock wants to say, "I'm sorry," but he just frees himself of the child, saying nothing. He feels confused. What does he think he's doing with this little boy? He's taken a liking, he might be smitten. Billy, he feels, is something of a mirror image. He knows he should deliver him, if not to Walsh then to his parents. If he can't complete the job he was assigned, he should do the right thing. Good people are waiting for him, worried. He stands back and keeps his distance, feigning as if to leave, but doesn't.

"Are you tired?"

"No."

"Would you like a nap?"

"No."

"Are you hungry? I am."

"No."

"Come on," says Skurlock. "I'm taking you home."

Just then, a snowflake falls upon the bridge of Billy's nose. Skurlock tugs at him, but the boy doesn't budge.

Presently, after a brief lull, snow begins falling in pristine sheets. People soon emerge out of nowhere, as if from beyond the pale of this world, stomping through the snow, delighted. Adults act as children, frenzied. Some carry torches, others lanterns. The faces the man and boy pass stream by, blurred, small and far away in the heavy shadow of snow. Billy might recognize some, for there are three that turn and goggle-eye after the tall man dragging him.

Billy wants to know, "What's going on, Han?"

They are singing, marching in lines of twos and threes, stolidly, as an army would march, only their clothes are weather-worn and sun-faded and grimed with mud, oil, and now a layer of snow, which upon contact with their skin appears as if melded with coal, splotchy gray. Their faces are craggy and gaunt. Many sprout whiskers so tangled that they're like wildernesses in miniature. Billy is about to bolt and grab one man's, but Skurlock, sensing mischief, strangle-holds him, yanking his hair so he shrieks. The passing men hoot with laughter. Skurlock agrees that it is humorous, straight out of a vaudeville theatre, so he laughs, too. Billy, however, would like more than anything to bury his head in the frozen earth and hide there for all eternity. For a fleeting moment this is what he does, tucks his head in his own shoulder so as to meet no eye.

"It's a strike," says Skurlock. A massive, citywide gathering in protest of workers' conditions in the slaughterhouses, which being as they are, abysmal, are in desperate need of alteration. Some think the approach should be peaceful, while others, including Mr. Walsh, tonight's ringmaster, think otherwise. Skurlock checks over both shoulders now, paranoid that one of Walsh's men, if not Walsh himself, might be after him. He was supposed to be here supporting the strike. The kidnapped boy was supposed to have been delivered to Mr. Walsh by now so that he might meet his ends—specifically, to parlay the kidnapping into a meeting with Potter Palmer, which would result in a future contract between the two gentlemen. Skurlock was supposed to have been with Fallon and Graft, searching the Electricity Building for spots to plant the dynamite, should it be needed.

"What's a strike, Han?"

By now, they're surrounded. On account of the hubbub, Billy doesn't hear Skurlock's response, which consists of a shrug and a mumble. For Billy it is something of an educational experience, striking. There are many men, many smells, many faces, and much, were he so inclined, to learn in terms of human oddity. By the looks on their faces, these men are either confused or enchanted or some mixture of both, having hours ago left their own boys or girls at home and trudged through cold and frost and now snow to stand around a makeshift fire, freezing.

There's a man saying (despondently) to another man, "Do you even know, let alone care, what is happening tonight? Do you know that tomorrow the whole world will know, and will be changed? Do you even care? We do. We know, and care, that, with the way things are going, the future will be horrible. Work, if it will even exist at all, will be hard to come by, and it will pay little. Mr. Edison may have elongated the day, but we won't let him take over our work as well. The White City—what is it but an illusion to ward off our fears? Think about it. They're relegated to their own building and are to keep quiet, and the workingmen, who left families overseas and came to America for the work, are now hard-pressed to even get in. If we even want to go see what we built, it will be our necks. How is that justice?"

Skurlock leads Billy deeper into the crowd of men. Soon, a few young, sprightly faces peek out from behind the shade of snow. Eyes dart about rapidly and without rest. Heads are covered, as seems the fashion, by hats that flop about in what little wind there is and that are weighty with fallen snow. These boys are about Billy's age, many older. Billy feels out of place, but oddly comforted. But when three boys close in upon him, right up in his face, he ducks behind Skurlock. After a time, one of the boys steps forward and offers a hand that's meant to be shaken, "Hello."

"Hello," says Billy.

"You're new," a second boy says. "Where are you from?"

Billy pays them little mind, his attentions being focused on the men who surround Skurlock, everyone laughing sinisterly and swilling from brown-glass bottles and smoking bent cigarettes. Eventually, Skurlock himself is swilling and also laughing sinisterly. Far away a few first hesitant chords are strummed upon a banjo, a tin canister is tapped for rhythm, and a rather stout gentleman without cap, half a Skurlock in height, twice one in weight, is singing in a transparent falsetto the song about the undergarments. Snow stops for a moment, but then, out of nowhere, the sky breaks, and soon everything, even the tips of men's noses, is blanketed by white snow.

Presently, half-a-dozen men escort Skurlock and the boy away from the wheel and to a site with a fire burning in a makeshift hearth. Men here look solemnly at the fire, yet, when they hear the music, everything changes, and these stony faces break into softer, jubilant ones. Soon everyone's singing. Skurlock and Billy sit side by side, right up next to the fire. Their bones warm; their snow-sopped clothes dry. No one has said another word to Billy Rockland, so he says nothing in return. He sits there watching the side-lit specter of Hannibal Skurlock. It's strange, watching Skurlock, because here's a grown man, whom Billy's never met before, yet he's more a father than Father Rockland's ever been. More present and more available, and for that the kid has grown fond of him and would one day like— is it possible?—to love Hannibal Skurlock.

"Here," in a voice that could be chinaware breaking. Billy's handed a tin bowl that steams with beans.

"Thank you," says Billy. He eats the grub.

Almost immediately, he's so thirsty that he's up, prowling about. The three boys follow him for no reason he can think of. He turns, catches their eyes, then turns back and continues on in search of beverage. An older, gray-haired man in suspenders approaches Billy and offers a green-glass bottle and says, "Here you go, son."

"Thank you," says Billy. He takes the bottle and sips. And as soon as he's sipped, his stomach turns, and he spits up the liquid, for it tastes like poison and sets his whole mouth aflame. He's instantaneously dizzy, and much colder. With his head teetering as if over a large abyss, he walks on past dozens of men, hundreds of men, all of whom are huddled around different fires and talking. He's overcome with tiredness and without further ado collapses into an especially comforting-looking mound of snow, but then every mound of snow appears especially comforting, warm, and welcoming.

Billy awakes, only to find that he's been buried in snow. Try as he might, he can't move a muscle in his body. Above him stand a half-dozen men and the three boys from earlier, all of them saying nothing. Oddly enough, roofed by snow, Billy isn't cold. He's lonely. He misses home, but also Skurlock. Before he knows it, the men have lifted him from his snow-blanket, and the boys snicker. Billy, whose hair has icicled, scopes about for his buddy Hannibal Skurlock. He finds the lanky giant right up next to the makeshift hearth, so close, in fact, the raw heat has burned the man's skin.

"Hey," says Billy. He taps Skurlock on the face.

Skurlock's eyes, when opened, are red and in the fading light of the fire might even phosphoresce. He looks partway confused, also scared. The skin of his cheeks has dried to a crisp and with each blink flakes off. His lips are severely blistered, discolored a pale green. Snow has crusted his beard, and icicles in miniature jangle as he presently sits up. Both of them, Billy notices with glee, are now half-living, half icicles. Billy checks Skurlock to see where he's looking and promptly looks there. Off to the far side of the hearth, by a rickety lean-to, men are gathered in smaller groups of twos and threes. Everyone is gesticulating as if in some mute pantomime. The music, for the most part, has died down. Skurlock stretches his arms and yawns, which sounds to Billy more like a roar. He giggles, but then, so as not to appear overeager, he stops himself and stares at Skurlock and twiddles his thumbs. At once, Skurlock flops back into the snow, feigning death, and for a split instant Billy is terrified. Fearing Skurlock might leave him, might actually have died, he stands on top of the icicled man, pounding away at the man's stomach. Nobody else seems to notice other than those three boys, who let out their snickering crescendo at Billy's expense.

With a lunge, Skurlock's standing. Billy, animated, screams, "Han!"

"Billy!" Skurlock shouts back playfully. He takes boy Rockland by the hand and leads him off. The bonfire behind them spittles and throws its final heat upon them before flickering out.

"Come on," says Skurlock. Billy begins to trot.

They're soon far from the wheel, Billy in front of Skurlock scurrying across the bridge and then past the fisheries. Skurlock knows exactly where they're headed, but he won't tell Billy. He thought of asking Billy where's home and taking him there, or turning him in anonymously, or even leaving him, so that he has to find his own way home. Instead, together they'll make a home, at least for the night. Tomorrow morning, first thing, he'll return the kid. Tonight, he'll spend his last dollar so that Billy may sleep in a cozy bed, and when he wakes, he'll wash the boy so he can return to his parents respectably. It is something Skurlock has always dreamed of for himself—to be taken to a home and not groped, but embraced. That Skurlock knows the owner of the World's Fair Inn can only help, but with respect to monetary matters Holmes is a stickler and despite his wealth squirrelly. The room, no doubt, will come at a price. They head west for Englewood, where the alleyways become avenues shaded by large elms and occasional oaks that are scarcely shrubs. Affluence has a way of creeping up slantwise and overtaking the whole world. The houses have become mansions, summer homes for the city's ruling class, but Skurlock, running behind Billy, hardly notices. Perhaps even Walsh has a residence here, a red-brick manse with a wide lawn and overzealous shrubbery. Skurlock wonders which would be grander, Walsh's or Billy's father's residence. It's simply an anonymous street with anonymous houses and anonymous people inside that leads into another anonymous street, which they follow. Skurlock checks to see if they're being followed. They are not. They, too, are anonymous, just a man and a boy, his son perhaps, out for a late-night stroll. Nobody would know the scenario, were anyone around to play witness. And if anybody did know, no one would care. Still, Skurlock's startled by sounds his imagination invents. He hears voices coming at him from the leaves in the trees. The wind would like Skurlock to know something, only it speaks an indecipherable tongue. The snow, falling softer now, comes at him like spears unleashed from some angry god. Skurlock feels as if he might faint, but doesn't. He'd like to collapse, but can't. Finally, exhausted, they arrive at the World's Fair Inn.

Above, the sky's opalescent, gray and dun and darkening.

It is a large building that sits fully over an entire city block. Just outside, to the left of the front door, there appears to be a corpse. Whatever it is, it's in the fetal position and wrapped in tattered canvass; its arms are twisted up and around its head, so that for an instant it appears to be dancing, only stilled. The smell's a rancid death smell, but perhaps that's just Skurlock. Flies gather around the mass of canvass. At first, Billy doesn't seem to notice. Skurlock tugs at the boy so they'll go in before the child recognizes it is a corpse. But it is too late. Billy buries his head in Skurlock's chest. He might be weeping, but his jacket muffles the noise. He opens the front door; the canvass mass jerks. Arms flail about momentarily, and a leg kicks out and then slackens. The corpse is but a wastrel passed out in the snow. Presently, it vomits, while high above, perched on a frail twig in a tree outlined by snow so white it glows, a bird chirps and flies away.

Twenty-Six

Inside, windows rattling, floor creaking, pipes clanging. Dr. Handley steps in and through a spiderweb that's so thick, it leaves her with something of a mask and the sensation of millipedes crawling across her forearm. The foyer funnels into a dim hallway that corkscrews around and empties into a large vestibule. The light's yellow with a tinge of orange-brown. There's a table at the far end of the vestibule, behind which, snoring, sits a beanpole of a woman dressed all in black with dark bags under her eyes. Dr. Handley raps twice on the table. Nervous, though she'd deny it, Handley takes note of her surroundings—the floral-print wallpaper, the ledger book open on the table, and a pen dripping ink across its pages. The curtain behind the caretaker falls, slanted and flimsily, so that the gas lanterns' dim light from outside creeps in. The caretaker has a nose that's crooked and a misaligned jawline, as though someone, or something, rearranged her entire face bit by bit. Her skin is so pasty, she appears, and for a moment Dr. Handley figures she is, deceased. Perhaps the Husker's latest victim. Impatiently, Handley raps a third time on the table, startling the woman, who pins her eyes, one green and the other blue, on the doctor and says, "No vacancy, I'm sorry."

Handley scans the open ledger for a moment. According to its contents, the inn has but four occupants accounted for. During this moment, the caretaker's eyes have sealed out the world's light once again, and she's taken to snoring, throatier than before. A gust of wind slams into the World's Fair Inn, and the whole structure buckles. The light stutters. The street-side window directly behind the caretaker rattles so forcibly now, its glass threatens to shatter at any moment. Yet even this doesn't rouse the caretaker from her slumber, so Dr. Handley slaps the table, saying, "I'm not looking for a room."

The caretaker, awakened, cackles, then, after loosening the phlegm in her throat, she looks at Handley, befuddled.

"The proprietor of this establishment, please. I'd like to speak with him."

Another cackle, and the caretaker says, "You're not the first." Handley's not certain what that means, so she rearranges herself, throwing the balance of her weight from one side to the other. A floorboard beneath her squeaks. At the same time, a pipe behind her clangs. The caretaker, who seems not to have noticed either stray sound, throws a thumb over a shoulder, motioning toward the avenue out front, but says, "Sleeping, he is. Upstairs and to the rear."

"Thank you."

As Handley turns to locate the stairwell, the caretaker says, "If you wake him, I'll be thanking you." Even though she hasn't moved, a floorboard under Handley creaks. The caretaker, coughing, cracks a knuckle. "My boy's at home with the snivels, see, and I should have been out of here hours ago, but somebody's got to watch the place when that man's passed out drunk for the third night in a row. Can't seem to help himself, he can't."

Handley nods and passes across the hallway and into an adjacent front room. This must be the lounging area, for there are countless couches and settees and tall-backed chairs with spindly legs and armrests that appear, only in miniature, as sailor-eating oafs. The upholstery that's not coated with dust is floral in nature and kaleidoscopes off into plant and vegetal before returning, wilted, to floral, as does the wallpaper. Colors have been mismatched, one presumes intentionally. Everything feels askew. The room's pitch-black save for a sliver of light escaped in from the hallway. On the far side of the room, there's a fireplace inside which smolders a log turned into ash hours ago. Periodicals have been thrown haphazardly across some of the furniture, and in the far corner, mostly shadowed, there's a white sheet over what Handley can only guess is yet more furniture. She lifts the sheet—yes, just another settee, although this one happens to be missing its upholstery.

Wind escapes in, repeating, *Yes yes yes yes yes.*

Dr. Handley, though she knows she hasn't, has the sense she's been here before once long ago. It is a primordial feeling, as if she's standing in a spitting replication of Grandmother Handley's living room. Perhaps that is where the sensation comes from, Grandmother Handley. And when Dr. Handley spots the painting above the fireplace, it's confirmed. The painting depicts an elderly woman with a beaked nose, sunken cheeks, ears that tent out, a forehead streaked with wrinkles, and piercing eyes in cavernous sockets that follow her as she moves about the room. The resemblance is strikingly chilling. The only difference is the nose—Grandmother Handley's was a button, not a beak. Still, Dr. Handley's skin crawls. She's perfectly aware that she must be imagining the resemblance, or willing it, creating some kind of familiarity, since she finds herself in such foreign surroundings. Embarrassment steals across her whole being. Presently, the feeling that she's standing on a floor made of glass so fragile that it might crack at any moment, dependent on whether or not she takes the right step, overwhelms her. She has no idea how to proceed. If what the Survivor said is true, if what she believes to be true is, if in fact the proprietor, Holmes, is Clemantis and Clemantis, Holmes, she's in his lair. She gazes at the painting as if searching for an answer. Grandmother Handley, or whoever it is, does not seem to know what to do either, so the doctor figures it's time to move on—this room's covered; no killer here—and so after a deep breath she's out a door at the other end of the room and back in the dimlit hallway, the floorboards beneath her now creaking almost in chorus.

Just down the hall, there's another room, about half the size of the lounging room, with a door cracked open and shedding an invitingly warm orange light. Handley enters. It's a library, every wall covered in books. Two chairs upholstered with leather that smells fresh, recently flayed, sit in the far corner by a curtained window. Handley lifts the curtain, revealing a paltry view—garbage receptacles covered with snow so thick, it's as frosting on a cake. Between the two chairs is a table with a crystal lamp and a sheet of paper but no pen. Handley inspects the paper. It appears, as far as she can discern, to be the start of a love letter: *Dearest Emma, I do not feign to understand what prompted me to act as I did this Sunday evening past, but there are—* Then there's a sloping streak, an aborted *S,* the letter's author interrupted in the heat of composition or his imaginative faculties hastily drained. She returns the letter to its place and peruses the bookshelves. As expected, there's little of interest—volumes by Aristotle, Copernicus, Kipling, Longfellow, Dickens, Poe. And then she spots the Doyle. It's her favorite, *The Sign of the Four.* She removes the book from its nesting and runs her fingers over the slick leather cover and the embossed faux-gilt lettering. Momentarily, everything's silent—no pipes clang, no floorboards creak underfoot. An eerie moment, to be sure. Handley flips through a few pages, the familiar words running wild through her mind. Soon, though, she opens to a hole that's been bored in the center of the book, a hidden safe that conceals no priceless jewels, only a paltry skeleton key. Handley places it in her pocket, just in case. With the hollowed Doyle back on its shelf, she inspects other volumes. Many, it turns out, are hollow. Why is she not exactly surprised? It's not that she was expecting it, but now that she's traipsed upon it, it makes a perfect kind of sense. Even *Gray's Anatomy*—an odd keeping in a hotel, to be sure—has been hollowed out by a crafty hand, but like all the other hollowed books aside from the Doyle, there's nothing in it—no jewels, no key. They're props. Dr. Handley's suspicious, so she starts removing books by the row, to inspect the bookcase to see if it, too, is a sham. She raps her knuckles against the back wall of the bookcase; it doesn't budge. A moment later, however, there's a muffled sound. She's still, placing an ear to the back of the bookcase as close as she can manage without breaking her neck or wedging her head between the shelves. At first, she hears nothing, and figures perhaps she only imagined it a moment ago. But then it comes again, positively, undeniably a human whimpering, only it's not coming from behind the bookcase. Handley trails the sound vigilantly as a dog on a scent. She locates a heating grate on the far side of the room, by the door. It is, as far as Handley can tell, the whimpering of a young girl or boy, high-pitched and petrified. Its source could be anywhere in the inn; at least she feels she's in the right place now—Clemantis is here, just as the Survivor said.

Above her, a pipe clangs. She jumps from fright and without looking back exits the library.

The hallway forks just outside the library. Handley considers her options. There are three: one is a stairwell that descends, the second is a stairwell that ascends, and the third is a corridor that leads to another snaking hallway. Since Handley's of the mind that one should never descend unless one has to, and since, according to the inn's caretaker, Holmes is upstairs, Handley decides to check the first-floor corridor first. But finds nothing, just a series of rooms. These, Handley figures, must be guest rooms. She tries the first door, but it's locked. Most likely they're all locked, everyone inside sleeping fitfully, exhausted after a long day at the White City. The killer might be behind one of these very doors, perhaps sleeping, but this does not correspond to the Clemantis Handley's developed in her mind. Even if he were in one of these rooms, he wouldn't be sleeping, and he wouldn't be alone. Even if the Survivor was right and Holmes is the killer, he wouldn't be here now—he'd be out, prowling, picking up his next victim. Just to be certain, though, Handley checks each door in turn. They are, it turns out, all locked.

The staircase up is narrow as a beam, and Handley, with her hoopskirt, barely makes it at all. The walls, on account of the pipes in them clanging with force, seem to be surging in, and the ceiling feels as if it's coming down on her. She has to duck. Before too long, she finds herself nearly crawling. The wires of her dress scrape against the walls. There's one long lantern at the very top of the staircase, her only guide in ascension. Since she can't see her feet, she trips, so that for every three steps up, she's pressed to take two back.

As she crawls out onto the second-story landing, she hears a faraway voice. It is a familiar sound, a panicked sobbing. A sound she's familiar with from her days at McClean. Once it might have been comforting, even encouraging. Now, though, it's a frightening, desperate sound. She rights herself and stomps down the hallway, no

longer worried about being so stealthy. She just wants to find the
source of the hotel, then the rear. The sobbing follows
she checks the front of the hotel, then the rear. The sobbing follows
as if hunting her.

When she reaches the end of the hallway, all's silent. It's an eerie
silence, the kind that comes just before something horrific happens. She checks each room, ear flush against the doors. There's
nothing, not even the sound of wind rattling the windows.

She looks left, then right. Still nothing.

Then abrupt laughter, symphonic and devilish. It's unbidden, rising and fading in volume without warning. It comes, she determines, from a room toward the end of the hall—a common area of
some sort, a place where conversations flow freely, greased by drink
and midnight fatigue and furnished with tattered chairs, a settee,
footstools, tables. A table for hundred-point billiards. Paintings that
appear to have been done by an amateur hand are hung crookedly
from dangling nails. The light's emerald on account of the emeralds
that pattern the lone lantern's shade.

"Sit down." His voice is cavernous, reverberating. He's seated,
legs splayed outward, on a dingy chair opposite her as she enters,
but she can tell he's tall and gangly. He's the only person in the
room, so far as she can see. And what a sight! His fingers are spindly
as twigs; his cheeks are sunken; droplets of dried blood dot his forehead. His hair's waxy black, and he appears to have been wearing a
hat, since there's the impress of a brim that causes his hair to wing
out, sticky with sweat. His teeth—the few that remain—are a particularly dark umber color, the tips appearing jagged as daggers. And
his sinister smile curves suspiciously upward. Despite appearances,
Handley isn't frightened by him in the least. In fact, based on first
impressions, she pegs him at once as a rather timid sort, a man who
once had a stutter and cured it at age fourteen simply by concentrat-
ing before speaking, an unresolved sort who has a low regard of
himself and fears and distrusts most men of regard. Dr. Handley can
relate.

She doesn't sit, not yet. She surveys the room once more, not
looking for anything in particular, then circles the billiard table, her

hoop dress scraping against the wall. With this the man laughs again. Handley stands over him and offers a hand in greeting. Instead of his hand in return, he offers the bottle he's been drinking from.

A pipe behind them clanks, but neither jolts. Handley mistakes a rushing of wind outside for trapped human voices.

"I couldn't sleep," he says, "so I thought perhaps I forgot to take my vitamins today." Here he flings the bottle across the room. It lands on the soft felt of the billiard table, so it doesn't shatter. "I just love this weather. Invigorating."

"I'm Elizabeth," says Dr. Handley snappily. "Are you staying at the inn?"

"There are nights I prefer to sleep with the window open, even in this cold." He's wearing a loose-fitting black shirt made of a wispy fabric—she can see clear through to his skin—that's unbuttoned halfway. A scar, still fresh, crosses his chest. "Do you know that feeling—of being pushed to your limits?"

"By any chance, are you the inn's proprietor?"

"I am in fact, yes," he says, "staying here, but, no, I'm not the owner."

"I am looking for a man called Holmes. Do you know him, or where I might be able to find him?"

"Do I look like the proprietary sort to you?" Here he laughs heartily, rattling a window, or perhaps it's just the wind.

"What do you do?" Handley, though she could easily sit in the chair next to him or at the least lean back against the billiard table, doesn't. She's not sure why she asked that; she truly doesn't care. He's either a laborer or a thief or perhaps—unlikely—he's a businessman of some sort. All is of little interest to her. In fact, as far as she's concerned, they're all the same—whatever their profession, they're men at base. It does strike her, though, standing over this strange person with the liquor breath, that she knows next to nothing about men.

"What do *you* do?"

Handley says nothing. She takes a step back, searching the pockets of her overcoat for the cigar she was smoking earlier, finding nothing.

He folds his hands on his lap, thumb rubbing thumb without stopping. Handley takes note of his fidgetiness. His body jerks about maniacally, whether or not he's talking. His hands graze his hair over and over. He sticks a finger up and in his nose, then scratches his knee as if he's trying to scratch down to bone. She wonders if he is doing this intentionally, to distract her or hide something. He might be on the lam, but if so, whatever it is he's running from is of no concern to her. He's not methodical or multifaceted enough to be the man she's looking for. There's a bit of laziness about him, either laziness or a kind of continual indecisiveness that would impede his killing anyone, unless by accident or randomly. Too reckless, she concludes, to be Clemantis.

Finally she says again, "What do you do?"

There's another snippet of laughter, intended to set Handley askew. He leers, his open mouth stretching almost to the side of his face as he speaks. "Rode Ferris's Wheel today." He pauses, to see if she'll say anything. She doesn't. "Man, is it a piece of machinery. Set my heart right on fire, I'll tell you. The thrill. The charge. It's the future, they say, flying." (Or did he say "flaying"? Dr. Handley might be hearing things.) "Each car, you know, is as big as a house, certainly bigger than any house I've ever been in. I don't see how the whole thing doesn't topple over and kill everyone out to have a good time." Here's another pause. Still Handley says nothing. "Actually," the man says, "I meant to ride it but never got to it."

"I haven't yet been to the Midway."

Crossing his legs and attempting to sit as if civilized, he crinkles his forehead together so that it appears sinister and meddling. He stomps his feet on the floor in rapid succession, delirious. Both it and the walls shake. The bottle on the billiard table rattles. He bolts toward her, very nearly snapping his neck, as if lunging at her jugular. But he will not assault her. Laughing, he says, "I do not believe you."

"It's true, I'm afraid," says Handley. Without warning, she laughs, just about choking on her own good humor. Spittle runs out the sides of her mouth, causing her only to laugh harder, laughing now in spasms and shuddering. The man begins to laugh also, only all at once he stops, and his face becomes as a statue's, cold and inflexible.

Even so, her laughter doesn't fade. At times, she surprises herself. All the stress of finding Clemantis, all the pressure—it all seems to fall away for a brief moment. It feels so good to laugh spontaneously and without restraint; it's as if a warm liquid fills her, rising inside her from her toes on up. She blushes.

"See, but that's exactly the problem. There is so much there. Strongmen, magicians, the Bewitching Bellyrina. But most fabulous of all," the man says, "is Buffalo Bill—you know, of Custer's Last Stand? He puts on a large show, far and away the biggest, most spectacular show I have ever seen. There are cowboys; there are Indians; there's gunfire. Everything a boy would ever want." He is beginning, Handley notices, to slur his words. As he talks, too, spittle flies everywhere—on the floor, on Handley's face. She doesn't seem to mind. And when he removes a second brown bottle and swills and then offers her a swill, she accepts, out of curiosity as much as politeness. When she hands the bottle back, his hand grazes her, sending trembles up her spine. Whatever it is, it tastes as coal, chalky and bitter. "MypoptoldmeaboutitoncebutIneverwentnowthatIhaveit'slikeI'makidagain."

The door behind her creaks open. She turns. It is a boy, his hair moppy and his eyes fatigued, rimmed with dark splotches. His clothes are tatters, a frayed, soot-stained shirt and threadbare trousers that seem three sizes too big. He is skinny, his skin pasty, his bones showing clear through—so skinny, in fact, that wrinkles scar his forehead, affecting him to appear a few years older than he must be, according to his mannerisms. He stands in the doorway, looking at Handley and then down at the floor, and then back at Handley, his hands digging hastily into his pockets.

"What are you doing?" The boy does a curtsey, then sprints toward the man, who, with a tenderness Dr. Handley doesn't expect, wraps an arm around the boy, squeezes him in a motherly fashion, whispers in his ear. Before too long, a particularly sinister laugh floods the entire inn.

The boy's cheeks flush sunset red. He hides his head in the man's side. A moment later, he peers out from the dark cavern, and he smiles, briefly, before burying his head once again. Then, suddenly, with a burst of energy only boys can summon forth, he sprints over toward Handley, offers a miniature hand.

"Hello, I'm Billy," says Billy.

"Hello, Billy." Handley has the feeling she's seen him before, once. Still, she can't place it. There's just something familiar about him—the droopy eyes, the crooked smile, the pointed ears. His face is innocent and carefree, just as any other boy's. He's lithe and limber, sprightly, but under all that Handley senses a desperateness, a confusion. She can't put her finger on it; it's just a first impression. Something, however, is amiss.

"Who are you?"

"Elizabeth."

"Elizabeth," says Skurlock. "I knew an Elizabeth once," and snickers. "Tough to the bone, she was. Rambunctious too. Had quite the mouth, she did. Swore like a sailor." Here booms a laugh, big and brawny. "I called her Ma."

Billy laughs, too. And then so does Handley. She worries they'll rouse the whole inn, but in contradiction to her nature she laughs nonetheless. Momentarily, in fact, she forgets they're *not* alone, forgets too that she's on the prowl for a killer.

All at once, the man's laughter ceases, and he stands and paces around the room once and then once again and then stands by the window watching the snow falling. His body in an uncomfortable-looking pose, with his legs as if twisted in on themselves and his knees buckling, he shades his eyes from the glare of the moonlight on the snow. It's almost as bright as high-noon sunlight, only with a bluish tinge. He removes a spindled protrusion from a shirt pocket and sparks it, inhaling deeply. The scent of its contents isn't familiar to Handley, so she assumes it's illicit and hunkers down on her haunches.

Suddenly, raised voices in the hall. First from far away, but then the sounds become louder, the voices and stomping nearer. Lanterns flicker. Right behind her, a man with orange muttonchops wearing a long black coat and a black hat and trailing a brisk arctic chill into the room enters. He says nothing. His face is devoid of expression, save determination. Handley can tell he's here looking for something specific. Behind him comes another man . . . and behind him yet another, totaling six, each man wearing a long black coat and a black hat, each trailing in the brisk arctic chill of outside and stomping snow. She recognizes none. It all happens so quickly, in a minute or less, that Handley's dizzy; she can't keep track of what exactly is going on; she keeps craning her neck about the room, trying to gauge what's happening. She grasps about for Billy, to pull him in and protect him, but he's not there; he's sprinting toward the man, hiding between his legs. He looks terrified, confused. His eyes are wide and probing. The men stomp in and head straight for Skurlock. At first, he doesn't turn, just remains at the window watching the snow falling outside with one hand upon the crown of Billy's head, mussing the boy's hair. For a moment, they seem as if frozen in time, man and boy in full understanding of each other. As the men approach, however, Billy screams out, high-pitched and truncated, then stands out from between the man's legs and faces the others full on. One whisks him up and turns to remove him from the room, but in the process of turning Billy has bitten the man's cheek. There's blood; the man shrieks and drops the boy. Handley lunges for him, but he slithers past her and out of the room, down the hall and away. In the meantime, the gangly man is surrounded. Handley stands, meaning to intervene, but she does nothing of the sort. He turns as if to confront the men but instead simply stands there, blank faced and saying nothing. Four men move in, two grabbing him by the arms and two by the legs. He's shackled and gagged. One man punches him in the gut; another lands a roundhouse-right on his cheek. The man does not put up a fight; he doesn't protest in any way; he allows them to drag him off, out of the room. As they pass, he and Handley lock eyes. He winks, grinning salaciously. Sometimes a wink's nothing more than a wink. Handley's not certain this is one of those times.

"Congratulations, Doctor." It is Tiggs, standing flush behind her. He stays but a moment and before leaving offers a hand, and when she doesn't take it, he says, "Delighted to have worked with you. Good luck."

Simonds, once Tiggs is gone, approaches Handley. "Without

Moreau trailing you, I shudder to think what might have happened," he says. "Are you all right?"

Snappily, "Yes. Why?"

"I don't know how you managed to do it," he says as he places an arm around Handley, as if to warm her. She shrugs him off. "Really, it's one for the history books."

Behind him various Pinkertons and policemen mill about, pacing the hallways frantically, searching—what else would they be doing?—for the disappeared boy. Oh, now everything's clear. Billy Rockland, the missing boy. She forgot about him, but here he was just a moment ago, in the flesh, living.

"You must have so much to say," says Simonds, "and now the world will hang on your every word. You're going to be famous!" That he says this excitedly and with a freakish glint to his eye is to put it mildly. Handley's embarrassed by the man's wayward enthusiasm. "I must admit, Doctor, that I wasn't fully taken with your methods, but you proved me wrong. You did it. You caught Clemantis!"

"But the boy . . . he's still . . ." She is about to say "living," but without her fully realizing it, Chief Detective Simonds has commandeered her off, downstairs and outside, where a moderate mob awaits her—curious Englewood residents and one lone reporter from the *Times-Herald*, who has neither pen nor paper. Later this morning, when at long last Tiggs fields questions from the world's reporters and one erstwhile photographer (from the *Times* of London) snaps a photo of the Husker on the sly, this original *Times-Herald* reporter will be heard to say, "And there I was, face to face with Beelzebub!" For now, however, snow swirls, wind roils, and soon sunlight will break over the lake. It's early morning, but for Handley it feels like midnight. She's so fatigued, she can hardly keep her eyes open, and her head's pounding, and her body feels slack, like it might just melt into a puddle at a moment's notice. By the time anyone notices, she's halfway up the stairs of the World's Fair Inn. Were she to turn around, she'd see, on the far side of the street, men in long black coats and black hats place Clemantis, shackled and gagged by now, into a carriage, the two horses, both braying, waiting for the crack of the whip, breath steaming in the air.

You are cordially invited to attend a Ball
To be given in celebration of the new P. Palmer Project,

the Cosmopolitan,

inspired by the White City.

⌐

Wednesday, the Eleventh of October, 1893,
at the elegant Palmer House

Twenty-Seven

Outside, snow falls violently now, the flakes as big as miniature planets. Inside, the air's a cosmic dust on account of the way the newly electrified ballroom floods the entire first floor with warm yellow light. Platters of miniature spiced Vienna sausages, Turkish delight, prune-stuffed hors d'oeuvres from Lapland and beyond follow. Music plays, soft and airy. It is a string quartet—two violins, a viola, a cello. The players, a man and three women, are imported from afar, and by the bags under their eyes, it appears they haven't acclimated.

One lone couple dances off in a corner. Enraptured, a server watches.

From the rafters supporting the gilded ceiling hang flags from around the world. In the center of the lobby is a sculpture in miniature of the White City and its distant cousin, the Midway, but since it's ice, it's melting quickly. The buildings, more transparent than white, are the first to go, their crested beaux arts crowns dribbling down the sides into a puddle. In the kitchen five chefs prepare hot meat sticks, tempura shrimp, clam and cheese dip, cold turkey glazed with jelly, fricassee of reindeer, monkey stew, boiled camel humps, jerked buffalo, and stuffed ostrich. While bakers, their toques weighted down with flour, bake various fried snowballs, wind doughnuts, crystallized frappes that are so wondrous and spindled they are in themselves feats of engineering. Others arrange everything on chinaware, the overall effect being one of synchronicity, Saturn melting effortlessly into Venus.

Upstairs, Bertha Palmer's at the window watching guests arrive outside. The pamphlet she's been reading while she waits, "The Reason Why the Colored American Is Not in the World's Columbian Exposition," dangles between two fingers. Its author, Frederick Douglass, should be downstairs, but she's here awaiting her dear friend Elizabeth Rockland, who's in the bath. It's been upwards of an hour since Elizabeth filled the bath, so Bertha's on guard, listening for the slightest signal of distress. On the other side of the mahogany-inlay, Versailles-style door, Elizabeth sits on the lip of a steaming bath that's been perfumed with lavender, rose hip, and a droplet of lemon. Before she slips out of her dress, she slides into the bath, plunging her head under and holding her breath for as long as she can. Then she crests the surface, gasping for air.

"Elizabeth!" Bertha Palmer helps her friend from the bath. Soon, as if by process of osmosis, Bertha, too, is sopping wet. With impressive dexterity, she unclasps Elizabeth's dress and brings her back into the other room, where a second, dry dress is chosen and quickly outfitted. This one has a red piping running along its seams and floral patterns stitched black on black upon the bodice.

"It's just— I'm sorry."

"Don't be silly," says Bertha. "I'm glad you're here. But we should go soon. Everyone's arriving."

"Where's William?"

"He's downstairs with Thomas. Shall I send for him?"

"It's best if you don't."

"All right, dear. Oh, that looks lovely." She's admiring the topaz stone Elizabeth Rockland just, it seems, pulled from the ether, pinning it to her bodice.

"It should," says Elizabeth pleasantly. "It's yours."

Bertha Palmer's on the verge of laughter when there's a rasping at the door. Before too long, it opens, and in stomp Potter Palmer and young Mr. Nix.

Jollily, "Here we are."

At first, she shows no expression of any sort. Then the corners of her lips drop, then her whole face droops. Elizabeth Rockland's cheeks go pale as if she'd just seen a ghost. Nix purses his lips, scrunches his cheeks together, and snivels his nose as to a tune of its own devising. A half smile, half sneer blooms across her face. It's a natural flinch; he's fully unaware he does it, but Elizabeth snickers, loud and wall-clanging, then ambles across the room and over to the boy, embracing him.

"Oh, Billy!"

The Palmers share a look of confusion. As Elizabeth Rockland moves toward the boy, Potter Palmer cuts her off, his beefy arm flung sloppily around her, saying, "You look very beautiful tonight. I'm certain your husband will scarcely recognize you."

He's downstairs in the hotel's library, waiting for her. There are dark orbs under his eyes, on account of lack of sleep. Before him is a settee with an ornate backrest of gilded mountain landscapes and on the velvet cushions furcating turquoise grapevines. In front of him at eye level is the scale model of the Cosmopolitan. It will be, when it's completed, the tallest skyscraper in the land—taller even than the Monadnock without being so broodingly erected. Rockland removes a cigar from his inside jacket pocket and contemplates it. It's his first skyscraper, the third building he's designed in its entirety; if it's built, it will be his second project to move beyond groundbreaking. That is a big if, since Palmer's yet to secure the land. They'd planned to go, early tomorrow morning, to scout a property not too far from the White City, but the plans were put on hold since Billy went missing.

The door swings open with such force that Rockland very nearly shrieks with fright. Once he sees who it is, however, he says calmly, "Hello."

"It's nearly time," says Palmer. He closes the door behind him. The smell of Madeira floods the room. Palmer steps toward his architect, pausing at the miniature Cosmopolitan, his body momentum continuing on so that he almost tips over. His face changes from a nothing face to a face at once joyous and solemn. He's been drinking. "It is incredible, William."

"There's something I need to speak to you about."

"All the world will flock back here once the White City's closed to see my . . . our building. I can feel it. This is just the very beginning."

"I know how to find Billy."

"There will be talk, there will be accolades. This is what the future will be."

"A man told me—"

"They'll find Billy," says Potter Palmer, his eyes still affixed to the model. "I've insured they have the best people working on the case." Here he deadeyes Rockland. "This criminal will be brought to justice. Trust in that."

But Rockland says, "I'm afraid there's another, faster way." Palmer's gaze returns to the model. "I was visited by a man the other night. He suggested he might know where Billy is."

"For a price. Yes?" Palmer's familiar with the sort.

"He would like," Rockland says, "for me to put him in contact with you."

"William." His voice is stern, rigid. Palmer steps directly in front of Rockland. Even with Rockland seated, Palmer's so squat, their eyes are level. "You don't think this happens all the time? It is called a bribe," says Palmer. "It's best, for now, if you don't intervene. That will insure Billy's safety."

Perhaps, after all, he's been a bad father; perhaps Billy wasn't kidnapped but left; perhaps if he'd been an attentive father, Billy would be here, upstairs with his mother, preparing for the party, and not another victim of the Husker. He's certain that's what's happened, by now. He'd never tell his wife this—she'd crumble—but his gut feeling is that Billy's gone. There are moments—flashes really— when he thinks perhaps that man knows where Billy is. Perhaps Billy's still alive, but he figures it is but a ruse, just somebody else wanting into Palmer's pockets. It was worth following up on, if only for his wife's sake. Even the smallest chance is a chance nonetheless. He can't seem to get the image of her face out of his mind. Sadness has rendered her unrecognizable. He's not sure what he should do.

He's not sure how much longer he can continue pretending everything will be all right.

"I'm not so certain," Rockland says in response to Palmer. With that he's up, pacing about the library. The spines of the books whirl past, mostly black with gilt lettering, in a blur. Rockland's dizzy but continues to pace, knocking into Palmer as he passes, headed for the door. There's bound to be food; now that he's hungry, food's all he can think of.

"I need a drink."

"Of course," says Palmer. He feels awful. He shouldn't have said what he did; it is none of his business, anyhow. He opens the door for William, saying, "Shall we?"

Rockland exits the library without another word. He marches off, leaving Palmer behind. The walls of the Grand Room are of a warm salmon color and the trellises of gold. The floor, checkered black-and-white, is cold and marble, perfect for dancing. As he locates the liquor man across the Grand Room, also on the lookout for Elizabeth, a soft melody whispers across the ballroom. Is it? Yes! The "Jubilate." He repairs a tumbler of Pernod and swills. On account of the lack of food and sleep of late, he's instantly buzzed and taps his feet on the floor with brio but nothing approaching rhythm. No matter. He is happy, elated. Billy, Clemantis, his wife's melancholia—all is forgotten, if briefly. Across the room, he spots a woman in a strikingly red dress that shimmers in the room's electric light. For a moment, he believes he knows her; just for the briefest of moments, he believes it is his wife, although he knows it cannot be. The woman is standing before the melting White City, one hand holding a champagne flute, the other twiddling midtorso to the "Jubilate." He decides he'll approach, but just as he steps toward her, someone wearing a suit that's two sizes too small for him cuts Rockland off.

"Dance with me?" For an instant, Rockland thinks it's Billy calling to him from the land of the disappeared. It is, in fact, Nix, tugging at the tail of Rockland's tux. The face is the same, the mouth, even the eyes. Rockland stares at the boy for a full minute. Scooping him up, he twirls the boy about, laughing heartily. To the amusement of those standing around and conversing, Nix shrieks. Mr. Douglass, his white hair a ball of frizz, and Mr. Adams, almost as short as Nix, stand beside Potter Palmer, who emerges with his wife and Elizabeth Rockland. At the sight of her, Rockland just about drops Nix. Elizabeth looks different. She appears to him as an entirely new person, not the woman he remembers falling in love with and not the woman he entered into God's provenance with. Her eyes are angry, with none of their usual, inviting warmth. She marches over and takes Nix by the hand, removing him as the "Jubilate" crescendos and fades. Perhaps it's her frightening leer, but Rockland, pink faced, dripping with sweat, fatigued, dizzy, turns and walks away briskly. Crossing the room, he weaves in and out of the crowd in search of the woman in the red dress.

Silence soon descends upon the entire Grand Room. Potter Palmer stands before the roast, talking to Mr. Field. Mr. Douglass and Mr. Adams wander off in search of more libation. Everyone's drinking and talking of politics, of van Gogh's *Landscape with Cypress Tree*, of *Don Juan*, of Jack the Ripper.

Father Rockland weaves the crowd, eyes peeled for the shimmering red dress.

Here are Mr. Douglass and Mr. Adams again, Mr. Adams saying, "Isn't capital just an extension of your self, in all its infinite curiosity and wonderment—a bridge to another world?"

Rockland, hearing this, chortles. The ice White City has all but melted. Rockland adjusts his tie, glancing about, frantically eavesdropping. He's started off, headed back toward the library, when he's approached by a strange little man in a stovepipe hat and black-on-black formal wear. The man's nostrils betray a pandemonium in miniature. The man moves abruptly, ineptly, and grasps Mr. Rockland by the lapels, saying, "I am sorry for your loss, sir."

Right then, the two violins, the viola, and the cello take their leave. Scott Joplin, a pale Negro wearing a pinstripe suit the color of charcoal, almost black but not quite, takes his place at the grand piano and begins his rag. A frenzied couple parts the crowd, limbs flying about haphazardly so that people move back, creating a dance floor of sorts.

"Mr. Walsh would like to speak with you in private, Mr. Rockland."

A large, portly man, twice the size and breadth of anyone else in the room, with skin ashen with soot, grasps Rockland by the left elbow and leads him to the library. En route, William Rockland catches his wife's eye. Even with the portly man pulling at him, he halts dead in his tracks. Her eyes are vacant, gaping. She turns her back on him and joins Nix on the dance floor. Nevertheless, he blows her a kiss before continuing on.

Walsh sits upon the settee in the library. Beside him is the woman in the glimmering red dress. She is, in person, simply stunning—her face as alabaster, her lips rouged, her hair the color of a flame—and her eyes, one of which is blue, the other a chestnut color, are piercing.

Rockland blushes, but Walsh says, "Sit down, Mr. Rockland."

Behind him emerges a chair. A rather large, unwieldy chair equipped with long, garbled armrests and a sloping back upon which have been whittled dancing nymphs and cherubs with flutes. He does as he's told. The door closes. The man with the stovepipe inspects the miniature Cosmopolitan, regarding it apprehensively, before sparking a cigar.

"We will need a guarantee for our union, and soon," says Walsh. "I trust you have worked out the details with Mr. Palmer."

Rockland goggle-eyes the woman in the red dress. He says nothing.

Walsh says, "Your son, I should remind you, is safe—as of now. But perhaps you are not aware of the gravity of your situation." At this, the large man reaches around Rockland and grips each wrist with such force they might crackle. The man's breath smells of a slaughterhouse, his hands are clammy, but his point is clear. "Your wife and your son . . . what a shame it would be, Mr. Rockland, if they just disappeared. Working in a factory, you learn accidents happen all the time, but the tragedy is not in their happening but when they can be prevented and are not."

Rockland nods, regarding Walsh solemnly. For emphasis, the large man removes a rapier from within his jacket and slashes Rockland's left ear. Rockland gasps, breathing heavily, heaving. Walsh and the woman in red remain stony-faced. Blood spurts everywhere. The slightest smile creeps across the woman in red's face.

"You have," Walsh says, "until noon tomorrow."

Walsh and his rogues now exit, the woman in the red dress trailing a scent of Woodbury's behind. It is a familiar scent—the same scent Elizabeth once wore in happier days. Rockland, though he'd like to, doesn't weep. He's too confused to weep. He's not sure whether to believe them. After they're gone, Rockland continues gripping the armrests of the chair as if the large man were still pinning them there, a bead of sweat dripping from his armpit and his own blood pooling around him. The threat seemed real, but then, of late, so much that appears real is not. Dizziness overwhelms him. He rises but then keels over, falling into the model of the Cosmopolitan, knocking it off the table and into the pool of blood. There's a ringing in his head so loud he cringes. Everything spins as he stands. He almost flops to the ground himself but makes it to the door and out into the Grand Room. People, previously dancing and talking, stop and stare. Some run; others just watch, captivated and confused. He must appear as a leviathan, blood spurting everywhere. There's a waiter with wind doughnuts emerging from the kitchen. No one recognizes Rockland at first; at first he could be anyone, certainly nobody anyone here *knows*. As he moves about the crowd, people stand back. Here's a man with a misshapen head. Here's a man with one leg shorter than the other. Here's someone wearing a tuxedo the color of a canary. Here's Mr. Roker, the renowned ocularist. Here's Mather Sprangs, the chief rubber at the Palmer House's turkish bath. A photographer takes a portrait of the Jatjat Jit Singh, the maharaja of Kaparthala. As the bulb pops, people shudder. Rockland isn't sure whether he's bleeding or it just feels like he's bleeding. Scott Joplin's midway through his rag. Rockland's feet squelch on the marble dance floor, but as he moves, it feels less and less that he's moving. The dancing couple dances on. He feels more and more that he'd like to sleep, just keel over right here and sleep for ages on the marble floor. Here's a woman in a red dress, but it's a different woman in a different red dress. Here's

Marshall Field talking to Alice Rideout, the sculptor. People are both familiar and not. Here are Jane Addams and, flanking her, Bertha Palmer and Elizabeth Rockland. What happens next is strange. He recognizes his wife, but he doesn't. When she sees him, she's all smiles. He hasn't seen her smile in days; smiling, she appears as an entirely different person, a happier, freer person. When she sees the blood, she looks troubled, but only for a moment, after which she returns her gaze to Jane Addams. That is all—a passing glance and nothing more. It's as if she hardly recognizes him, but perhaps this is what passes as love these days.

Rockland walks on, headed for the melted ice White City. Here he finds Potter Palmer and Nix. Palmer, seeing Rockland, stands there, pop-eyed, his jaw dropped. Rockland ignores Palmer for the moment and heads for Nix, who leaps right up and into Rockland's arms as if expecting to be twirled. He is. Meanwhile, Palmer busies himself finding a doctor. If Rockland doesn't stop bleeding and soon, who knows what might happen. The Cosmopolitan might be compromised.

Then Palmer spots one. Dr. Tanner, Palmer's personal physician, stands on the far side of the Grand Room, champagne flute in hand, a cautious smile breaking across his face. In the time it takes Palmer to commandeer the doctor, Rockland twirls Nix, arms flailing, blood streaking the boy's cheeks and neck, and a young newsboy, not much older than Billy and trailing a checkered scarf long as a python, runs in screaming.

"They've caught him! They've caught Clemantis!"

MURDERER NABBED IN MELEE!
NO APOLOGIES.
IN HIS RESIDENCE.
MURDERER PROCLAIMS INNOCENCE.
PRESS SWARMS.

Twenty-Eight

All around her, Pinkertons swarm. They flood the first floor, searching for Billy Rockland, overturning furniture, ransacking each room in turn. Nothing is left untouched, but then again nothing is found, no evidence revealed. The inn's caretaker has been taken off for questioning, so Handley searches the front desk for the ledger of guests. But the ledger's missing. Every pursuit, she knows, constructs its own system—that is, the ledger, though missing, still indicates something. But what? Billy could be hiding, or Holmes may already have found him. She must move on, which she does presently, checking each room of the first floor in turn, jostling the brutish Pinkertons out of the way. They work by sheer vigor, overwhelming whatever is in their way, while she works with a certain kind of poise, attuned more to the smaller aspects of the investigation.

"What are you doing here? No women allowed."

The Pinkerton, in a long black coat, black gloves and with a stern grin, towers over her, his hair brilliantly white, even in the dim light. Clearly, he has no idea who she is, that she's working on the investigation; all she has to do is show him her identification papers or drop a name, and the situation will be rectified. But that would waste valuable time. Rather than refute him, she simply nods and pretends to vacate. In fact, she dawdles in the hallway a moment until the Pinkertons have been summoned upstairs—apparently, they've found something.

When they've gone, she decides to check the basement, since its door is ajar. Behind her, though, the door slams shut. Just to be sure, she checks it—as suspected, it's locked. It's so dark that she cannot see the hand she places just in front of her face, to guide herself. Halfway down, she bumps her head on a pipe. It occurs to her that this is her last chance to change her mind; even if the door's locked, she can pick it and escape. But no, she's so close; she has to see her search through to its terminus. The stairs empty into a large, cavernous room with turrets that impede passage and shadows that appear as demons and dust so thick and rife it's as snow, only its opposite. A lone window, halfway covered with snow, allows in a sliver of moonlight. The wind outside howls. A wayward door rattles in its frame.

All around her, pipes clang. Steam hisses. Dust swirls.

She steps through soupy cobwebs and over scuttling rats. She feels dizzy, for the darkness expands in all directions, and the ground beneath her softens as she passes over it, as if it were a swamp. Perhaps she is sinking. Perhaps this is, in fact, a swamp, for it smells as if she's waded into a sewer or into an underground garden pregnant with the smell of wilting flowers.

Above her, she hears footsteps. Behind her, more footsteps. Another door slams. Steam hisses. Sweat drips off her nose; her head throbs; a burning sensation jolts up her spine. Gasping for air, she drops to her knees. Her eyes sting with dust, and her throat fills so that she can hardly breathe; soon it hurts to breathe. Perhaps, she feels, she has been drugged; perhaps the libation she swilled upstairs with the man they apprehended as Clemantis was an elixir or a sedative; perhaps the rank air she is breathing has been infused with a gas or a chemical. Perhaps she is hallucinating, for there, emerging from a shadow at the far end of the cavernous room, she spots the shadowy figure of a boy. Moonlight streams in around him, exposing a man who's neither tall nor short, neither slim nor stocky, with strangling arms. This, she believes, is Holmes. She cannot make out his face but can see that he's wearing a steam-pressed suit, black with white pinstripes; even in the dark, she can make out the white pinstripes. Rather than move toward them, she remains crouched down, hoping they haven't seen her. Stealth she needs now, as much of it as she can muster. She needs to follow and hover; she can't let him out of her sights; he can't know she's here. He places a hand as big as a globe fully over the boy's mouth, muzzling him. The boy bites his hand, drawing blood. And then he stares right at her. She holds her breath. Does he see her? After a moment passes, he drags the boy around a corner, disappearing into the darkness.

She feels her way along a brick wall, unsure of where she's going. Her whole back is sopped through her blouse. Her throat is parched, and she feels as if she might faint at any moment. Perhaps it's the steam; perhaps it's the gas or the sedative; perhaps it's fear. To her immediate left, a rat screeches. She begins to think, the longer she's down here, that she won't find them. She'll only be lost, and nobody will come looking for her, or if they do, it will be too late. She'll die of suffocation; she'll die of starvation; she'll die alone, or Holmes will find and kill her. She has, she fears, already failed. She will not find the boy alive; he'll be dead, and Holmes will have disappeared. There's so much dust in the air, she inevitably swallows some. She strips herself of her winter coat, unclasps the neck of her dress, gasping for air.

A pipe clangs, startling her. After a moment's silence, there's a faraway wailing, and at the far end of the corridor, she sees a flickering orange light. She stops breathing, trying to determine if she is hallucinating the wailing and the orange light. She blinks; she rubs her eyes of dust; she pounds her palm against her forehead—but there it is, flickering. It could be a beacon of some kind, a summons meant to lure her. She deliberates whether she should follow it. Just then a pipe directly above her bursts and steam hisses out, burning her face. A moment later, there's another wail, this one shrill and lingering. She walks faster, stepping through pools of water. Something (broken glass?) crackles under her boots, which are saturated with sewage water. Cobwebs drape across her face, but she's running now and soon runs into a wooden wall that shifts upon contact, the wooden planks splintering. A liquid of some kind streams out, soaking her. Her skin burns. Before she can turn, something grasps at her—a hand. A hand, cold and slimy. Not a living hand, a *dead* hand.

Behind her, a corpse dangles out of a vat. Its hand grasps for Handley, tearing her blouse. In the scuffle, the band of her timepiece snaps, and the timepiece itself falls into the sewage. There's another wail, and she runs faster down the passageway, then left into a brick wall. She's breathless, dizzy, nauseous. But there it is again, the flickering orange light. It appears to be swaying, as if it's a lantern on a boat at sea. Yes, that's what it is. It's a lantern. Could Holmes be ensnaring her? Perhaps, she thinks, this is all part of a grand scheme; perhaps she's a pawn in a puzzle. Somewhere in the darkness, something creaks. She searches the pockets of her dress for a cigar and matches, so that she may light it and spark her way back to the stairwell and out, but she finds only the remains of a cigar, no matches. Hands trembling, she decides there is nothing she can do, so she follows the lantern down a passageway that gradually declines into a small corridor, in the center of which there's a fountain. The infrequent drip of water calms her, if briefly. Here, too, the air's cooler—perhaps there's a draft from an open window somewhere. For a moment, she loses the lantern; when she relocates it, it appears to be ascending. More distant cries . . . after a brief search of the corridor, she locates a ladder, which she quickly climbs. It funnels up into a smaller room with two doors, one of which is opened. Light escapes out the bottom of the other door. Handley pauses, considering her options. Holmes is in the locked room; there he will torture and kill Billy, if he hasn't killed him already; this is her last chance to save the boy—if she waits a moment longer, he might be dead. She approaches the locked door, bangs on it, kicking it, ramming it once with her whole body. Holmes does not come to the door. Perhaps, she thinks, it is a soundproof room; she's heard of them, but it's a bit extravagant. Anything's possible, and time's running out. She gives up, pacing about, frustrated, and then decides to try the other door.

Inside, just darkness. It is so narrow—about two feet—she figures it is a passageway of some sort. But it is not. At the far end, there's a brick wall, blocking passage of any sort. She is, she fears, trapped. The frame of her dress blooms out, and the walls squash in on her. Once inside, she can hardly maneuver herself. She can't turn left or right, only glide about sideways. Cramped quarters disturb her, and these are the most cramped quarters she has ever been in. Almost immediately she's hyperventilating, whacking the wall before her with both hands, kicking it, trying to remove herself. It does not occur to her that she could easily skid out, as she did in. Her mind is reeling. Panic trounces her. The silence is deafening—no pipes clanging, no steam hissing, no wind. She screams out, but her scream echoes, disquieting her more. Either she's weeping, or that's just sweat running down each cheek. Her heart rattles her rib cage, her chest expands so fully that a button on her dress bursts, and she rakes her fingernails into the wall in front of her, loosening a panel of some kind. Due to the placement of her arms and her inability to reposition them, she can only move the panel partway. It reveals the other room, a room bathed in blinding light.

At first, she sees nothing, just the light. The walls of the room are white. There's a slice of shadow on the far left of her vantage, but then it disappears. A moment later, another shadow appears projected on the wall—a line that jags up, then down. Initially, she thinks nothing of it. But then it strikes her. This, she fears, is the shadow of Billy's legs, a suspicion confirmed when two other elongated shadows—a grown man's arms—reach down, fastening a strap. Handley bangs against the wall. Presently, the silhouette of a man comes into view, and then a moment later the man himself appears, Holmes. His face in profile, he appears to be freshly bathed and scented, his cheeks lightly powdered. A spotless bowler hat sits snuggly atop his head. He turns, facing away from her. She jostles for a better vantage, her forehead flashing clammy and hot. Certainly Billy is there, dead or alive. It occurs to her that it might be too late, but still she bangs against the wall. Holmes's head bows down now, as if in supplication. A vertebra prods out of his neck. His hair is a dark scarlet color, closely sheared. A few pimples line the back of his neck. His ears, from her vantage, bloom out, and his earlobes appear overly droopy. *These* are the earlobes of a murderer? She's not sure what she expected—draconically pointy spikes?

Holmes bows down, facing away. It appears that he is talking to himself. Handley cocks her head so that her ears are flush against the wall, but she hears nothing. She shifts her head to the left, but sees only the tip of one of the child's shoes. She shifts her head to the right, and sees the edge of a shelf. It's empty, but she imagines it contains tools—bottles with spindly necks, daggers, knives of all sorts, also saws, cattle prodders, whips, a branding iron.

Presently, Holmes turns and faces her dead-on. Handley looks away, as if hiding, but she cannot bear not to look. In the electric light, his skin is pasty, ghoulish. His face is slack, but his eyes are troubled, panicky. A slight blemish just to the left (his right) of the nose draws her attention immediately. He does not appear to be possessed by the Devil; he appears calm, collected; he appears to be rather attractive, even handsome, with bony cheeks, eyes set far back in their sockets to be mysterious, full lips, a fuller mustache, and bushy eyebrows. Calmly, he stares straight ahead, eyes closed now. He does not appear to be in ecstasy so much as reprieve, calming himself for the act he is about to commit. He is not, she thinks, looking at her, only through her, if he sees her at all. After a moment, he drops his lower lip, exposing yellow, uneven teeth—the mark, she discerns, of someone who grew up in poverty, or overseas. She realizes she's too late; Billy's almost certainly dead, or will be very soon. Still, she cannot bear not doing anything, and she maneuvers herself out of the small room and tries to open the other door. It's locked. With a hairpin, Handley tries to pick the lock. The hairpin breaks. Anxious, she returns immediately to the narrow room. She must see what is happening; she must know what Holmes is doing, how he is doing it.

Still, her vantage is obscured because of the panel. She can see Holmes circumnavigating the boy, an arm stretched down. But then Holmes disappears. When he returns, he is standing farther back, on the far side of the boy. This time he does not look at her. Instead, he looks down, his eyes as if closed and his lips quivering ever so slightly. The muscles of his cheeks tense up for a moment, then relax; tense, then relax; and his forehead, after a moment, creases. She can hardly feel her body now. Her knees jerk spasmodically. She must be imagining things, or willing them. Every other moment, the muscles on one side of his face tense up, then relax, causing his mouth to appear momentarily disfigured. He is not sweating, even in the electric light.

Blood, from her bruise, drips over her left eye and into her mouth. A strand of bloody hair affixes itself to her cheek. It itches. She tries to remove it, but cannot. Her throat is parched, her heart's racing, and her stomach stings from acid. She feels light-headed. Her blood's boiling. Her skin's cold. Everything's numb.

When Holmes tugs at his right earlobe, leaving a smear of the boy's blood, she gags, the acid in her stomach splattering up her throat. His sleeves, she sees, are rolled up, and blood splotches his white shirt. In a moment, he disappears again and returns with a bottle labeled CANTHAR, the contents of which he appears to empty into the boy's mouth. A hand flails up, then drops instantly from sight. Holmes leans over farther, gagging Billy. His hair falls forward, veiling an eye. When he looks up again, his lips are moving, he appears to be talking, but she can't hear anything. After a moment, he disappears, returning momentarily with a knife so long it's almost a saber. His face is still calm—eerily so. His cheeks, by now, are relaxed, though his shoulders stand rigid. He's talking to himself. But otherwise he appears tranquil, perhaps euphoric. Again, he disappears from Handley's vantage, only to reappear a moment later, still talking to himself. Handley forces herself to concentrate. She needs to know what he's saying. She has never been able to read lips, but she needs to make out what he's saying. *Over easy.* She blinks, trying to focus. *Under mother.* She tries, but she cannot make it make sense. All of a sudden, he stops and stares at her intently. This time, she knows, he's seen her. He looks, Handley thinks, frightened or betrayed, his lips curled slightly downward and his eyes saggy. He could, of course, kill her; he could slash her throat; he could rape and torture her—and for a moment that is what she determines he will do. But his limbs shake, his jaw clenches, his eyes blink without stopping. And then, without a word, he flees. She maneuvers herself out of the narrow room, but her dress catches again on a nail, fabric tears, and when at last she's out, he's gone—down a darkened passageway, around a corner. She could follow the echo of his footsteps and be lost, or she could check on Billy. The door's open, light glistening off the blood that streams out into the hallway. As she passes, she lifts her dress so as not to ruin it and steps over the blood, and then, without even a glance, she's off, down a series of passageways, some of them dead ends, until it's so dark she cannot see the hand she places just in front of her face, to guide herself.

Epilogue

All over Chicago, roiling black smoke. It cloaks the city as a fog, hanging stagnant. It's a muggy July day, with temperatures in the high nineties by the lake. A fierce gale blows from the southwest, fanning the fire into a conflagration. By sunrise, a massive crowd has gathered. Some suspect arsonists, others mischievous children. Nobody knows exactly how it happened. Speculation's rampant. It started, some say, at the Terminal Station but leapt acrobatically across the plaza, sparking the Administration Building. Within minutes, its crested dome crashed to the ground with a boom. A gigantic cloud of soot and ash funnels upwards and north, over downtown. Burning cinders ignite Mining and Electricity and the Chocolate Menier. The statue of Benjamin Franklin turns to ash within seconds, as does the Hayward Restaurant. Even Columbian Fountain burns, its gold leaf easily combustible. The orange flames engulf Transportation to the north and the Stock Pavilion to the south. Those gathered run for cover as Manufactures catches ablaze—its roof, eleven acres of glass, shatters instantly. By noon, every wall of every building has collapsed, and by dusk the White City is in ruins.

Handley watches the burning from the pier at North Avenue, jostling her way through the mob to gain a better vantage, but all she can see are the plumes of black smoke moving quickly north. Though it is just past noon, the smoke has stamped out the sun, and

the only thing visible downtown is the skeleton of a future skyscraper, the Cosmopolitan. All around her people stretch skyward
in search of clean air, while pickpockets take advantage of the darkness and tricksters hover. Beachgoers, thinking they'd enjoy
another blisteringly hot summer Sunday, tie towels around their
heads like turbans, to keep the soot out of their hair. Nobody can
believe what they're seeing—it appears, from here, that the whole
city has caught on fire. When the smoke plumes approach North
Avenue Beach, everyone disperses, some charging inland, others
leaping into the surging lake.

Handley, however, stands transfixed, not so much frightened as
baffled, until a voice calls out behind her, "Clemantis . . ." She turns,
startled, only to find a newsboy, all floppy hat and sad eyes,
approaching her, waving a copy of this noon's special edition in her
face. HANGING TONIGHT, in gigantic type. Speaking of which,
she will be late if she does not get a prompt move on, so she flips a
coin in the air for the boy to catch and takes a paper, which she
tosses in a refuse receptacle as she vacates the pier. She walks, heaving on account of the smoke, a mile inland to the El. There, she
impels herself through the waiting crowd and at the very last
moment onto the very last car, elbowing a woman in her Sunday best
out of the way. As the train pulls out of the station, the woman grabs
at Handley's dress, slitting it. On account of the Pullman strike, the
ride downtown, usually half an hour, takes three times that. Frustrated en route, some jump out onto the tracks and try their luck by
foot—many plummet through the elevated rails—while those who
remain curse each other at random, when they're not choking on the
smoke.

Central Station, as expected, is mobbed. Many are here to meet
the first train allowed into the city since the strike began in May, now
arriving on Track 4. Handley's train arrives on the elevated rail, but
it, too, is packed with people hanging over the railings, some on the
verge of falling in search of clean air. People propel themselves up
the stairway to Central Station, stampeding those who wish to
descend. Inside, high above, soot blankets the all-glass atrium; wind
screams in the rafters, which is where the pigeons have gathered. As

she steps onto the platform, a white dropping splatters her left shoulder. Even inside, smoke stings her eyes. It's so muggy, her skin crinkles and her spectacles, which are oversize and threaten to fall off the bridge of her nose if she so much as breathes, fog up immediately so that she can't see even a foot in front of her. In the darkness, she reaches her hand out and grabs whatever she can, which happens to be the lapel of a willing gentleman, who gladly leads her outside.

"Dr. Handley!" Inspector Moreau is exactly where he said he'd be, on the corner of LaSalle and Adams. She is late, but he does not appear flustered. He is, in fact, grinning widely. She notices, at once, that he has changed markedly since she saw him last nine months ago—where once Moreau was chunky, now he's gaunt, his forehead more prominent and his cheeks as if chiseled. Since she's wheezing, he places a handkerchief over her mouth, saying, "This will help," before directing her into a waiting phaeton. Before the carriage door's closed behind her, the driver's whip cracks, the horses whinny, and they're off speeding through the smoldering city.

"There has been a new development in the case, Doctor," Inspector Moreau says, clasping his hands together in his lap. "Remains have been—"

"I have retired, Inspector," says Handley. Which is not entirely true. While she is no longer involved in the Holmes investigation actively, she has been writing about it, in her spare time, in the room she rented last November in Lincoln Park, over the horse stable. At first, nothing of substance came into her head and what she wrote was like a journal filled with haphazard, unimportant recollections. Over and over again, she'd search for the exact way to describe her long night in the cellar of the World's Fair Inn, but she found and finds still that she cannot recall much of anything—she concluded that she was, in fact, drugged. The book languished. Inevitably, a bird chirping outside or the piercing winter sun would distract her, and her thoughts would wander down less-malevolent alleys. To pay her rent, she established her own practice in psychotherapy, based more on the writings of Dr. Freud than on those of her mentor Dr. James, placing an advertisement in the *Tribune;* aside from her landlady, however, nobody responded. As for Billy Rockland, she has forgotten about him almost entirely. "I'm sorry," she says, "but I do not wish to hear the specifics."

"I will respect your wishes," says Moreau. "To be honest, I was not certain you'd attend today's festivities, but it is good to see you."

They ride in silence, Dr. Handley gazing absentmindedly out the window. She can see, nestled between the skyscrapers, orange flames swirling up as far as the eye can see, fracturing the smoky blackness. As they cross State Street, she can see that the windows of Marshall Field and Company, which were damaged by the strikers, haven't been replaced. The streets have been cordoned off so that authorized vehicles may pass, and policemen stand guard, keeping the public at bay, but still some stream alongside the phaeton, slapping it as it passes. A few hop aboard, only to be thrown off a moment later by sheer momentum.

The phaeton comes to a halt at Michigan Avenue. A tent has been set up for certain dignitaries and those involved directly in the Clemantis investigation. Outside stand three policemen, each twice as tall as Handley. Moreau escorts her through the smoke and inside and over to a table at which Theodate Tiggs, the government agent, sits with folded hands and weary eyes. Handley checks Moreau for an explanation, but he does not return her gaze. Tiggs says, "Too much attention is being paid to the strike and the burning of the White City, but this is good. Dr. Handley, a body was found a month or so ago. The manner of death was consistent with the Clemantis killings." Here he pauses. "Needless to say, it hasn't been announced publicly yet. I am not certain how, but around this time it occurred to Potter Palmer that perhaps we had the wrong man." In fact, Dr. Handley passed along an anonymous note, but she hadn't told a soul and certainly won't now. "At first we were hesitant, but Mr. Palmer eventually persuaded us to have an open mind in the matter. The man we apprehended, Hannibal Skurlock by name, is a ruffian, most certainly, but is he capable of skinning a child? Interviews with the captive suggest, no. In fact, when told of the child's death, he even showed remorse, seemingly earnest. Gratefully, Mr. Palmer concurred with our wishes not to make his personal views public. And despite the strikes, he contributed and continues to contribute

to the investigation. Times are tough, but a Palmer's still a Palmer."
Which is true. Since last year's panic, American securities, because
of the exportation of American gold, have liquefied. European
investors, once the exposition closed, sold American securities at
rates that soon shut the Illinois Steel Company and the Grant
Locomotive Works, which in turn caused silver mining in Colorado
to stagnate and the New Bedford and Fall River mills and, in May,
the Pullman Palace Car Company, to close indefinitely.

Here Tiggs pauses again, raising an eyebrow.

"The man will hang tonight, as planned. Public fears must be
calmed. If they want blood, blood we'll give them. Finally," Tiggs
standing, "a sense of closure, for every one of us. As far as the public's concerned, Clemantis will be hung tonight." He circles the
table and stands before Handley. "Our own investigation, of course,
will continue, but nobody will know this. There is a man, Holmes,
who has disappeared. You may know of him. He owned a hotel
many people checked in to, but few seemed to check out. We have a
Pinkerton tracking him, but your expertise in these matters is
unparalleled, Dr. Handley. There are suspicions of fraud and possibly murder, although no boys were linked directly to Holmes—until
now." Here he glances at Moreau, who nods. "We have found the
remains of a child in Holmes's inn, specifically eighteen ribs. Also,
several adult vertebrae, a shoulder blade, and a hip socket were
uncovered, as well as bloodstained clothing. A rug in Holmes's private quarters was found to be woven with human hair. It appears
that in his cellar he had constructed rooms out of lead, so as to be
soundproof." Tiggs pauses here so that Handley may gasp, but she
doesn't. "We have already canvassed the Englewood area, speaking
with local merchants and people who knew Holmes. The task of
hunting down former lodgers of the World's Fair Inn has been more
difficult, but progress has been made. Of those to whom we spoke,
nearly all claim to have been swindled by Holmes. He is something
of a serial deceiver. Those Holmes knew personally have all disappeared. Here," he says, "is where you come in."

"I don't see how," Handley says. "As you may know, I have retired
myself from the case, or from any cases for that matter."

"You are a huntress, and for people like us, Dr. Handley, there is only the hunt. You would be interested to know that the president has specifically requested you," Tiggs says. "Perhaps you will change your mind."

Moreau removes a velvet sack from a pocket and hands it to the doctor. She inspects it cautiously, determining its shape and heft, and recognizes it at once as the timepiece she lost in the World's Fair Inn. They know, for if they turn it over, an inscription on the back reads, *"To Elizabeth, the best of all Handleys."* So they know—that she was there; that she witnessed the child's death but did nothing to stop it; that she has told no one because they would think her guilty, as guilty as Clemantis; that she watched a child die to appease her own thirst for the knowledge of a killer's mind. Although she is, in truth, shaken, she does not show it. In fact, as she places the velvet sack, without opening it, in the pocket of her dress, she grins.

"I have made up my mind," she says. "I will not vacillate."

Tiggs says, "It's almost time, Dr. Handley."

Outside they are chanting, "The Devil must hang! The Devil *will* hang!"

She follows him out, Moreau in turn following her. The wind has shifted, gusting the smoke, thicker than before, farther inland, over the gallows, which have been set up in front of the Art Institute. Various guards and functionaries scamper about, insuring that everything is in order. Skurlock is being kept in a small cement structure that resembles a mausoleum, guarded by a dozen troops sent here by President Cleveland to stymie the strike but today given orders of an entirely different nature. As they pass by, Handley loses herself in the gaggle of reporters waiting impatiently for their chance to question the man the world thinks is Clemantis. Just momentarily, she glances at the mausoleum, wondering what would happen if she just burst in. Would he remember her? Would he know it is she who is responsible for his death? Just then, Moreau finds her in the smoke and escorts her through the reporters over to a grandstand of sorts—in truth, three benches placed one atop the other—that has been erected to the immediate left of the gallows. Tiggs is already there, sitting in the first row toward the middle next to the Palmers and—she recognizes him even with her spectacles grimed with ash—Mr. Rockland. As she sits, she avoids eye contact. Presently, however, Mr. Palmer, after talking to Tiggs, says to Handley, "Hello," but that is all. Handley glares out at the crowd, which stretches from the gallows as far as the eye can see in every direction—north to the river, south to Glessner House, and west to the stockyards.

"Hang him! Hang him! Hang him!"

Easily half of Chicago is here, as well as many who have taken the rail in from New York and Philadelphia, just to witness the hanging. Fathers place sons atop their shoulders, eager for them to see the Husker's last moments. Families have brought picnics and lounge on patterned blankets as ashes shower down, sticking to skin and garment. Groups of women, supporters of Jane Addams, hold placards that say, JUSTICE, NOT JUDGMENT, while groups of men—they appear, Handley thinks, as strikers—brandish railroad ties, a few of them improbably ablaze. After a while, the crowd grows restless. The sun, if it could be seen, sets, and as it grows darker, bonfires begin to burn in every direction, until the crowd itself, Handley thinks, resembles a firestorm, a sea of flickering orange flames under a charcoal sky. Two bright electric lights, hanging from rafters directly above the gallows, come on, blinding those seated in the grandstand. "Hang him!" Applause. "Hang him!" The chanting grows louder. Just after eight, they bring him out. The crowd explodes. People jump up and down, waving the smoldering railroad ties and chanting louder. Skurlock is led to the center of the gallows, wearing a black hood. The executioner emerges from the rear of the gallows now and removes the hood, then places the noose around the man's neck. Just then, he looks at her. She is not certain if he recognizes her. Even with the glaring lights and the smoke, with her grimed spectacles, she can make out his face, but perhaps he can't make hers out. His face is haggard, gaunt; his teeth are yellow; and the whites of his eyes have been flooded with blood, and his lips are engorged—an effect, no doubt, of being summarily, frequently beaten. She is not certain what to do, or for that matter why she was brought here in the first place, other than so that she will feel guilty—if not for turning over the wrong man, then for not rejoining the investigation. Guilt is exactly what she feels now, and for a moment her dislike for Tiggs turns into revulsion. But then, a moment later, into a kind of self-hatred. Perhaps, through the distended eyelids, in the blazing light and through his bloody eyes, Skurlock can see it written on her face.

She looks at him full on and feels, for the first time, repentant. She was so focused on Holmes and her own vain quest for knowledge, nothing else mattered, even an innocent man's freedom. But here he is, face ravaged, body savaged, unable to hold even his own bile.

As the noose tightens, his lips move. He appears to be talking, only she can't read his lips through the smoke. She stands and starts running toward the gallows. Perhaps, she thinks, he's telling her not to repent; he harbors no ill will; he has forgiven her, and now she must forgive herself, but before she can reach the gallows, the rope falls taut.

A wintry wind blows off the lake. The chanting becomes a cheer, which soon erupts into one big, deafening roar as the body of the man the world will forever know as Clemantis falls and the Husker is hanged. Some weep from elation, but most scowl, whistle, hoot, and scream as they rush the gallows. In the grandstands, they are slow to realize that they are being charged, but when they do, everyone flees, the Palmers and Mr. Rockland trampling over Handley, even Tiggs and Moreau running for cover. Handley herself is almost trampled, but at the last moment she's thrown off the edge of the grandstand, landing under a fallen pole, trapped. From here, through the smoke, she can see them dousing the corpse and igniting it. The chanting becomes louder, deafeningly so. In the melee, the corpse disappears. Despite an extensive citywide search, it will never be recovered. The smell of burning flesh hangs in the air, masked only by the smell of the burning city. In the distance, a few last orange flames break the black city's skyline.

Note on the Distortion of the Historical Record

During the writing of this book, certain liberties were taken with the historical record, embellishing, exaggerating, and tailoring. The only actual building left standing from the White City is a reconstructed version of the Palace of Fine Arts, now the Museum of Science and Industry. October 8, 1893, was indeed "Chicago Day," the anniversary of the Great Chicago Fire of 1871; on that day alone, the exposition welcomed 751,026 curiosity seekers. A Parade of Nations followed by fireworks was on the schedule, but boys' corpses were not that day or any other day found littering the White City. As far as real personages are concerned, George Pullman, Frederick Douglass, Henry Adams, the comte de Paris, the maharaja of Kaparthala, Thomas Edison—all attended the exposition, as did 27,539,000 others. The most liberty was taken with the life of Herman Mudgett, alias H.H. Holmes. Events were shifted around to better adhere to the novel's dramatic arc. Potter Palmer, the day's Donald Trump, never visited the World's Fair Inn, located at 701–703 63rd Street at Wallace, a surprising distance from the White City. Clemantis, the Rocklands, Thom Nix, and Hannibal Skurlock are all entirely fictitious characters. The Palmers did not own a Winslow Homer, though they did own many Monets. Nor did the Walsh Gang ever exist. Elizabeth Handley never studied under William James, although she might have written an account of the Clemantis killings; if so, the manuscript was lost.

The survivor never again surfaced.

Institutions used in the research of *The White City* were as follows: Joseph Regenstein Library at the University of Chicago; the Chicago Historical Society; the Chicago Public Library; the Newberry Library; Chicago; Butler Library of Columbia University in New York; the New York Public Library; the Library of Congress. Texts used in the research of this novel, which provide further information on the 1893 World's Fair, include John Moses and Joseph Kirkland's *History of Chicago*, 1895, by Munsell & Co; Bancroft's two-volume *A Book of the Fair*, 1893; *A Week at the Fair Illustrating Exhibits and Wonders of the World's Columbian Exposition*, 1893; *World's Columbian Exposition, Plan and Classification*, circa 1893; *Laird's and Lee's Standard Pocket Guide and Time Saver*, 1904; *The Education of Henry Adams; Two Little Pilgrims' Progress: A Story of the City Beautiful*, 1895; back issues of *Leslie's Monthly Magazine* and *Halligan's Weekly World's Fair; The World's Fair: Being a Pictorial History of the Columbian Exposition*, 1893; *The Columbian Gallery: A Portfolio of Photographs for the World's Fair; World's Columbian Exposition Illustrated*, 1891; Frederick Douglass and Ida Wells's *The Reason Why the Colored American Is Not in the World's Columbian Exposition; The World's Columbian Exposition: First Annual Report of the President*, by Lymon Gage, 1891; *The White City, Being an Account of a Trip to the World's Columbian Exposition at Chicago in 1893*, 1933; Louis Sullivan's *Autobiography of an Idea; Fairground Fiction*, edited by Donald Hartman; *All the World's a Fair*, by Robert W. Rydell; *Depraved: The Shocking True Story of America's First Serial Killer*, by Harold Schechter; *The Trial of Herman W. Mudgett, Alias, H. H. Holmes, for the Murder of Benjamin F. Pitezel; The Holmes Castle; Sold to Satan; Holmes—A poor wife's sad story, not a mere rehash, but something new and never before published; Murder in All Ages*, by Matthew Pinkerton; Herbert Ashbury's *The Gem of the Prairie: An Informal History of the Chicago Underworld*; Arthur Schlesinger's *The Rise of the City: 1878–1898*. And *Lives of the Most Remarkable Criminals Who Have Been Condemned and Executed for Murder, Highway Robberies, Housebreaking, Street Robberies, Coining, or Other Offences: From the Year 1720 to the Year 1735, Collected from Original Papers and Authentic Memoirs* (London: Reeves & Turner, 1873); and *Holmes's Own Story*, only one copy of which exists in the Library of Congress.

Acknowledgments

I'd like to thank Michael Cunningham, Peter Gadol, David Wojahn, Jim McManus, Rick Moody, Jonathan Franzen—for helping whip me into shape; Bill Duffy (R.I.P.) and Marie Stone at Parker; Bill Brown at the University of Chicago; and my friends Alex Hall, Mary Wharton, Spencer Schilly, Darran Foster, Touré, Dave Moon, Dave King, Peter Vilbig, Christopher Shinn, Kevin Chong, Emily Chenoweth, Hannah Chandler, Michael Krauss, Dave Ladik, Rami Djemal, Jennifer Dorr, and everyone at Columbia and VH1. Thank you.

Becki Heller, you made the prose clearer and the story stronger. Above all, you were the right editor for this book. Thank you.

Kim Goldstein, your wizardry verges on the extraterrestrial. This book simply would not exist without you. A writer couldn't dream up a better agent or friend. Thank you.

Mike and Rick, thanks for keeping me real whenever—frequently—I flew off on flights of fancy. Mom and Dad, thanks for everything. Everything.

Thank you. Thank you. Thank you.